Obedience

By Michaela Laws

Obedience

This is a work of fiction. The story you are about to read resides within a fictional replication of Chicago, Illinois and its surrounding suburbs. As such, all characters, businesses, and events that occur within these pages are wholly imaginary.

Many thanks to Bryan Bibiano, Evan Bremer, Katie Radocaj, Loucius Bell, Kristi Jimenez, and Martha Coleman for being the best alpha readers a writer could ask for!

Obedience

Content and Trigger Warnings:
~NSFW (18+) Sexual Content
~Golden-Retriever Millionaire Boyfriend
~Pleasure Dom Boyfriend
~Morally Grey Tragic Hero
~Mafia/Syndicate
~BDSM (Bondage, Blindfold, Rough)
~FULL Consent (No SA)
~Threats of Violence
~Witness to Assisted Death (Suicide)

Dedication

For my love, Bryan, who stood by me in my darkest of times.

For my family, who believed in me ever since I could walk.

For my friends, who inspired me every day to keep going.

For my followers, who cheered me on in wild fervor.

For myself, in defiance of impostor syndrome.

Fuck you, impostor syndrome.

Table of Contents

CHAPTER 1

Acknowledgment

"She almost died, Jerry!!"

"I know!! But what do you want me to do? Take her keys and keep her locked up in the house!?"

"I'm not saying that! Don't put words in my mouth!"

I could barely understand the shouting around me. I couldn't even move without feeling something tug at different parts of my skin. My vision, hazy from some sort of anesthesia aftermath, made shapes and colors and slowly tried to carve out details. Still, I was as lost as I could be.

Where was I, and what had happened to me?

Focus. Take a breath and rewind.

I remained still and recollected everything I could. My name was Maya Augustine. I was a twenty-five-year-old online blogger who wrote about food trends and recipe opinions for money. I lived with my parents, lucky enough that they were willing to shelter me after college. My dad, Jerry, worked extremely hard at his mom-and-pop auto shop. On the other hand, my mom Sarah climbed up a steep corporate business ladder and was now the head of Human Relations at her office. Compared to most of my friends, I was one of the lucky ones to have both parents in my life and together.

Yet I kept hearing their voices bounce back and forth with anger. Did I do something wrong? They barely ever fought- at least, in front of me, they never raised their voices. What was different now? I had to remember what happened before I ended up here.

~ ~ ~

"Are you sure you're going to be okay? I can come with you if you want." My dad was always worried about me. I was more-or-less a shut-in, electing to only go out if necessary due to not caring for crowds and living my best life working from home. That day was one of those days I needed to see through outside my office. I was tasked with reviewing and writing about a very complex curry recipe that was said to be flavorful but not spicy, which was hard to believe. There were so many ingredients in the roux that I knew a good quarter of the spices I needed to import-buy. Still, I was twenty-five. I knew I could handle a grocery store run on my own. I had done so just fine before, or else my business would have failed long ago.

"I'll be fine. It's just a trip to the grocery store for spices. I think I can handle that much," I replied reassuringly. My dad didn't look like it, but he was a significant worrywart when it came to me. Even when I was a kid, he would protect me from anything he could because I was his little girl. He'd try and sway me from going out with friends, seeing sports games or shows my school put on and even had to be convinced by my mother to let me go to prom. I often thought my love for staying indoors spawned from his over-protection of me, but it wasn't harmful. After all, I was safe, and he didn't lock me away like some tower princess, bound to never see the outside world.

My dad sighed and stood from the dining room table, walking away from the bills he was counting off to hug me gently. "I know, but I'm always gonna worry about you no matter what."

"Cause I'm your little girl. I know. I love you, and I'll be home soon, okay?"

"I love you, too."

He was sweet, waving me off as I walked out the front door towards my old ride. I had a pretty crappy car, but it was a car that served me well ever since I got it at sixteen. That car got me to high school, college, and back home with only an oil change and a light repair needed to keep it running. Maybe it was my rare usage of it that kept it alive, or possibly my dad had maintained maintenance on it in secret from time to time. I would honestly never know.

I hopped into my car and slowly drove off to the nearest international grocery store in town, which was about fifteen minutes out toward the city. I lived in the beautiful northern suburbs, where the hustle of urban life calmed to a steady, negotiable beat. I went through the list in my head of everything I needed, tapping my phone that was resting in the cupholder in the habit of checking off each item I remembered. My eyes were glued to the road, ensuring I took every precaution to get from point A to B and back without an incident.

When I arrived, I was relieved that not many people thought of shopping at the same time I was. That meant less chance of random rude customers ruining the mood for everyone. Thank God. Even parking with two empty spaces on each side of me made me sigh out in contentment as I exited my car.

Taking a grocery basket and nestling it in the crook of my elbow, I made a beeline toward the spice aisle. It was daunting as hell to see more spices than someone could imagine lining a wall, but when you have a list in your head, and the herbs are in alphabetical order thanks to the labor of the store stock employees, things just safely fall into place. The collection then became a smooth conveyor belt with my hand going from the shelf to the basket, with something becoming scratched off of my mental list.

What stopped it was a hand softly bumping against my knuckles, causing me to drop the bottle of ground fennel I had almost wrapped my fingers around.

"Oh shit!" I gasped, reaching out to catch the falling bottle with both hands. Despite my clumsy release of it, I managed to catch and cradle the bottle in my palms. However, a large hand was nestled beneath both of mine as secondary support. Another was softly laid against my upper back. For one second, I was relieved that I had caught the bottle. The next second I froze in mild fear. Who was touching me?

I quickly looked over to meet the gaze of a rather handsome

gentleman staring at my hands in worry. The third second passed and had me falling mentally into his soft jade eyes. How could a set of eyes look so gemlike? He wasn't looking at my gaze as he kept his focus on the mini-rescue mission in our hands, yet I couldn't pull away from staring into his eyes.

The fourth second had him finally meeting my stare, his expression melting from worry to soft concern with a smile. Then, finally, the fifth filled my ears with his voice.

"Are you okay? I didn't mean to scare you."

I was at a loss for words. My life was devoted to writing and expressing my thoughts and feelings publicly and proudly, but I could not speak a single word in reply. Was it due to my surprise or my confusion about the situation? My mind was spinning slightly, even as he gently pushed his hand up against mine and guided me to stand up straight. After I let in a breath, I slowly let myself mentally center and nodded to the stranger. As I did, he released my hands and removed his other hand from my back, taking a step back from me in understanding.

"Sorry about that," I mumbled in embarrassment. "I guess I just got into my own head and wasn't paying attention."

I looked at the stranger again to see him chuckle and brush a couple strands of black hair across his hairline. It allowed me to look at his entirety and note his black sneakers, simple dark jeans, brandless zip-up hoodie, and a band t-shirt I didn't recognize. He was a typical stranger, yet something made him stick out to me. Had

I seen him somewhere before?

Whatever. It was just a stranger.

He nodded to me and looked at the shelves, obviously looking for something. "I feel that. No worries, okay?"

I nodded, and that was that. The stranger reached up and took hold of a bottle of fenugreek powder before stepping back and walking around me out of the aisle. I let my mind linger on him for a bit longer, trying to pin down his appearance with anyone I had seen before and swearing there was a reason I recognized him briefly. After a moment, I shook my head and resumed my gathering of spices before going to collect other ingredients for my curry review.

I walked out of the grocery store fifty dollars lighter, but I knew my work would replenish the expenses over time. I loaded the three bags I carried out into the backseat of my car before stepping into the driver's seat and driving out of the parking lot towards home. I went through the setup in my head, knowing that curry was temperamental despite just being a spice mix turned sauce.

I swore the light was red. As I approached an intersection, I knew I had seen a red light and immediately pinned the color to the potential angry emoji I'd have to use if the curry failed.

I guess I really got into my head, not noticing a large vehicle that would suddenly crash into the back of my little car, causing me to quickly skid forward into the middle of the street. I felt my skull and brain shake as the side of my head collided with my steering wheel, but all I could see was black immediately after.

I could softly hear car horns and police sirens wail all around me, muffled by my dizzying mind. I knew someone had taken hold of me and dragged me out of my car, but I couldn't remember any other details beyond that.

~ ~ ~

It took me all that recall to realize I was in the hospital, covered in IVs and bandages from a car crash I didn't even cause. I was so careful, and yet I was there, injured with a fuzzy memory. The shouting match was all I heard around me, barely softening the sounds of the heart monitor's incessant beeping, signifying my life.

At last, I slowly opened my eyes and took in the bright light of my hospital room. I was right. I was laid on a hospital bed with my parents shouting back and forth over me. I could only let out a groan, signaling them to stop. I needed quiet, but my jaw was too sore to form words.

"Ah! Maya!" My mother gasped before dropping down to her knees beside me and taking my hand into both of hers. "Thank God you're awake..."

My father said nothing and gripped my other hand, staring down at it with gritted teeth. I could tell both of my parents were frustrated, but all that mattered to them was that I had opened my eyes. I took the sight of both of them in, letting out a small sigh before forcing myself to speak.

"What happened?" I mumbled, barely moving my lips. My mom grimaced and placed her forehead against my hand while my dad shook his head.

"Some car thief tried to speed through a light while getting chased by the cops... you were in the way and ended up in a crash," my dad confessed, squeezing my hand softly. "It stopped the thief, and he's been arrested, but... I'm sorry. I should have gone with you."

I was at a loss once again. This time, my mind was saying a million things, but I physically couldn't say them aloud. I was so careful, and yet...

A knock on the room door captured our attention, making the three of us in the room stare at the entrance. A muffled voice echoed behind the wood, barely audible enough to hear. My dad, however, had excellent hearing.

"Come in."

The door swung open, revealing a nurse motioning someone out of sight to enter. My brain suddenly fell silent as the stranger I had met before walked into the room with a bouquet of assorted flowers. Him? Why was he here?

My dad took a step forward, holding a hand over me in some form of protection while my mother pinned her eyes on him, standing up slowly.

"I'm sorry to disturb you, but... wait..." the stranger began to say before looking at me and letting recognition paint over his face. "You're the woman I bumped into at the grocery store."

I could barely nod in confirmation, surprised to see him in the room, much less with flowers.

"Who are you?" My dad asked, taking another firm step forward. The stranger shook his head and held out the flowers as a gesture of some kind.

"I'm the owner of the car you helped stop the thief from taking. I know it's not a lot, but I wanted to say thank you somehow." When my dad didn't step forward to take the bouquet, the stranger made his way toward my mother and handed her the flowers. She took them and placed them on the nearby table before turning back to the stranger in some form of awe. Did she know him? The stranger continued. "Also, please know that I'll cover any and all hospital expenses, so don't worry--"

"You can do that?" My father asked, a hint of skepticism in his voice. It was fair; hospital bills were not small by any means. The stranger looked like an average joe. How was he going to cover everything?

Suddenly, my mom practically hissed, "Jerry! Please!" I was stunned. Why was she so hostile all of a sudden? My dad stared incredulously as my mom cleared her throat and walked over with a smile. "Thank you kindly, Mister Hunter. We really appreciate it."

Hunter? The name, the face, mom's sudden business behavior... it suddenly clicked.

The company my mom worked for was created and owned by Liam Hunter. He was a genius in technology and business, placing stock in new ingenuity and betting his mind on projects meant to change the technological world. So many companies begged him to work for them, but he started his own business from literally three-digit numbers in his bank account. Blogs raved about him. He was praised for his intellect, drive for future technologies, and ridiculous charm that captured the heart of every male chaser alive. His face was plastered all over social media and news outlets for being part of the Forbes 30 Under 30 list as well as being a candidate for America's Top 20 Most Handsome Men.

And he was the guy I bumped into at a random grocery store? In the spice aisle, no less?

I could only gawk in surprise at Liam-- assuming he was indeed the Liam I was thinking of. My dad did the same, now understanding that this man could undoubtedly cover the hospital expenses needed.

Another knock at the door caused everyone in the room to look over, seeing a nurse quickly let herself in. "Excuse me. The doctor would like to speak to both of you, Mister and Missus Augustine. It's just about Maya's eventual release."

My parents looked at each other and nodded in mutual understanding before excusing themselves from the room with the nurse. I was alone with Liam, unable to speak and still lost in the fact that I had met such a famous figure AND stopped a criminal from stealing his car. Of course, it was at the expense of mine, but at the end of the day, crime was stopped, right?

Liam smiled at me and walked over to my side, reaching into his pocket and pulling out his wallet. I watched as he pulled out a small, partially transparent business card and placed it on the table beside the flowers.

"You're Maya, right? I know you can't speak right now, or else you probably already would have. If there's anything else I can do to repay you, please give me a call, okay? Just mention your name, and whatever you need or want is yours," Liam said with a smile. I was flattered that he somehow seemed to be in my debt, but he was already paying for my hospital bills. I didn't want to look a gift horse in the mouth, but it was perplexing to imagine being so grateful that one would offer 'whatever I needed' in exchange.

I slowly formed a smile of my own in return, causing Liam, for some reason, to stare at me for a moment. I could tell something clicked in his brain, but seconds later, he simply chuckled again and shook his head. Liam then turned and made his way to the door, only stopping at the entrance to look back at me and say, "Get well soon, Maya."

He's rather... interesting, no?

Something inside of me begged to learn more about him. Some strange curiosity prodded my mind in need. He had suddenly come into my life and offered me something compelling. How powerful was this seemingly unlimited wish? Were there any hidden limitations that I would learn about later? How would this man get certain things if I asked for the unobtainable?

Liam clung to my mind for my entire hospital stay. I barely remembered to post about my hospital stay on my blog, lost in simply researching Mister Hunter when I was able to get my hands on my laptop. My followers were sympathetic, and my sponsors were more than understanding of my delay on the curry review. Still, ninety percent of my browser tabs consisted of tabloids and news articles.

I just needed to know more before I obtained my unlimited wish.

CHAPTER 2

Control

It had been two weeks since I met Liam. I recovered quickly due to just suffering a head and neck injury and was released within days. I then spent my time listening to interviews, feeding my internal curiosity about the businessman. Was this healthy? I wasn't stalking him; I was just learning about him beyond just being my mother's boss. So, I was justified, right?

Of course!

I decided against arguing with myself. The internal struggles I had never really worked out well and just made me want to snack on junk food in comfort at the end every time.

I slowly worked through recovery with Liam factoids circulating in my mind. Even working through my curry assignment was a trip with spice and trivia colliding in my head. Make sure to combine the spices for the roux. Liam was six-foot, two inches in height. After cooking the chicken, add the carrots and potatoes. Liam was listed in the top ten young-and-successful entrepreneurs in the country. Wash your rice and measure one-to-one water to rice before cooking it. There were rumors about Liam being single, but nothing was confirmed.

It was a natural yet slightly concerning mixture of thoughts that seemed to sit together without much chaos; another reason to justify how sane I was in researching Liam. After all, he apparently owed me some sort of unlimited wish. I didn't want to nab it from someone sketchy or unreliable. Best to know as many details as possible.

The only thing to break me from my regular train of patterned thoughts were my online friends and colleagues. Word of my hospital visit spread quickly because of my delay in posts and my public disclosure to my followers. I was more than grateful to know the world was sympathetic to anyone suffering from an accident. Part of me wanted to disclose my encounter with Liam, but I knew better than to entice his fan base into my world, where food should have been my focus, not men.

A simple ping broke me from my typical mental vegetation. The blip emitted from my chat program ushered me to open it both to see who was contacting me and to remove the annoying visual notification from my taskbar. To my surprise, however, the message was from a close friend I had known since high school, still living in my area and willing to consider me their friend in return.

~~~

ToysAreBetter: Hey sweet thing! Are you available to chat right now? :D
MmmFoodQueen: Somewhat? What's up?

ToysAreBetter: I'll be quick I promise. Just tell me what kind of person you like. Any little detail >:)

MmmFoodQueen: Danni...

ToysAreBetter: Now hold on!

ToysAreBetter: Before you block me, know that I'm being serious! I have tix to an art show and wanted to invite you and someone you might like.

MmmFoodQueen: I'm really not interested in dating anyone right now.

MmmFoodQueen: Still recovering, you know?

ToysAreBetter: I understand, but you can't fully heal staying cooped up in your house all the time. Your mental and social health is important, too.

MmmFoodQueen: I know, I know... How about I go, but no date?

ToysAreBetter: Really?

MmmFoodQueen: Danni.

ToysAreBetter: Fine! Fine. No matchmaker, I promise.

~~~

I was genuinely grateful that my closer-to-home friends still wanted to interact with me. Despite having an overprotective father, I still went to school and made friends. Many of them branched off into their own paths, but a few stuck around and kept in touch with me. It was a breath of fresh air to remain connected to my environment.

An exchange of information and I was set for an art gallery exhibition later in the week. I never dressed formally to impress anyone; a simple pair of slacks and a dress shirt were enough for me. Sometimes, I even threw in a scarf or headband to be less bland, but that was only if I felt like it at the time. However, simple was never out of style and sometimes made more of an impression than fancy garments and attire.

I sat in my chair and soaked in what had occurred. Maybe a break from the routine I had set for myself was needed. This was a step outside my house that most likely wouldn't end up with me in the hospital. What was the likelihood of being in a car accident twice? Probably less than five percent.

Maybe.

Besides, this would be a way for me to not constantly think about Liam. I knew my digging was becoming almost fangirl-ish, and it was a little embarrassing to think about. I wasn't interested in being with him. I just wanted to know more. A powerful man had offered me a very ambiguous wish, anything I desired. He could have simply kept it at paying my medical expenses.

Why the wish?

I sighed and rubbed my face, digging the pads of my fingers into my cheeks and pressure points to relax further into my seat. This was ridiculous. It truly was. This man was charming, and I had fallen into the honeytrap of him. Enough was enough.

Art gallery. Right.

The rest of the week was me perfecting my curry review and doing side research into the art gallery I was going to. It was a simple gallery with pictures from multiple artists hoping to get further in the art world. While it was not my area of expertise, I still appreciated the work and dedication of anyone pounding the pavement for their craft. Some of the photos sampling the gallery's wares made me purse my lips in impressed surprise. Too bad many of them would have four-digit prices.

Of course, I wasn't going to go without a typical concerned conversation with my parents.

"Are you sure, Maya? It's only been a couple of weeks since you left the hospital. Maybe you should rest more..." my father mumbled, chowing down on the leftover curry I had made the day before. I shook my head with a reassuring smile.

"I'll be okay. Danni is going to drive, and she is an excellent driver." I explained, knowing I had to make triple-sure that my parents were satiated before I could go anywhere. After all, they had taken it upon themselves to obtain and seal away my car keys. It wasn't like I was going to go anywhere without them stepping in anyway.

Still, I wasn't some broken doll. I wasn't incapable of doing anything I wanted to do on my own.

My mother pressed her finger to her temple and rubbed circles into it.

"We're just concerned for you, sweetie. That's all. Are you absolutely sure?" My mother pressed. I persisted in return.

"I'm sure. It's just an art gallery show."

~ ~ ~

The ride was careful, as Danni knew not to test the speed limits with me in the passenger's seat. It was another precaution, but I understood why. At least I wasn't being denied an experience for my injuries.

"Your head okay after the accident? Sorry if I'm prying, but mama had you in her prayers. Gotta ease her mind, you know?" Danni asked, making me chuckle softly. Her mother, the gem she was, became like a second mother to me when I was out of the confines of my home. She snuck snacks to me and treated me like one of her own. It was quite a blessing as I also knew the woman had the fear of God in her heart and contained the rage of several demons within her fists, saved only for those who threatened her family.

"Tell her I'm okay. It was just a bump on the head." I replied, taking the situation lightly. Danni laughed and shook her head. "What?"

"A bump on the head landed you in the hospital. Nuh-uh, I'm not dumb. Mama's not going to accept that." Danni preached. "That

19

woman knows too damn well how careful you are, so she knows only the Devil himself could have done something to put you there."

"I'm serious! I'm okay, I promise. In fact, tell her God saved me if that helps ease her mind." I defended, trying to move away from the subject by bending to her mother's need for religious explanation. Danni shook her head with a wry smile of her own. I knew she was worried about me too, but she wanted me to be out and about and not trapped in a bed, not that I was to begin with.

"Yeah, God gotcha..." Danni muttered, refocusing on the road.

"What do you want to hear, Danni?"

"The whole story. Girl, like... I may not be like you-- all introverted and crap--, but that doesn't mean I don't care about you. I read your blog and stuff. I guess I just didn't expect to learn that you went to the hospital on your blog."

"Oh... right. I'm sorry. I guess my job really set me in the mind of putting my audience first, friends later."

"That means you need to take a damn break. When was the last time you went on vacation? A staycation?"

"Uhh..."

"Uh-huh. Exactly. This accident was God saying you need to stop and step away from the blog."

"Oh, now you believe in God?"

"Never said that, but I ain't gonna question obvious signs. Life will knock you flat on your ass if you don't pay attention."

"...or land you in the hospital."

Danni wheezed back a laugh. "Goddamnit, Maya."

We both finally laughed together. Danni was indeed a dear friend of mine. I was perhaps the luckiest woman to still be her friend as she didn't keep people close for long. She was a rising star, grinding pavement to excel in the business. Her skill required a lot of social grace, which was natural for her. I wasn't sure what she saw in me, but I valued that she cared in her own way. It made me internally cringe at being introverted enough to be often forgotten by people I knew, yet she still accepted me and tried to remain close.

I relaxed into the car seat and stared out the window as Danni settled into the drive. The lights of the city always managed to entrance me, despite me never really going into the city at all. It was fast for me, the drum of energy that zipped between the buildings like a lightning bolt. Everyone was expected to be quick and unrelenting in getting from point A to B and back again as if their lives demanded it. I was certain, however, that the smell of the city's trash and unfortunate homeless made people walk as fast as they did.

A combination of both disgust and determination seemed to be the right mix.

My peace was broken by Danni's voice, her teasing tone escaping into the air between us.

"So, I gave my extra tickets away to a couple of friends, and they may show up. Don't be afraid to talk to them, alright?"

Oh no. I knew what that meant.

"Danni--"

"Look, I said no matchmaking, so no matchmaking. But goddamn, don't be a damn prude if one of them makes you lick your lips, alright? Enjoy yourself."

I sighed. That was not part of the plan. My enjoyment was going to be in the air conditioning and art in a city gallery, not in some guests who probably didn't really need to know me. Besides, what was I even going to talk about?

Hello, I'm Maya, and I just got out of a car crash while trying to buy stuff for curry!

Yup. That was bound to go well.

CHAPTER 3

Appreciation

I didn't expect anything from the art gallery besides a slew of art pieces and high price tags. Yet, that was precisely what I got; a simple maze of a gallery with every wall and panel covered in art pieces ready to be bought and taken home.

Walking through the front door, I was impressed by the crowd. You could walk around without bumping into anyone if you were walking side-by-side with a friend. Many potential buyers and art critics looked around in either interest or boredom. You could practically hear the judgment that ran through each brain as you walked by. Not every piece was going to appease everyone. It was the same in my world: not everyone liked food reviews. I could only hope the artists themselves had the confidence to stand tall with their pieces despite the words of critics.

Despite my own perception, I felt a little out of place standing at the crowd's edge. The slacks and dress shirt seemed to be the bare minimum, as everyone else had taken the art gallery show as an excuse to show off their jazz bar and club attire. Part of me was thankful for wearing my mini sunhat, or else I would have been confused for some of the gallery staff.

Though the mini sunhat did give me a slight coven vibe that I was grooving with, easing my nerves a bit more.

My internal vibe was interrupted by someone calling out Danni's name, causing me to look over and spot the source. Two gentlemen, suited up with smiles on their faces, walked over to us with glasses in their hands. The blond gave his extra drink to Danni while the redhead offered me his extra glass.

"Alex! Ty! God, you both clean up well! Barely recognize you two!" Danni gushed, taking her drink and sipping from it. Out of politeness, I took the extra drink and nodded in acknowledgment. The men chuckled and nudged each other before looking at me.

"And who is this?" The blond inquired. Danni opened her mouth to speak, but I decided to take the reins this time.

"Maya. Food reviewer and blogger." I introduced myself, keeping it simple and stupid. I knew food reviews weren't fascinating, so I only hoped they would become disinterested. The redhead pursed his lips, impressed at my words, while the blond looked at Danni in surprise.

"That's pretty unique. Any works we might recognize?" the redhead asked, taking a sip of his drink. I shrugged.

"That depends. My market is a niche one with independent fans, and it's not like a branded review chain. It's just me talking about food." I kept myself at a low bar, despite speaking pretty much the truth of my job. Danni knew how I played my games and laughed.

"It's okay. She's a really good friend of mine but keep your paws off of her. She's like a sister to me, and I do not want to have to kick both of your asses for making her feel uncomfortable. Got it?" Danni instructed, wrapping her free arm around my waist and walking me forward into the gallery. I followed, mainly to not fall forward, but I was glad that she wasn't going to force me to interact with them. The gentlemen laughed in reply and followed behind us to join our exploration.

"Work friends?" I whispered, leaning over to keep my volume low. Danni nodded and squeezed my waist before releasing me and simply walking beside me.

"Alex and Ty work in my department. Alex handles tech support, and Ty is our main runner." Danni acknowledged.

"Runner?"

"Coffee boy. But he's got a good head on his shoulders, so he won't be stuck getting my coffee forever." Danni joked, looking over her shoulder at the redhead and causing him to blush. If I didn't know any better, she was the one both men wanted, as the blond Alex chuckled and kept his eyes on Danni's lower half.

We approached a panel covered in paintings of beautiful people and scenery. There were mountain cliffs, rivers, and still forms of hikers and campers decorating each canvas on the wall. Each had its own voice, but none of them conflicted with one another. It was a perfect harmony set on the wall, almost harmonic enough to justify buying all the pieces at once. That was probably the idea.

Danni let out a small breath of awe. "You know, I could never be as good an artist as these people. How do they come up with these??" She muttered, staring up at the paintings.

"I mean, they do have art schools, you know? Takes years to do this." Alex added, stepping up beside Danni to gawk at the paintings. I wasn't sure if he was genuinely interested or just wanted to be close to Danni, but I didn't let my curiosity linger. Instead, my focus was called once again by the paintings down the line, a new theme on another set of panels with more art to explore. I gently separated from Danni and made my way down the line of paintings, letting my eyes take in all the paints and oils adorning the makeshift walls.

I eventually found myself in an emptier part of the gallery. While other pieces enticed and called others to gaze upon them, one wall had a few passing eyes glance at the paintings in almost shy embarrassment. To me, however, the pieces welcomed me to look upon them in a show of my own, despite feeling a little dirty looking at them alone.

Adorning the wall were paintings of women, each nude as could be but in positions one could imagine in erotica novels. One had a beautiful blonde woman leaning against a bedpost, erotically wrapping one of the bed curtains around her stomach and staring up at the empty black ceiling. Another had a gorgeous black woman sitting on a balcony-- the night sky bright behind her-- like a queen presenting her nude body to the world.

Not many other paintings in the gallery had nude bodies, but these had the same scribbled signature and theme. These all somehow represented feminine beauty, and, despite the disinterest of the general crowd, I felt myself appreciate the attempt.

"Got a favorite?" A voice asked beside me, snapping me out of my thoughts. Turning my head, I was stunned by an even more brilliant and unbelievable sight standing next to me.

"M-Mr. Hunter?" I barely let out, stunned at the idea of the man who had been on my mind being in the same place as me. Yet here he was, dressed in a simple pair of dress pants and a deep red button-up. Liam's sleeves were rolled to the elbows, presenting his already toned forearms to me as his hands were sunk deep into his pockets. He seemed so casual in such an event, but my mind was more focused on the coincidence of him even being in the same place as me. This was the second coincidence. How was that possible?

I didn't want to see him be another prelude to an accident that sent me to the hospital.

Liam turned his head to me and smiled, locking his gaze with mine. He was genuinely charming, making my heart melt ever so slightly in my chest at the sight of his happy expression.

"It's good to see you again, Maya. Have you fully recovered?" He asked, turning his body to me for a conversation. While I was more than excited to finally speak more to Liam, I didn't want to be seen as a fangirl or obsessed info-miner. I took a breath and nodded, giving a smile of my own.

"I have. Wouldn't be out and about otherwise, hehe." I

answered, shrugging a bit into my relaxed joke. Liam chuckled, emitting a sound that rang in my head as something I personally found utterly sexy.

"That's quite fair," Liam remarked before stepping forward towards the paintings, looking up at them in examination. "So, got a favorite?"

"I, uh..." I stumbled over my words, or lack thereof. While the paintings were absolutely gorgeous to behold, I didn't have any desire to claim them or have them anywhere in my home. Besides, I wasn't rich enough to obtain any of them, even if I wanted to make a purchase. "While these are really beautiful, I'm not sure I'd take any of them home."

"I see. Quite a shame, but that's fair. These pieces really do set a tone." Liam remarked, stepping up to one and running a finger over the frame. I stared, watching him slide the pad of his finger against the crevices of the frame in slow motion. Both lost in his intimacy with the picture and entranced by his simple gesture, I stood there with a shiver running up my spine. "I'd probably do better selling these at an auction."

"Are these your pieces?" I instinctively asked, wanting to break out of my trance and genuinely curious about his close demeanor to the paintings in question. But instead, Liam shook his head with a small smile before turning to lock eyes with me again. I had to stop letting him do that, but would my body listen?

"No. These are my sister's. She's a brilliant artist, but she can be rather... 'open' about her sets." Liam confessed, stepping away. "However, I knew all of the models she hired."

"You did?" It was not surprising to learn. According to how the artist painted, these were all absolute goddesses of women. A charming man like Liam certainly had to have had a connection with them, as they were the subjects of his sister's work.

"Yes. Many of the subjects work for me at my company, and they all applied when I was helping my sister look for models."

"What about those who don't work for you?"

"I helped my sister vet through contracted models my company hires for marketing. Those picked have been helping with advertising for a while, so I trusted them." That made sense. Liam turned around and walked toward me, stopping at a surprisingly comfortable distance. "Are you sure I can't interest you in one? Free of charge, of course."

I could only laugh and shake my head no. "It's alright. These pieces belong to someone who can appreciate them much more than I can. They truly deserve more than my simple gaze." I commented, looking down at my feet at the realization of my words. These were fragments of time, still images of a moment exposing these women to the world without shame. Would I ever have the courage to do the same thing?

Who knew?

What broke the line of sight to my feet was a hand reaching for me. I followed the arm up back to Liam's gaze of... concern? Was he... saddened by what I said? I didn't say anything truly self-deprecating, did I? Out of instinct, I placed my hand on his, unsure what he would do.

My heart almost popped as he slowly lifted my hand to his lips and kissed over my knuckles.

"No painting or person here is worthy enough to have the pleasure of your gaze, Maya..." He whispered. I couldn't tell if he wanted me to hear him, but after his lips left my knuckles, his gaze somehow managed to burn into mine with some sort of passion, his irises dilating to form thin jade rings around them. An unfamiliar warmth radiated inside of my chest and began to grow up through my neck and into my cheeks. I could tell I was blushing from the heat my face felt.

I took a breath, trying to center myself without looking like an utter fool. Liam's words and gaze would have been the death of me. "You've got quite a silver tongue, Mr. Hunter." I only half-hoped that he didn't hear me. It shouldn't have been surprising that he did, yet I silently gasped as he chuckled once again and lowered my hand, releasing it from his.

"Please, call me Liam." He requested. I obliged with a nod, slowly coming down from my internal high back to reality. Still, a small smile stretched across my face.

Liam... what a name to say...

Knowing this man on a first-name basis seemed like a gift on its own.

"Okay, Liam," I replied, letting his name roll off my tongue and savoring it for a moment. At that, I barely caught Liam's shoulders shuddering a bit at my calling of his name. Huh.

Before I could think further, my name echoed across the air, but it wasn't Liam who spoke it. It was Danni.

"Maya! Where did you run off to-- Oh! There you..." Danni's words trailed off, the volume of them indicating that she had found me and walked up to stand beside me before I could turn my head to her. As I did, I witnessed her staring with an impressed expression at Liam and knew immediately that she had turned on her infamous flirtation mode. Oh, dear.

"Oh, hey, Danni. I just wanted to see these paintings. They were pretty well done, don't you think?" I spoke aloud, not really knowing if the paintings would distract her mood or if Danni was fully locked in on Liam. The latter seemed accurate.

"Before that, Maya, who is your friend?" Danni inquired, lowering the pitch of her voice to an unmistakable bedroom tone. It didn't go unnoticed by Liam, who simply smiled and held out his hand to Danni.

"Liam Hunter," Liam answered, watching as Danni promptly placed her hand in his before lifting it to his lips. Maybe it was my imagination, or maybe my carnal thoughts were so focused on Liam, but I barely caught the difference between how he kissed her knuckles and how he did mine. Liam's kiss seemed deep and loving to me as if he was kissing a crown jewel ring resting against my knuckles. With Danni, he was barely laying the skin of his lips against her knuckles. If Liam had not kissed my hand before Danni's, I would never have known the difference of intent he seemed to have for us.

Some strange part of me felt relief.

Danni gave out a cute giggle and a smile that would have hooked any lady-chaser to her whims. "What a pleasure it is to meet you, Mr. Hunter," Danni remarked, a purr melting into her words in apparent approval. "How do you know Maya?"

"Wait, what?" I felt myself say aloud, surprised that her flirting now involved me. Usually, when she went after someone, she focused on making the world around them disappear. So why was I involved now? Liam and Danni turned their gazes to me as the former released the hand of the latter.

"I actually owe Maya quite a bit," Liam stated. He stepped towards me and effectively wrapped his arm around my shoulders, placing a soft hand on my upper arm. The warmth in my chest and cheeks reignited at his touch and closeness to me. I could only let my gaze lower to the ground in mild embarrassment as Liam softly laughed under his breath. "You might even say that she saved me."

That's when my brain stopped working. What? I saved HIM? How? When? What? My mind became so confused that I didn't even notice if Danni's expression had changed. Her voice was the only indicator I had, and even that barely phased me out of my stunned state of mind.

"Well, how about that? She never told me anything of the sort, and she and I have been friends for a long time." Danni remarked with a soft chuckle. I couldn't tell if it was genuine towards me, out of mild anger for the lack of knowledge on her end, or if it was out of insult for not being the one praised by him. My thoughts were on the fact that he paid off MY medical expenses. How was paying for debt saving his life?

"Regardless, I owe her quite a lot. She just has to say the word; anything she wants is hers." Liam continued. His voice felt louder as if he leaned into my ear to emphasize his words. Was it to remind me of my seemingly unlimited wish? What was the goal? Was he... flirting with me in front of Danni?

"Maya?" Danni's voice finally broke through my mental obstacle, causing me to look up at her. I expected to see a look of mild jealousy from my friend, but instead, I saw her smiling kindly at me. It took me back a bit, as I was pretty sure I was in the way of her getting more out of her interactions with Liam. I was incorrect.

"Yeah?" I finally replied, curious as to why I was taken out of my introverted demeanor. Danni laughed and walked over to me before tapping my nose with her finger. "Uh?"

"Maya's a good woman. You'd best give her exactly what she wants, Mr. Hunter, or you'll have an entire food blog community plus some wanting to make a recipe out of you." Danni playfully warned, a sly smirk growing across her lips with a gaze at Liam, whose face was indeed very close to my ear. Whatever red color was on my cheeks only intensified at Danni's protective statement.

"Indeed. I will take your statement to heart, miss...?" Liam said as he finally released my shoulders and held his hand to Danni again, positioning it to shake her hand rather than kiss it. Danni reached out and accepted his hand, giving it a small up and down of acceptance.

"Daniella Carter. Marketing Specialist for Anderson Toys. Perhaps we can come to you about increasing the reach to our audience with new tech." Danni formally introduced herself. She went immediately from wanting to bag Liam to forging a potential business relationship. It was definitely a first I had seen from her. Her intention was sealed as she released Liam's hand and reached into her clutch, taking out a business card and passing it to him. "Our CEO would appreciate a conversation."

Liam took the card and nodded with a polite smile, sliding it into his pocket. "I'd be happy to assist in any way I can, Ms. Carter." I smiled. I was glad to see that Danni and Liam were going to get along, yet I felt a little happier that Danni didn't seem unhappy about giving up a hot target like Liam.

Wait, did I just think of him as a hot target? I quickly shook my head and rubbed my face to break this dumb line of thought. I needed to step back into reality.

As I shook my head, Danni gave me a wink and walked over to wrap her arm around mine; softly pulling me away from Liam. I almost instinctively pulled back but felt my brain ease my reactions down to merely a fleeting thought. I had to admit that I had an attraction to Liam, but now was not the time to allow myself to fawn over him.

"Now, if you'll excuse us, we have a whole section of the art gallery waiting for us to observe and view. I'm sure you understand." Danni said coyly. I opened my mouth to interject, wanting to spend more time with Liam, but as I turned to speak, a woman dressed in a full suit stepped up to Liam and whispered something to him. Liam's expression went from friendly to almost stone cold as the woman delivered her message. What was going on? What was wrong?

Liam cleared his throat and smiled at us. "I understand completely. Please don't let me keep you." Liam replied before stepping up to me and taking my hand. He quickly lifted it and gave another kiss over my knuckles, locking eyes with me to ensure he had my full attention. He took another step toward me as he released it and leaned in to whisper in my ear. "I meant it: anything you want is yours, Maya."

With that ringing in my head, Liam stepped back, smiled at me, nodded to Danni, and left with the mysterious woman. I watched him go, stunned by his words and curious as to why he also had to leave.

He was interested in me. It took me a moment to realize that, but I wasn't dim enough to ignore such signs. In the heat of the conversation and the instinctual emotions running high, I was indeed foggy about the subtext, but standing there, I was able to steady my thoughts and piece together the complete picture.

What needed his attention away from me?

"Maya? Hellooo?" Danni's voice echoed in my ear, causing me to turn to her. She tightened her arm around me and wiggled her eyebrows, a Cheshire cat-like smirk across her lips. "So, when did you plan on telling me about him?"

"About Liam?"

"No, the Pope. YES! How do you know him?"

I grimaced, not wanting to paint the picture of him being involved with my hospital visit. Still, Danni deserved to know.

As we toured the rest of the art gallery, I painted her the story of how I stopped a thief from stealing his car. My heroism landed me in the hospital with no worries about paying expenses and an unlimited wish. Danni hung on my every word, clearly fascinated at the turn of events that led to me meeting Liam. Still, as I retold the memory, a part of me could only whisper doubt.

Why would Liam be interested in me? We met ONCE before crossing paths again in the gallery. I wasn't any high figure in business or society. I was a food blogger who lived with her parents and barely went outside of her own choice. I wasn't an ugly woman, but I was not going to be scouted for my looks. I was average, at least to my judgment of beauty and interest.

So why on Earth would Liam Hunter show interest?

CHAPTER 4

Initiation

It had become days since the gallery when I settled into a conclusion with myself: I had to meet up with Liam. I honestly did wish to know him more, which might help me determine what to ask of him. But what if he took my request for his time as my actual wish? I had to be clever about how I wanted to approach this situation. I was smart enough to figure that out, right?

I sat at my desk, clacking away at a new blog post as I let my mind wander to Liam. First, I had to confirm my memory. He did indeed say *anything* I wanted was mine to ask for. He was rich enough to fulfill that, I supposed. A car or maybe even a home was nothing to him. However, I didn't want anything as superficial as that. I was pretty minimalistic to begin with; simple to please.

Maybe... a date was a good idea? I had to consider it: a date with one of the most successful young entrepreneurs out there? I was barely two years younger than him, so it wasn't awkward to think about. I'd learn more about him, and if he was genuinely interested in me, we'd get something out of it. My logic and my emotions could shake hands on it in camaraderie.

Yeah. That was the answer.

I took his card out from its previous home inside my desk

drawer and palmed my cellphone in my other hand, ready to dial the number required to contact him. It probably went to his office.

What if a secretary answered? What if it was a cruel joke? I felt my lips purse at my doubt, and I was half-tempted to listen.

No. Just call.

I took a breath, let my doubts clear from my mind, and dialed the number he gave me onto my phone. Then, bringing the phone to my ear, I listened and waited for the phone to connect.

Ring.

Ring.

Ring--

"Thank you for calling Labryintelligence. This is Louis speaking on behalf of our President and Chairman Liam Hunter. How may I help you?" a voice answered on the other line. I felt my body freeze up slightly, but I forced myself to speak through it.

"Oh, hello! Uh... Mister Hun--... Liam gave me this number to contact him. My name is Maya Augustine." I began. Before I could continue, however, Louis gasped on the other end.

"Miss Augustine! Mister Hunter has been waiting very much for your call. Would you like me to schedule a meeting with him for you?" Louis chirped almost too happily. I could only guess I was keeping both Liam and Louis on their toes. I smiled a bit before nodding despite Louis not being there to visually see me.

"I would like that very much, thank you," I replied. I moved my phone and initiated the call through its speaker before tapping my fingers on my mobile calendar. "When would be best? I am available whenever it would be of convenience to him."

I faintly heard Louis giggle before he cleared his throat. I barely caught the rustling of clothes as well. What was happening on his end of the call? A wide smile was brimming in Louis's voice.

"Well, Miss Augustine, Mister Hunter has a fully open schedule tomorrow night if you would be so kind. Do you have any dietary restrictions?" Louis inquired, a small huff in his voice as if he was quickly moving while on the line.

"I do not. My job would be rather limited if that were the case, haha!" I joked, trying to brush off my curious confusion. Louis shared my laugh.

"Very good! Very good. Well then, if I may have your address, we will have an escort retrieve you. Is that permissible?"

"Oh, uh... sure. That sounds nice, thank you." I felt a slight spider-like chill run up my spine. An escort? Retrieve me? Where was I going to be taken to? I gave Louis my address, letting the question linger in my mind for a moment longer.

"Excellent! Please be ready by five o'clock tomorrow afternoon. If I may be so forward, you should know that Mister Hunter adores dark red."

"Pardon?"

"Ack--! Very good! Have a wonderful day, Miss Augustine!! Ta-ta!" Louis almost shouted, his voice a short distance from the phone, before the call ended abruptly. I stared at my phone, even more concerned about what I had signed up for. Was... Louis being a wingman? Was Louis his secretary? What on Earth was going on?

Liam liked dark red.

I let that mental note solidify in my brain before feeling my body automatically stand and walk to my closet. Did I have any dark red clothes? Opening the doors to peer into the interior of my closet, I quickly ran my gaze over each article of clothing I had. I didn't have many outfits, but I wasn't caught off guard by the idea of going to a formal event.

Alas, no dark red.

I sighed. Was I going to spend money on an outfit just to impress Liam?

I stood for a moment in thought.

The next, I was dressed in a casual outfit, grabbed my keys, and drove out before my parents could spot and stop me.

It took me hours to find a dark red dress in my size, going into different department stores. It was bad enough that I wore outside the typical fashion line size, but apparently, the color was also out of style. Yet I did secure an outfit that I thought flattered me. It was a simple dress, barely cutting past my knees, but with a nice open slit on the side to give a peek at my thigh. Was I hoping to entice Liam? Yes. I couldn't lie to myself, but it fit the dress design so naturally.

This was for a date I could only hope would go smoothly. A first date with technically a stranger. Would it go well, or would it end with me swearing him off? Only time would tell on the matter.

~~~

"So you're meeting with Mister Hunter?" My mother asked, a nervous energy in her voice as she cleaned the kitchen for what seemed like the fifth time that day. I had informed my parents of the matter when I returned with my dress, but their concern didn't seem to boil hard until the morning after. I sighed as my mother resprayed the kitchen counter with disinfectant spray and began to polish it down.

"Yes. He is coming to pick me up at five. It's nothing crazy, I promise." I swore, wanting to soothe her nerves.

"Maya. You can't promise me anything. You're meeting with the man I work for, assumingly for a date by the look of your dress." My mother grumbled, finally pausing her cleaning to look up at me with tired but concerned eyes. "What am I supposed to feel?"

"I just want you to not think I'm going to die when I walk out the door." I simply stated, organizing the interior of my purse. I mentally checked everything I thought I needed: wallet, phone, chapstick, emergency pain medication, pad and tampon, a stylus that doubled as a pen and self-defense weapon. I was content with what I had, despite my mother's second sigh.

"It's not like we expect you to get into an accident, Maya. It's... just that we don't want to get another phone call saying--"

"I know, mom... I'm sorry. I promise to be absolutely careful." I

41

surrendered to comfort. Understanding both worry and concern was surprisingly hard when you wanted to be independent, but only the truly lonely didn't care one-hundred percent of the time. I walked over and took one of her hands, warming it between mine. "I'll be home tonight."

"You will?"

"Yes. If that helps you feel better." I did not expect anything to happen beyond food and drink. This wasn't the situation to demand a one-night stand or a runaway plan into the sunset.

My mother finally nodded, relaxing her shoulders at last. A mental weight was lifted from my shoulders at the sight. However, a quick look at my phone urged me to be ready. 4:58 PM. I leaned in and kissed my mother on the cheek before making my way to the front door.

"Maya." My mother's voice caused me to turn to her in curiosity. Her lips formed a gentle smirk. "If he does anything, I'll fight him. Boss or not, no one disrespects my daughter."

I raised a playful eyebrow, knowing she was ferocious, before continuing my path to the front door.

I wasn't expecting to see a luxury car parked in front of the house. I had barely taken a step out of the door, but I froze in place, stunned at the sight. Why was there a luxury car parked on the curb? Was this Liam's escort?

A woman exited the driver's side, dressed in a nice suit with her blonde hair in a clean updo. I faintly recognized her as the woman who whispered something to Liam at the art show, but I didn't linger on the recognition. She walked around the front of the car and stopped at the passenger's side, opening it and looking up at me expectantly.

This was the escort. I was going to ride in a luxury car to meet Liam. A part of me that only knew the lower half of middle-class as extravagant was screaming internally in excitement. This was a dream for the younger me.

I shook my head and stood up straight, trying to give off the impression that I expected this escort to be lavish, before making my way down the stairs of my home and towards the passenger door. Might as well get to know my driver.

"Hello. Can I ask who you are?" I inquired. The driver smiled and nodded her head.

"My name is Emily, Miss Augustine. I am Liam's personal driver and will be escorting you tonight. It's nice to meet you." Emily replied, passing me a business card with Labryintelligence's logo on it. I felt a smile of my own grow on my lips. She seemed very nice. It was a little surprising to see a female chauffeur, but she seemed confident enough to hold the job title with pride. With a nod, I lowered myself into the car and almost melted into the leather seats.

Emily closed the passenger door and returned to the driver's seat, settling in before beginning the drive towards my meeting spot. A part of me was curious as to where Liam wanted to meet. With the diet question I got from his secretary Louis, it had to have been a restaurant. However, there were plenty in Chicago or even the surrounding towns. Maybe it was one of Liam's favorite places? Perhaps it was something typical. Who knew?

Well, the only one who didn't know was me.

I felt myself sink into my thoughts for a moment, trying to dissect where I was going without any hint or clue from the tinted windows. My thoughts were broken by Emily's soft voice.

"Would you like some music?" I looked up at Emily's reflection in the driver's rearview mirror, seeing her look at me with a curious stare. Perhaps I was getting too much into my head. I nodded.

"That would be great, thank you," I replied, relaxing back into my seat.

"Do you have a preference?" Emily asked, turning her gaze back to the road.

"Well..." I trailed off, trying to think of what I was in the mood for. Then a thought hit me: this was the perfect chance to learn more about Liam. "What does Liam typically listen to?"

Emily chuckled softly before lowering a hand and pressing some buttons on her dashboard. Soon, the sound of a piano began to play some jazz, followed by an accompanying bass, drum set, and saxophone. Liam liked jazz music. Huh.

"So, Liam likes jazz?"

"Very much. Mister Hunter sometimes wishes the jazz era of music would return."

"I'm surprised to hear that. He seems like someone who keeps looking forward rather than looking back."

Emily laughed softly. I felt like I was prying too much, but Emily didn't seem like she was going to be tight-lipped about her boss. "Mister Hunter is quite a mystery."

I let the silence that followed disappear into the music playing in the car. The song that played was unfamiliar, but it somehow captured me all the same within its melody. There was indeed something about jazz that made me want to see it return to modern media, but at the same time, there was beauty in its age. I closed my eyes and let the music lull me into a relaxed state.

I barely noticed how long the drive took, but before I realized it, we had driven into the heart of Chicago and arrived at a giant skyscraper. As Emily parked along the curb of the building, the music faded out almost perfectly and roused me from its lullaby.

"We've arrived, Miss Augustine." Emily softly announced. I barely heard her leaving the car and opening my passenger door. I slowly stepped out of the car and stretched, taking the chance to look up at the destination as Emily passed the car's keys to a nearby valet.

While the building itself was impressive, the doors into it made my eyes widen, waking me from my lulled relaxation. The archway was carved with gold and stone, welcoming each entrant with an obviously elegant flair. I could hear my wallet screaming to run the other way, knowing that this was the dining hall for the rich. I forced my legs to lock into place, as this was where Liam wanted to meet up. I was not going to run.

I took a breath, felt energy rev back into my chest, and nodded to Emily. "Thank you very much. Shall we?" I said before walking forward towards the building. I was up to the door by the time Emily rushed up beside me. She took the door handle and opened it for me with a smile, ushering me to enter first. With a grateful nod, I entered the building with Emily following behind.

The interior was just as extravagant as the exterior. There were red and gold accented carpets, chandeliers, and paintings across the ceiling and walls. Marble busts and plants decorated the lobby, and many people in suits and fancy attire roamed the floor, chatting or slowly making their way to where they needed to go. Again, I felt out of place. I did not grow up wealthy, so this was a foreign experience.

Emily, however, extended her arm out to me. "Would you permit me to lead you, Miss Augustine?" Did she sense my discomfort? If so, she was very good at her job. I nodded slightly before tucking my arm under hers. I allowed myself to be led towards a set of elevators, where a man in a suit looked at Emily with a raised eyebrow. Without missing a beat, Emily spoke to the gentleman, "The Hunter Reservation, please."

The man quickly pressed a button for the elevator. Within moments, the elevator doors opened, and Emily led me inside. Then, with another button press from the man in the suit, the doors closed, and up we went to who knew what floor. I looked up at the elevator floor screen, seeing the number rise. Soon it became double digits. This was indeed a skyscraper, so I had to guess it had over fifty floors, but just how high were we going to climb?

Emily gently placed her free hand on mine, which was nervously clinging onto her arm, and gave it a slight squeeze. "Are you alright?"

"Yeah! Of course! I'm just slightly nervous, that's all. Can't help it, you know? First date and all..." Did I really call this a date? Yeah, it was a date, but to say it out loud with my chest? Emily giggled and pulled out her phone, unlocking it to show her home screen. On it was a picture of her and a beautiful Muslim woman in wedding gowns, holding the same bouquet of irises and sunflowers. I stared in awe at the picture as Emily explained.

"The first date I went on with Ameerah, I couldn't stop shaking. After meeting at a bar in Boystown, we went to dinner at a fancy restaurant a little further south of here. I thought for sure she wouldn't show up, but sure enough: she came to the table in a gorgeous purple dress. The rest was history."

My heart swelled a bit from the sweet story. "How long have you been married?"

"Five years now. Our anniversary is coming up next month." Emily was beaming at the mention of her marriage, and I couldn't help but internally coo at the happy occasion.

"Congratulations!" I cheered for her. Emily blushed and slid her phone back into her pocket.

"Don't be nervous, okay? Mister Hunter is a good guy deep

down. None of us would work for him otherwise." Emily stated, straightening her shoulders and looking up at the elevator floor screen. I did the same, letting her words sink in.

You didn't often hear praise for an employer, especially in our economy. So to hear such was a surprise to me. My mother barely spoke of him other than stating who he was in society. The only time she seemed to be in awe of him was when he came to the hospital to visit me, but I figured it was typical to kiss up to the boss when you worked in a cubicle.

Floor seventy-seven. The elevator stopped at last.

The doors opened to reveal a small hallway that led to a pair of black doors guarded by a man and a woman, both in matching suits. Was the security really needed? Where was I being taken? I could have sworn the hints laid out that I was going to have dinner with Liam.

Emily tilted her head to her shoulder opposite of me and whispered, "We have arrived." Was she speaking into a mic? Before I could question it, Emily gently led me forward into the hallway towards the doors. As we stepped past the halfway point, one of the doors opened, revealing a black man in a nicely tailored suit and a big smile. He made his way to us, tapping his fingers on a tablet attached to his hand via a velcro strap, and gave me a slight bow.

"Miss Augustine, thank you so much for coming! Mister Hunter is waiting inside." the man chirped. I suddenly recognized his voice.

"Glad to be here. Louis, right?" I inquired, causing him to place his free hand on his chest and coyly smile at Emily before turning his politely joyful gaze back to me.

"Yes indeed, Miss Augustine! A pleasure to meet you at last," Louis replied before holding out his hand to me. I took it and gave it a shake before Louis gently pulled away and turned to lead Emily and me further down the hall. "Follow me, please!"

Emily and I followed Louis to the doors, where the two guards eyed me up and down. Emily held up her hand to both guards as Louis opened both doors into the room beyond them.

<u>CHAPTER 5</u>

Proposition

I stepped inside to witness a small suite with windows covering eighty percent of the walls. Where there wasn't glass, there were marble and gold trimmings and wallpaper. Black, reflective tile decorated the floor; spotless and almost glimmering. Near the far window-wall was a table with two very comfy-looking chairs. The best sight, however, was the man who stood by the table.

That man was dressed in a finely tailored suit with a dark red undershirt and black tie. A part of me could not handle how visually handsome he was; his hair slicked back to accentuate his jade eyes. However, I could faintly catch how nervous he seemed to be as he fiddled with one of the cuffs of his sleeve.

I was thankful I wasn't the only one who was nervous now.

I released myself from Emily and continued forward, walking up to Liam with a smile.

"Liam." I greeted. Liam's eyes never left my form, and I felt almost naked under his gaze as he looked at me up and down. He was clearly dazzled by my outfit but gently held out his hand and smiled back.

"Maya." He replied as I placed my hand in his. Once again, he kissed over my knuckles, and I felt my heart swoon a bit as he kept his eyes locked with mine. I rolled my shoulders back, maintaining my composure as he came back up to his full height. Liam gestured to a chair at the lavishly set table with a nod. "Please."

I followed suit and walked over as Liam pulled out the seat for me. I was a bigger woman, so I slowly lowered myself down onto the chair and felt it being pushed under me. Liam knew, and I mentally thanked him for saving me the embarrassment of scooting the seat up myself, not knowing if he was strong enough to push me in. Liam walked over to his seat and sat down, returning the smile I was giving him. Before I could blink, a waitress walked over with a tablet and a polite bow.

"Welcome to the Gold Nest. It is a pleasure to serve you both." I became stunned as I heard her speak the restaurant's name. The Gold Nest? I had only heard of it from the food blog community, and it was an extremely rare chance to be able to even sample its offerings. Those who were able to practically chanted their praises of the meals they had, claiming it was a gem hidden away from Michelin's ever hawk-like rules and regulations. Yet here I was, about to have a hopefully delightful dinner at that very same establishment. Liam continued to surprise me. "Can I start you two off with anything?"

I looked to Liam, wondering if he had access to a menu I hadn't seen yet. He chuckled. "Let's start off with water with, perhaps, lime and lemon wedges on the side?" He suggested. I nodded, earning a smile of approval from the waitress. Her fingers clacked on her tablet. "And would you be so kind as to provide a menu? Miss Augustine is a first-time guest, and I did not reserve the set meal."

I giggled nervously, a blush washing over my cheeks as the waitress cooed and nodded again. "Right away. My apologies!" She replied before rushing towards a door in the corner of the room, most likely the restaurant's server area. Within moments, she returned with a menu decorated with gold trimmings, our glasses of water, and a saucer with lime and lemon wedges. "Here you are! Please, take your time."

I took the menu and looked it over; not surprised to see no prices for each item offered but also impressed at what was offered in general. "Oh wow..." I let those words escape my lips.

"They also allow substitutions if something doesn't suit your taste," Liam remarked, making me smirk a bit. Did he forget who I was or at least what my profession was?

"Why substitute anything I haven't tried first? You never know what you will like until you give it a shot." I mused, focusing on my menu and contemplating what I was in the mood for.

"Spoken like a true food critic." Liam complimented. My smirk turned into a grateful smile. "Might I then suggest the blue lobster thermidor? It's quite delicious."

"That does indeed sound as such. What do you plan to get, if I may ask?" I inquired.

"Perhaps the lamb loin. I'm quite a fan of the chef; she always swears by her lamb dishes." Liam mused. I tilted my head. Who was the chef? I quickly scanned through the menu, attempting to find a credit to their name, but found none.

"You know the chef?"

"I do indeed. She's not particularly a fan of publicity, but if you'd like to meet her, I can arrange that." Liam offered, causing me to lower the menu onto the table and shake my head. I did not want to impose at all. Besides, the evening was meant to be for Liam and me. A meeting with a mysterious chef could wait another time-- if there was another time.

"I'm sure she has her reasons, so there's no need." I looked back down onto the menu and nodded at my choice before looking up to the waitress, who stood dutifully waiting for our order. "The blue lobster thermidor, please."

"Would either of you like a drink to accompany your meals?" The waitress asked. "The chef would recommend a rosé or chardonnay for the lobster and a malbec or light red wine for the lamb loin."

"Maya?" Liam caught my attention, most likely wanting me to answer first.

I thought for a moment before finally replying, "The chardonnay sounds perfect, please." Liam nodded and turned his head to the waitress.

"A pinot noir. Have both of our drinks from the best bottles available. Thank you." Liam answered, earning an affirmative nod from the waitress.

"The blue lobster thermidor with chardonnay and lamb loin with pinot noir. Thank you so much! We'll be out with your meals soon." The waitress stated before taking the menu and walking away, leaving us alone.

With the conversation of food over, the music took control of the air, piquing my curiosity. It was a mixture of jazz and almost tango-style music dancing in the air, and it somehow made sense.

"Now, Maya, I have a question to ask if you don't mind," Liam said, setting his elbows on the table and lacing his fingers together, leaning over slightly so as to give me his full attention. My heart stopped for merely a moment. Was he going to confess a dark truth? Was my unlimited wish limited after all? I could tell he considered this a date just like I did, but where would he lead me?

No choice but to follow for now.

"Of course. What's the question?" I answered, sitting up in my chair and trying to prepare for anything he might have said. Liam relaxed his shoulders, reminding me that I was not the only one in the room who wasn't sure where the night would go.

"Would you allow me to explain myself before deciding on what to ask from me?" Liam's eyes seemed genuine in concern. I, however, became confused. What did he mean?

Was this about him mentioning how I saved his life? I couldn't piece together what he meant, but it seemed like the only question he could answer with such a request. I honestly couldn't see anything else that needed to be clear between us at the moment, and

I was okay with him explaining.

"Okay."

I slowly sat back, ready to hear some sort of story. Perhaps something happened while I was unconscious in the hospital? Or maybe he knew the thief who stole his car, and I was able to stop them from taking some sort of revenge on him? A couple of theories quickly zipped through my thoughts as I watched Liam lower his hands and take in a breath.

"When I say that you saved my life, I truly meant it. The car that was being stolen-- the one that ran into yours-- well... It is a very important car. It doesn't actually belong to me, but it belongs to a friend of my late father, and I had volunteered to retrieve it from the shop it was being worked on instead of one of his employees," Liam began. "Now, saving a car shouldn't mean much, but to the owner: the car has extreme value since it belonged to his father. This man is wealthy enough to own multiple cars, but the one I was tasked to get was the first his father ever purchased."

"I see... I didn't get to see it, so I wouldn't have known its significance." I joked, hoping the hilarity of it would land. As Liam chuckled, I mentally gave myself a high-five. Liam relaxed further afterward, leaning back in his own chair before continuing.

"Still, it was important that it didn't get taken. A car can always be fixed, but if it is taken, it may never be recovered. So while it was insanely unfortunate how the theft was stopped, I'm still grateful that you stopped it from happening. The owner is not exactly a forgiving man." Liam seemed very serious about his description of the owner. It was nice of him to get the car, but then a thought hit me: why was he at the store then?

"Wait, then..." I mentally recalled meeting him in the grocery store that day. If the car was that important, why did he not just drive it to the owner? "Why were you at the grocery store then? I remember us meeting in the spice aisle."

Liam's lips grew into a goofy smile as he rubbed the back of his neck. It was like I had caught him in some sort of hand-in-the-cookie-jar situation. "I made a stop on my way back to the owner. I was supposed to make and have dinner with him and others, but I was missing a key ingredient. I figured one stop wasn't going to hurt." He confessed, making me laugh.

"Well, I mean..." I began before stopping myself and stifling another giggle. It didn't hurt *him*, but it did hurt enough to send me to a hospital. I had to stop. While I found my jokes funny, this was still a date. Who knew if my joking continuously would be a good or bad thing here?

He somehow caught on and laughed as well. I listened to it and felt my heart patter at how attractive it sounded, despite it just being a laugh. I couldn't control myself and let myself continue to laugh along with him with a grin stretched from cheek to cheek. There was some relief in my chest, but as we laughed together, I felt my introverted demeanor sink into my thoughts. Enough now, Maya.

I slowly came down and let out a sigh, back down to earth as

Liam seemed to do the same. He gave a slightly toothy smile.

"I knew I would like you the moment we got to talk at the art gallery." Liam professed, suddenly turning my mental state of relaxation to stunned shyness. What? That came out of nowhere. How did he determine that from my laugh? My joke that he understood without me even vocalizing the entirety of? My face became red as I stared at him in timid confusion.

"What do you mean?" I let myself ask. What did he mean, Maya? He liked me. Duh. Anyone could have seen it. Yet some part of me didn't understand. We met only a handful of times, but he claimed to know his feelings about me within that span. I did as well, but I could tell my emotions were more curious and willing to experiment rather than confirming genuine affection versus whimsical fantasy.

Liam gave me a charming look and slowly placed his hand towards me in the middle of the table. I looked down at his open palm, knowing he wanted my hand in his, and let myself oblige. Then, as my hand rested on his, I watched his thumb caress the back of my hand before I looked back up at him.

"You're a beautiful woman. Beautiful and kind, I can tell. The way you speak comes from the heart rather than just out of manners or practice. I admire that a lot." Liam said, letting each word of his compliment melt into my mind. I sat there silently, listening and allowing him to dissect me in adoring praise. "There's no doubt that you're quite intelligent; enough to find a passion and make it a career. Your sense of humor is brilliant, and it matches mine. There are many more things about you that I find intriguing, and that was from only knowing you a short while."

"You're too kind..." I could only mutter back, truly astonished at his words. Part of me wanted to believe that this was all a ruse for a one-night stand, yet the other half didn't think a one-night stand would need a private escort, dinner, compliments up the wahzoo, and an unlimited wish. He flattered me enough to make intentions up to me and how far I myself was willing to go.

My mind had to remind me that this was the first date. Don't make a volcano of an ant hill. This could go south in many ways, no matter what compliments he gave me. I had to feel this out from beginning to end.

I took a breath and finally settled down before returning the compliments with a squeeze from my hand to his. "Well, you are just as charming. Well-spoken, a genius of your own right-- enough to have a business that towers above so many others. You're very impressive, Liam." I returned the praise, making Liam's eyes go slightly wide in surprise. Did he not expect me to say what I said? Did he think I was going to keep silent the whole time and not reciprocate?

After a brief moment of silence, Liam smiled and chuckled, lowering his head and relaxing. He returned the squeeze I gave him and placed his free hand over mine. "How on Earth did I get so lucky enough to meet you?" I barely heard him mutter to the tabletop.

"I'm the lucky one..." I muttered to myself, practically uncaring if Liam heard my words. However, the truth ultimately melded between both of our confessions. If both of us were even content with this encounter, we were both equally lucky to be together at that moment.

Liam slowly looked up, the thin rings of jade once again taking over his eyes. It was familiar, and I knew well enough: He wanted me. But would he ask? Would he impose such a desire on a date like this, the first time we sat down together? Or would this be a slow burn that would work its way into my body to where I would give in and demand it? I knew the power I had in that moment, which was intriguing.

The world around me became dark, with only Liam being illuminated for me like a spotlight was on him to keep my focus on him. My thoughts wandered to the soft feel of his hands around mine. I felt protected yet beguiled by a simple pair of hands. The simple caress of his thumb over my skin sent tiny shivers up and down my spine. My already strange attraction to him continued to increase, a desire to know becoming more of a craving to get closer in mind and body. How did he make love? Did he make love at all? Was he a man who just had sex without the need for romance? How would this man feel above, below, or even behind me?

My curiosity was never-ending, which was always my weakness. I was not a fool or stranger to sex and love, despite choosing not to frivolously fuck. Anyone who liked sex would have the imagination to fantasize about things they've not experienced yet, including people they never shared more than a glance with. I even collected erotica to read in my free time, embracing my desires and being unashamed of spending my liquid funds on supporting dark romance writers of all kinds.

My mind painted a dark room, like one of his sister's paintings, where the ones illuminated by the moon were Liam and me. Entangled in the sheets, we held on to each other like the night would end sooner than our passions would have allowed. Liam's soft hands ran up and down my sides with possession and adoration as his lips graced mine with passionate kisses. My moans echoed into the air as his lips trailed down my cheek and neck, gentle yet powerful licks peppered between each kiss.

How much harder could he go? My thoughts imagined him occasionally gripping my sides as his teeth only ever so slightly grazed over my skin, teasing me to potential danger but holding back with no permission. A perfect tease. My hand gripping the back of his neck and scratching down his arm was enough to push the boundary even farther. I could play with him in my mind, balanced to my personal tastes.

A voice was the only thing that broke me out of my mental contemplation of sleeping with Liam.

"Li-- uh, Mister Hunter. A call." Louis's voice timidly interrupted. I barely took notice of his frame stepping up beside

Liam as I kept my sights locked on target. Liam seemed to refuse or not listen to Louis, keeping his wanting gaze at me. The world had become ours, but still, Louis tried to invade. "A call from Mariana."

"Tell her I'm at a very important dinner," Liam replied, a hint of irritation buried beneath his response. Still, he refused to turn away from me or release my hand, seemingly finding comfort with my touch and my eyes. I couldn't help but question who Mariana was, but I could only mentally list her as someone not worthy enough to break Liam's focus on me. My confidence definitely got a boost despite a small voice in the back of my mind growing ever curious about who Mariana was. Louis's breath hitched slightly as if he wanted to speak more, but Liam continued. "Unless it's an emergency, I am not available."

Louis stepped back, and I felt the world slowly return. Perhaps the voice in my head got louder. What if Mariana.... no. Who is she first? A friend? A lover? Family? What if I misinterpret the situation? I did not want to fall into a hole that would end with me being embarrassed. Nevertheless, my tunnel vision disappeared. I took a breath and let my mind completely clear, not wanting to hear my doubt and sacrificing my pleasure at being emotionally alone with Liam in order to silence the former.

Liam let out a small sigh and slowly released my hand, sitting back up and running a hand over his hair. I also sighed, saddened that my fantasy was broken but settling into reality. I readjusted myself in my seat and rolled my neck, feeling it needed a slight stretch. As I did, the smell of food entered my nostrils and caused me to look around for the source. Our waitress wheeled a cart with two covered plates over to the table. With a smile, the waitress revealed the dishes with a flourish of steam. I was floored by my blue lobster dish before it was even placed on my side of the table. I barely even noticed the drinks being placed meticulously as well; my sight locked on the delicious meal in front of me.

Liam's chuckle broke my attention. "Will you be writing about this on your blog?" He inquired with a slight smirk. I half-forgotten that I was a food blogger but laughed softly.

"Maybe. Not many people get to post about the Gold Nest. It would be quite a privilege to do so." I noted as the waitress bowed silently and rolled the cart away from us, not wanting to disturb us. Liam took up his glass with me following behind with my own.

"Well then, I'm sure the review will be fair and tantalizing," Liam stated, raising his glass to me. "Please enjoy."

I raised my glass in return before sipping at the same time as him. I wasn't a big fan of alcohol-- only drinking it in pairs with food or mixed for small cocktails-- yet the flavor was refreshing. I was mildly taken aback by the experience. The chardonnay was unbelievably good. Was the care behind the price point the reason? I didn't hesitate to ride the positive start. I lowered my glass to the table and started on my lobster. It was an ocean of pleasure in my mouth, and I felt my body melt into the flavors. My head fell back on its own as a moan escaped my lips, the experience on my tongue overtaking me.

As I lifted my head back up to look at Liam and recenter myself, I noticed a tiny hint of red glow on his cheeks with the already thin jade rings in his eyes thinning even more. My moan must have gotten to him, and I felt myself internally go crazy from embarrassment. It wasn't my intention to tease him, yet there we were. Before I could react, however, Liam began to eat his lamb loin; a smile on his face as if I had done nothing of the teasing sort.

<u>Chapter 6</u>

Intoxication

We took our time to eat, and I had to thank every star in the sky for the ability to do so. My mind was going at insane speeds, trying to dissect and enjoy my meal. It was a new experience for me, and I wasn't even sure how I was going to write about eating such a delicious meal. But, then again, did I have to? This was a date. Should I have been so focused on work? Why not just enjoy the meal?

Our talking was brief, as we both were absorbed in the pleasure of dinner. Still, I was able to glean small bits of info from Liam as he did from me. I had been working on food blogging for almost five years, starting in college with simple hack recipes for college students and evolving into home tips and reviews for cooking. He surprisingly wasn't at the top of his class when he graduated but had started his business immediately after throwing his graduation cap. Our conversation helped slow our eating pace, letting us take in every spice and flavor our meals had to offer.

With my plate cleaned, I let out a sigh and sat back, taking in the aftermath of a truly indescribable meal. Liam finished quickly after me, finishing his glass of wine.

"I take it you enjoyed your lobster?" Liam asked with a

conspicuously raised eyebrow. I nodded, unable to form words in reply, and earned a chuckle from the handsome gentleman across from me. "Very good. I'll make sure to let the chef know."

"Do you eat like this all of the time?" I asked, letting the random question out to find some form of conversation mid-euphoria. Liam's chuckle became a laugh as he shook his head.

"Very rarely. You'd be surprised how rarely I eat out like this." Liam confessed. I raised an eyebrow of my own, surprised that my brain's image of luxury didn't exactly match reality.

"Truly?"

"Yes. In fact, I try to cook on my own more often than not, and it's not often that I cook for others unless it's for my family. It's easy to feed one mouth when it's your own."

"So, you live alone?"

"I do. Are you interested in moving in?" Liam's teasing remark stunned me for a moment. His smirk indicated it was a mildly flirtatious joke, but there was something I was sensing behind his words that was genuine to the curiosity.

If it's a game he wants, a game shall be played...

For some reason, I felt like playing along. Something in my mind ushered me forward.

"That depends. Would you count it as my wish if I was?" I replied, matching his flirty tone with my own. I caught his eyes widening ever so slightly, but his expression remained calm, only his smile becoming a confident smirk. I grew bolder and felt my spirit's shy uncertainty lower its volume in my head.

"Is that what you wish for? I did indeed say anything was yours if you wanted it." Liam repeated, slowing each word to emphasize how serious he was. My mind immediately pointed at him as what I wanted at that very moment, but was it a fleeting sexual desire, or was it something else that made him the object of what I wanted to wish for? I tried to think about it, but some train of instinct pushed me farther into the charm of the conversation.

"Anything, huh? You seem very insistent about that. What if I asked for something ridiculous?" I pressed, wanting to test his limits. I took a moment to truly observe Liam as a man. He was handsome and perfect for my fantasies. Something about him wanted me to both know him more and tear his clothes off. Maybe this conversation was the chance to let me decide how I wanted the dice to fall.

"Like what? Tell me what you want." Liam's voice dropped slightly, causing some sort of tingle to resonate in my core in desire. It was like a command, and I instinctively felt like following it to please him and my own mental submission to him. It was him I wanted at that moment, and I stopped giving a damn why. I just needed to figure out how I was going to close the gap between Liam and me without it becoming a one-and-done night of romance. Why give up something that seemed like a good time for a long time, just for a one-time fling?

Keep going.

"I would, but I did want to ask how much you'd be truly willing to give," I pressed even farther. I was playing with fire in multiple ways, but I had to press down the introvert deep into my chest to let my inner charmer out. The shy woman was silenced for now. "The word anything is too vague. I could ask for a country, a fantasy you can't make real..."

I felt myself slowly stand and walk around the table. I knew I had to be confident to play the game, but I did not expect my body to immediately lean into the role I was putting up. The back of my mind desperately tried to pound the abort button. This was too much. I was diving into territories that might have turned him off. What if I was playing with a fire that wasn't burning for me? What if I was painting a picture that wasn't real?

The carnal part of my brain said no and didn't care. It was done being polite, shy, and cute around this man who intrigued me so much. I somehow *needed* to know how deep the hole was that I was diving into, and the only way I was going to learn was if I took the leap without hesitation.

Liam also stood from his chair and met me halfway, looking down at me and burning his gaze into my eyes. His irises were fully blown out, only a thread of jade color circling them. Full lust. Was it real? His breath was slow but heavy as if he was controlling something within him. I wanted to see him break at that very moment, but I pushed forward, unrelenting if he did or not.

"Are you sure *anything* is on the menu?" I asked, letting my voice drop low and leaning in to barely be inches away from his face. His cologne caught me and only enhanced the hot spell I was feeling in my body. I was so close to the water of this dangerous ocean that my body almost pressed up against his chest in need to close the gap.

"Yes." Liam's voice was deep and low in reply, almost making me quake at his singular word. What was happening? I had lost control. "Tell me."

I felt myself lick my lips slightly, immediately wanting to say it was him I wanted. How fast would he grab me and devour me? Would he fuck me on the table, pushing everything out of the way and having me in that room? Would he tease me further? I looked up at him from under my eyelashes, tearing the last bit of resistance I had in my mind with my words.

"I want you."

I said it. I said it out loud, and now it was in the air.

And I didn't give a fuck.

The second my wish left my lips, the world became still.

The next, Liam grabbed my waist with one hand and the back of my neck with the other, pulling me into a deep kiss that felt like fireworks. I moaned hard against his lips and wrapped my arms around him in return, pouring my desires into the kiss. My fantasy painted an idea, but reality was much better in feeling his lips on mine. I was more than happy to have this and more.

Liam's hand on my waist slowly dragged itself down to my hip and gave it a firm squeeze, making me bring up my leg to his waist and push myself against him harder. His hand followed my leg and hooked itself under my knee to support me with his thumb happily caressing my skin under the slit in my dress on the way. I kissed him with as much passion as I could give under such pleasure, taking precious milliseconds of breath between each kiss he laid on me.

How could this man completely intoxicate me with just dinner and some words? Was I indeed in need of him? Nothing in my body was protesting anymore, not even as I slowly dragged my hand up and ran my fingers over his coarse hair. The feeling earned me a slight growl from him, shooting a shiver through me that made me weak in my one standing leg.

I completely fell into his arms, powerless against Liam, and felt him hold me up without a struggle. He was strong enough to keep hold of me, making me swoon harder. I almost whined when he pulled away from the kiss we shared ever so slightly. We panted for air, only then realizing how out of breath we were until he spoke.

"Shall we go to my place?" Liam whispered, the intent perfectly clear and agreeable for both of us. I nodded, my face flushed with pleasured fever and my mind full of eager excitement.

With my arm in his, Liam quickly led me out of the room and towards the elevator. My mind barely had time to catch up to me being led into the underground parking garage and guided into an even fancier luxury car, where I was driven to another building. All that mattered to me was every kiss we claimed on each other's lips, heated and full of fire. His hands were teasingly slow, keeping me on the edge of madness and euphoria with every stroke of his fingers on my waist and arms. Liam definitely knew how to keep me wanting and eager to follow.

The ride became a blur as we came up on another skyscraper. The car drove into the underground lot and, soon enough, I was guided out of the car and into another elevator. We didn't even wait for the doors to close and for the box to ascend before Liam pinned my arms above my head against the far wall and ravished me with more heated kisses. I tossed caution to the wind and hopped up, wrapping my legs around his waist. Liam easily caught me with one arm under my thigh and his body pinning my body against the wall to keep me up.

I could feel his desire for me rub up against mine, making me moan wildly against his lips. I knew he was going to fill me up just from how hard he felt. I could barely hang on enough, only being patient in knowing the pleasure would be worth the wait. Liam slowly began grinding his hips into mine, almost growling in need against my lips. I moaned back in kind, feeling my throbbing pussy quiver with each rub of his crotch against it.

"Maya..." Liam moaned as he trailed his kisses across my lips and cheek to my neck. I let out a guttural groan of pleasure as his tongue ran over my skin. Shivers rippled down my spine from the sensation, and I could not hold back my voice in praise of Liam's touch. His lips, his tongue, his *teeth*... I was melting into the euphoria of it all against my neck. As he ran his hand down my arm and side, I shook involuntarily before gasping when his hand reached to grasp my ass cheek. His hands were large enough to cup a good portion of it and massage it, forcing a pleasured mewl to escape my lips.

This man knew exactly what he was doing to me.

The elevator doors opened to a new space, but I did not care to take in the sights of where I was. Liam quickly pulled me from the wall, wrapping his free arm around my back to support me as I instinctively wrapped my arms around his shoulders.

What surprised me was him softly biting down on my neck as he began to walk out of the elevator. I gasped and squeezed myself around Liam in reply as he marched in fervor through the ample space, down a hallway, and only turned to shoulder-shove a door open to a bedroom. It was huge, but the only thing I cared to take note of was his large king-sized bed covered in soft black sheets.

He lowered me to the edge of the bed, pulling up the bottom of the dress to expose my legs and panties and seat me skin-to-sheets on his mattress. As he settled on his knees between my legs, his hands continued to slide my dress up my body and dance each finger against my skin. I quickly pulled the dress off, tired of having it on and needing air to cool against my burning body, and tossed it away into some secluded corner of the room.

Before I could let Liam do anything else, I grabbed his head and kissed him again, running my teeth along his bottom lip and biting down softly to pay back the bite on my neck he gave me. His breath hitched, and I could barely contain myself at the sound of him growling hard against my lips. His fingers had flexed and dug themselves into my sides in pleasure, making me grip his head tighter between my hands. The sounds he made drove me nuts, and I wanted to hear more as I was sure he wanted to listen to me as well.

Liam's hands quickly slid up and unlatched my bra behind my back, allowing it to slack down from my chest. He followed the straps of it down to slide it away from my body before grasping it and almost whipping it around one of the bedposts instead of just tossing it into the dark of the room. How polite of him.

As he freed me of my clothes, I let my hands wander down his neck and shoulders, pushing away his suit jacket. Liam obliged and moved his arms to help me remove the jacket in question, using a hand to toss it towards a set of chairs as I used mine to release each button of his shirt beneath his tie. This was a damn tease on its own. I wanted to feel more of his skin on mine, and it took every ounce of control I had not to rip the damn shirt open. Liam took care of his tie, throwing it off his neck and letting it fly to where his jacket was discarded.

At his last button, I practically shoved the shirt down his shoulders and arms just to see his chest. He was toned and strong, enough to carry me through his apparent home. I swooned at how his chest swelled and sank with each heated breath he gave. I leaned back, watching him remove his shirt and toss it away, and drank in the sight of the man who was going to rail me into his mattress. A smirk danced itself onto Liam's lips as I licked my own.

"Like what you see?" Liam asked. I nodded, obviously impressed and eager. He chuckled before kissing me hotly and trailing kisses down my chin to my neck and chest. I tossed my head back, allowing every moan in my body to freely escape my voice as Liam kissed and licked over every sensitive spot on my skin. He took his time with each breast, massaging and squeezing one as he gave oral praise to the other before switching and giving fair love. He only gave a slight pause to speak before kissing down my stomach. "I absolutely want what I see."

His fingers latched onto the straps of my panties and began to tug them down my thighs. I lifted my hips, allowing it to be stripped off my body and down past my knees. As it fell past my toes onto the floor, Liam gently cuffed my ankles with his fingers and slowly lifted them to his shoulders. I could only lean back at the angle, gasping as his eyes peeked over the curve of my stomach with glistening lust and intent.

Then his face ducked down, and I felt it, his tongue teasingly dancing over my heated and already dripping pussy. I let out a helpless gasp and mewled at his mouth, feeling him kiss, lick, and suck over each centimeter of my heat. My body shivered when he brushed the tip of his tongue over my clit. He knew exactly how to please and continued to massage and rub my sensitive button, occasionally lowering his tongue to lick up and down the slit of my pussy.

I gripped the top of his head with my hand, running my fingers through his hair and combing my nails over his scalp in ecstasy. He was making me feel so heavenly, and I could do nothing but buck and bend to his touch. I happily welcomed his finger inside of me, only held down by one of his hands on my thigh to keep my legs open to him and moaning without restraint. He was meticulous as he caressed each crevice within my core with his fingertip, easing and teasing me to the prospect of something bigger coming soon.

I was his and allowed myself to simply feel pleasure. I was already soaked and ready for him, but he made sure that I was on the edge of begging. I became breathless by the time Liam slowly began to rise from the floor and unbuckle his pants. He slid down his pants and boxer briefs and bent forward to tuck his arm under my back. I grasped his shoulders and felt him lift and slide me farther up the bed to where my head rested against the softest pillows I had the pleasure of laying upon.

I was happily stunned at one thing: his cock. It rested against my crotch as he lowered me to the bed, and I could tell that I was going to be stretched perfectly by him in length and girth. I licked my lips in excitement, practically purring as Liam gyrated his hips and let his cock slide over my clit in stimulation. I barely noticed one hand slip by my head and into another pillow, only turning my head to see his hand pull out a condom from the pillowcase.

Fuck, he was considerate too?

I looked up at Liam to see him raise an eyebrow at me, panting in the heat of his own desire. That's when I noticed it: he was barely hanging onto some sort of internal control. It was commendable, and I felt a twinge of curiosity about what he was holding back, but I knew he was waiting for me to give a go-ahead of some kind without directly asking and breaking the line of passion we were building.

I nodded. Better safe than sorry.

Liam nodded in return and leaned down to kiss me hotly as he quickly opened the condom packet. It took me biting his lower lip again and leaning up to make him pull away softly with a slightly confused look. I wasn't going to be the only one pampered tonight.

I took the condom with one hand and slowly traced down his chest with the other, only softly scratching at his skin with my nails. His body shuddered, and a pleasured sigh escaped Liam's lips at my touch. When I finally reached his dick, I let my fingers glide over the length, earning more shivers and a groan of joy. He was perfect in my hand, and I was doubly assured that he would rock my world with what he was given.

I happily took my time, wrapping my hand around his hard-on and pumping him slowly to keep him hard and hot. He was practically thrusting against my hand as his own almost scratched against my sides in need. He was barely hanging on, and so was I, but I could tell we both were going to be rewarded for our patience. I finally slipped the condom over his cock, tapping it at the base to mentally secure my doubts, before laying back and lifting my legs with my hands gripping the back of my knees.

All it took was a wink from me to make Liam lean into me and kiss me deeply, sliding one hand beneath my shoulder to support me and the other to guide his dick to my pussy and line up the tip to the entrance. He was smart enough to know where to aim, and only moans escaped us as he finally pushed into my body. I was right. He was absolutely perfect. He took it slow, but he gave me every inch to stretch around, and I felt full.

"Liam!" I cried out happily, feeling ecstasy from the single thrust and wanting to feel it rail me down. Liam growled with a pleasured smirk, staring down at me and making me instinctively squeeze over him.

"Maya..." He lustfully replied, slowly starting to thrust back and forth in and out of me. God, he was hitting every pleasurable spot within me, and my body could do nothing but grip onto his shoulders and back. I didn't even care to hold back scratching over his skin from the ecstasy. His muscles flexed as he tucked his arms beneath me and cupped my head before fucking me faster. He made sure to make me moan out to each thrust, each inch that brushed inside of my pussy over and over.

My mind was filled as perfectly as my sex with Liam. He was perfect. He felt so good, and I didn't care for anything but to have this man inside of me for as long as possible. I wrapped my legs around his waist, pulling him even closer before pulling his head down to kiss him hard. Our moans muffled against each other's lips as he fucked me harder into the mattress. One of his hands slid down to wrap around my waist, and it practically held me in place to let him thrust from tip to base, only intensifying the pleasure between us.

I was quickly climbing to my orgasm, shaking wildly beneath him. It wasn't hard to cum when the buildup was teetering you over the edge, and the sex practically tossed you over without mercy. I eagerly let myself drown in the pleasure and felt it ripple through my body, shaking as I came. I screamed Liam's name and felt my entire body tighten around him.

It was glorious.

I felt breathless as he held me close in his arms and let me cum over his cock. As I settled, he began to slowly thrust again, igniting my pleasure once again from the bottom. He got me to cum, but was he satisfied with being within me? His moans and grunts of pleasure seemed to signal such, so I let myself fall back into his rhythm. That night was ours, and I was more than willing to ride him until sunrise.

His speed increased, as did his passion. His fingers gripped onto me, and I could feel him flex to ensure we both felt amazing. Still, he kept his eyes on me, and I felt helpless beneath him. He happily watched me moan and wordlessly beg for more of him with my hands and legs. He obliged my kisses and returned each with passionate desire in kind.

He was a perfect partner.

Time slipped away, and all I could feel was pleasure and the ache of euphoria. I didn't care how long our sex was, but I rode with Liam until he finally began to rut roughly against me in his orgasm. I quickly gripped his head and kissed him hard, wrapping my other hand around his back and pulling him against me. As he reached his climax, his body tensed, and he let out a roar of a moan, vocalizing my name in his pleasure.

Fuck, he sounded so hot, screaming my name.

I held him close and let him rut against me as he spilled into the condom. As we finally calmed our breaths, Liam slowly and carefully pulled out despite my mewls of protest. I felt empty without him within me, but I knew better. He gently shuffled to the side to discard the condom in a wastebasket near the bed before laying beside me and opening his arms. I happily slid between them and cuddled close to his warm body.

I was happy and content. Would more come? Maybe, but the night was perfect for me. I looked up and smiled at Liam, allowing him to know my contentment with the wish I had made.

Liam stared deep into my eyes and softly smiled as if he had read my mind. He brushed my hair with his fingers, and I could feel myself fall into the depths of slumber.

<u>Chapter 7</u>

Realization

I felt myself naturally open my eyes, sleep finally releasing its claim on me. My body was covered with a soft black blanket, and the sun was peeking in from a window across the room. Slowly waking, I took in my surroundings. The bedroom I was in was pretty lavish; a table with matching cushioned chairs sat by a small digital fireplace while a closet and mirror stationed themselves across from the opposite wall. The walls were a darker color, but the room somehow seemed bright, perhaps because of the window.

One thing was missing: Liam.

I looked around, wondering if he was in the room, but found myself alone. However, one glance at my side revealed a thornless rose and a note. A blush crossed my cheeks as I lifted the message to read it.

'In the kitchen making breakfast. Robes are in the closet.'

I smiled. At least Liam was considerate enough to let me know instead of just leaving me in bed alone. I crawled out of bed and walked to the closet, opening it to see an array of fluffy and silky robes to wear. While they weren't fit for a plus-size woman, they looked comfortable just looking at them. I took one of the silky robes and tried my best to cover my body with it. A little cleavage spilled from the top, but at least I wasn't bare.

I made my way out of the bedroom and followed my nose down the hall. It was a very lavish studio loft just from the decor and structure alone, but the kitchen was easy to find. The soft sounds of bossa nova music emanated around the corner of the hall, dancing with the smell of bacon and pancakes.

As I turned the corner, I felt myself smile at the sight of a shirtless Liam swaying to the music as he fried some bacon. There he was, the man that would destroy any future man's attempts to pleasure me. How lucky was I?

Very.

I silently walked to the counter, not wanting to disturb Liam's musical number, and waited for him to notice. As the song ended, Liam turned his head and chuckled.

"Good morning, Maya," he greeted, turning to slide some bacon from his pan to a paper-towel-covered plate. "Did you have a good night?"

I playfully pursed my lips at his question. How cheeky. I shrugged and leaned against the counter. "I mean, *I* had a perfect night. I don't know about you." I teased, looking up at the high ceiling with a coy smile.

Liam laughed and set the pan down on the stove before walking over to me and gently lifting my hand. I watched as he kissed my knuckles, locking my eyes with his loving gaze. "Glad to hear it. How do you like your eggs?"

"Over-medium, please. Also, where's your bathroom?"

To my surprise, Liam lifted my hand and gently spun me around, making me giggle as he faced me towards the hallway I emerged from. "Down the hall, second door on the left," Liam whispered into my ear before releasing my hand and walking to the fridge. I smiled back at him before making my way to the bathroom to freshen up.

As I looked at myself in the mirror, I noted the love bites and hickeys he had left behind. Of course, there were many perceptions of sex and the aftermath. It was a thrill when you stood after a night of passionate fucking, relishing the memories and taking mental victory laps at your experience.

Still, a small ping of worry took hold of my thoughts: was this a one-night stand?

Sure, he was making me breakfast, and he was charming, but was this all he was willing to give as the fulfillment of my wish? I did say that I wanted him. Was this how he interpreted it? What happens now? Any lover has or would have felt this doubt. I just wished that I didn't have to know the answer.

A sigh escaped me before I gathered myself up and returned to the kitchen to see Liam plating up some bacon, pancakes, and the eggs I asked for. I smiled and moved to sit on the counter stools but was stopped by Liam taking my plate and a second plate full of food towards another open area with a dining table. He placed the plates down at two chairs hugging the corner of the table and pulled out my seat for me.

"Thank you," I said with a polite nod before sitting down.

He moved a small container of condiments nearby and took a step away from me. "Any requests for a drink?" He asked with a simple smile.

"Do you have any orange juice?" I inquired, only to earn a wink and nod in return. I watched as Liam, clad in only a pair of sweatpants, obtained a gallon of orange juice and two glasses before returning to me. He poured us both a drink and set the gallon by the condiments before sitting beside me.

Before I could even start eating, however, he spoke.

"You know last night doesn't count as your wish, right?"

Thankfully I didn't put any food in my mouth, or I would have spat it out in surprise. I shot my gaze at Liam in shock, confused about what he meant. He did fulfill it, though. I wanted him, and I got him the previous night. How was that not fulfilling my wish at all?

"W-What do you mean?" I stammered in confusion. Liam chuckled before cutting out a piece of his fried eggs and eating it.

"Your wish was... *too vague*." Liam playfully replied, a smirk dancing on the edge of his lips. He was using my argument against me. How dare he? It was cute as hell, but the audacity of the man sitting beside me was enormous. "Besides, I also had a wonderful night, and your wish should absolutely be selfish to only your desires..."

I let out a sigh, stunned that my playful banter was being fired back at me. My face was red from the fact Liam also desired and loved my company, but still. So, I had to make another wish. Well, that wasn't bad, but the prospect of me doubting the night was moot now. He seemed content to have had the night with me, so another free wish was fine by me.

"Very well, Liam. I'll be more specific next time." I tossed back at him, puffing out my chest before eating breakfast. I barely caught a small smile on Liam's lips before he began eating. Breakfast was nice, especially when I didn't have to cook it myself. Liam's cooking wasn't perfect by any means, but I still liked every bite.

Simple was good. The feeling in the air was simple joy, and I melted into it. It was nice to imagine every day like it for a while, even as my plate grew emptier and emptier. Could I have something like this? With Liam?

My thoughts broke at the sound of a mambo ringtone echoing between Liam and me. Without hesitation, Liam reached into his pocket and pulled out his phone. One button was pressed, and the call was answered.

"Good morning, Louis," Liam spoke, using another finger to turn the speakerphone on.

"Liam, let me up. I have Miss Augustine's bag." Louis declared. I went pale. I left my bag at the restaurant. I was too busy smacking my lips against Liam's to care about my personal belongings, but who could blame me?

Then I remembered: I was supposed to go home. I could practically hear my mother's heart attack in my head. Did she call me? Did she call the police?

Oh no.

Liam stood from his chair and jogged to the other side of the room where the elevator to the garage was, leaving his phone on the table.

"Um, Louis?" I meekly called out to the phone, unable to process the panic rising in me. "My phone is in there, right?"

"Miss Augustine! Oh yes, your phone is in the bag. I have not touched anything." Louis replied, a mild one-eighty in energy from Liam to me in his voice.

"Could you check to see if it's been ringing?" I asked, preparing for the worst. After a moment of silence with some minor shuffling noises later, I got a reply.

"Oh... oh dear. You have thirty missed calls."

I'm dead.

My panic festered into my hands as I began to shovel food into my mouth. I needed to eat, then I needed to leave. I had to find my clothes, get dressed, grab my bag, and get to my house before I became a picture on a wanted poster. I knew logically that my mother would never do that, but after the accident, who knew where her panic would take her?

I barely finished eating as the elevator doors opened to reveal Louis. Somehow sensing my panic, Louis rushed past Liam, practically shoulder chucking him, and held out my phone to me. It was already ringing for my mother. Bless him.

I took the phone and got it up to my ear before hearing her voice.

"Maya!?" Her voice was hoarse and tired. I knew I had screwed up.

"Mom, it's me. I'm alive. I'm sorry." I began, not knowing if my words would convince her to be calm or ignite her rage. "I forgot my bag at the restaurant Liam took me to--"

"Maya." Her voice dropped hard with stern seriousness. I stopped talking. I listened as she took a breath.

I was an adult. There wasn't anything to be ashamed of. Yet here I was, worried beyond reason that I was giving my mother a heart attack when she had already seen me in a hospital bed not long before.

"If you were going to sleep with my boss, a text would have been nice."

I practically snorted at her words. I covered my mouth and nose in case, but I stared at the floor, unbelieving at what my mother spurted out. "MOM!"

"You are safe, though, right?"

"Yes, I'm safe. I just finished eating breakfast."

"Where?"

"...Liam's place. He cooked."

Silence. Liam and Louis looked at me with a mixture of concern

85

and held-back laughter. This situation was hilarious, but I wasn't in a position to laugh with my worried mother on one end of the phone and the man I slept with standing near me with his secretary.

"Well then. Please come home when you're done. Your father was worried as much as I was, and the last thing we need is to put him in the hospital after you had just recently gotten out of it."

I grimaced. I wasn't a child, but it was sort of irresponsible to let them worry for no reason. I had my hands full of Liam and simply forgot. "Alright, I'll be home soon," I answered.

"Alright. Be safe. I love you."

"Love you too, mom." I hung up and slumped into my chair with a sigh. Louis slowly walked up and placed my bag beside me on the dining table before turning to Liam with crossed arms.

"And you didn't think to grab her bag on your way out?" Louis scolded Liam with a raised eyebrow. Liam and I both blushed deeply at the incident, though I was a little shocked at how Louis was acting.

"Well... you see--" Liam started before Louis cleared his throat and held up his hand to silence him.

"I'm no stranger to cleaning up after your messes, but don't get *her* into trouble over *your* dumb mistakes. You know better." Louis lectured before turning to me with a smile. "I'll go ahead and arrange a car for you, Miss Augustine." Louis finished before spinning on his heel and walking back towards the elevator. "And call Mariana before she kills you, Liam."

As Louis disappeared behind the closing elevator doors, Liam let out a sigh, and I couldn't help but giggle at his worn face. The charming CEO had an imperfect face, after all. At my laugh, Liam lifted his head and looked at me in surprise. I shrugged with a coy smile.

"We both messed up, I guess. I left my bag, and you ignored a call from... Mariana?" I repeated, curious as to who the mysterious woman was. Liam nodded and rubbed the back of his neck.

"Mariana is my sister. She's also the artist who painted the pieces at the gallery." Liam confessed, moving to the table to retrieve his phone. As he scrolled through it, he brushed his hair back. "Probably another piece needing a model or financing."

With a nod, I felt my heart release its fear of a potential rival. Wait. Rival? Liam wasn't mine. We had sex once. That wasn't a commitment. He wasn't claimed.

I closed my eyes and let out a small sigh before gathering my bag and repocketing my phone into its interior. "I should probably gather my things then. Wouldn't want to keep my problem waiting."

Liam's shoulders slumped slightly, but he walked over and took my hand. "I would escort you home myself, but I should follow my secretary's instructions. The last thing I'd want is to anger my sister further before having the chance for a second date with you."

That took me aback. Liam wanted a second date.

"A second date?"

"Is there a problem with wanting that, Maya?" Liam inquired, lifting my hand to kiss my knuckles with his gaze locked on mine. My heart fluttered, but I was able to keep myself together despite his lips on my skin. "Perhaps then you'll have a deep wish I can grant."

I smiled up at Liam and nodded, but not before a soft giggle escaped me. "You really need to be careful with how vague you are."

Liam raised an eyebrow and smirked playfully. "What do you mean?"

"You just handed me another wish without any limitations. That's dangerous."

I meant to lighten the mood, knowing that this was goodbye for now, but Liam made me gasp as he pulled me close and wrapped an arm behind my back. He slowly laid his forehead against mine and gave a low chuckle, vocally prodding at my infatuation with him. I instantly looked into his eyes to see a more profound desire than the lust he initially stared me down with.

"Perhaps... but I like a little danger..." Liam whispered in the sexy low tone that drove me crazy internally. For the first time in my adult life, I mentally damned my mother to hell for her promise and damned myself for being a good daughter.

~ ~ ~

To think a man could burn an impression into my soul. I didn't want to leave, but I went with a whispered promise in my ear. *"When you want me, we'll arrange a second date."*

I sat at my desk, mentally swooning over the potential of a second date. Liam was indeed handsome and charming, so a second date with him, even without the promise of more, was a desirable treat any man-chaser would have drooled over. The fact that he wanted me in return was an added bonus for my confidence.

However, I couldn't help but admit to myself that he was also a distraction. I was sitting at my desk for a reason: to write down my review of the Gold Nest, not daydream about Liam... and the kiss we had... and the sex...

"GAH! Maya, snap out of it..." I vocalized, my internal responsibility popping out to scold me verbally. I tapped my desk several times with my fingers before looking up at my word document program, seeing only a couple of words written into it. Then, with a groan and a mental slap on the wrist, I lowered my head to the desk in disappointment at myself.

The knock at my door didn't push me enough to lift my head, despite me calling out permission to enter my office. The door opened, revealing my father with a cup of tea most likely made for me.

"Hey, sweetie," He began, a slightly nervous tamber in his voice. "How are you feeling?"

I had forgotten about returning home that day with a scowl on my face. When I left Liam's suite, I was calm, but on the ride back, I was buried in my own thoughts. I felt like a spoiled brat, but Liam was worth the grumbles I had returning home. Why did I have to run home like some sheltered princess when her parents called?

When I walked back into the house, my parents were waiting for me but stopped smiling in relief when they saw my face. Was my scowl really that prominent? I barely remembered.

Apologize. They did nothing to warrant anger.

I felt a ping of regret hit me as I looked over at my dad and witnessed the look of friendly worry on his face. Sighing, I sat up and turned to him in my chair.

"Yeah. I'm sorry, I just... I guess I didn't really want to leave, you know?" I replied. My dad smiled a bit. I was rarely a girl who let people in, and he knew that well enough to know that someone had to be very important for me to enjoy their company for an extended period of time. I lowered my head, a blush growing on my cheeks at the practical confession. Liam really made an impression on me.

"Well, your mom is in the kitchen and wants to talk to you." I furrowed my eyebrows. What did she need to talk about? I already apologized.

I stood from my chair and made my way out of my office with my father following behind me. My mother was preparing dinner early in the kitchen, so I sat at the table and let out a sigh to alert her of my presence.

"Maya, I need you to be completely honest with me about something. Alright?" My mother began, keeping her eyes on the cutting board in front of her.

"Alright." I agreed. My mother stopped chopping the vegetables in front of her before turning around to me. My father stood beside her, taking a sip from the mug he was holding and listening as well. "What is it?"

"Are you serious about being with Mr. Hunter? Or was last night a one-time thing?" My mother pressed, raising an eyebrow. I grimaced hard, staring down at the table. Where did I stand with Liam? He was fantasy worthy as a gentleman and lover. Any person would have been lucky to have a conversation with him, let alone be in his bed. Still, something about him sparked a connection, and I couldn't deny that he liked me somehow. Was it purely sexual, or was he legitimately interested in me as a person?

I took a breath and finally spoke. "I honestly didn't know what to expect last night. I thought it was just going to be dinner, but something about him... really charmed me, you know? Enough to say yes to sleeping with him, okay?" My mother went pale with a very soft blush across her cheeks, while my father's entire face turned tomato-red in embarrassment, causing him to turn around to hide his expression. I continued, nonetheless. "Still, he is charming and took excellent care of me. He made breakfast, for God's sake. So yeah, I may be thinking of being serious with him. I need a little time to think about it."

The professional approach was best. It laid out the details in plain words without any animosity or bad feelings. Still, my mother rubbed her cheeks, trying to regain some color on her face from hearing that her daughter wanted to be with her boss. Then, after an awkward moment of silence, my mother finally spoke.

"Thank you for being honest with me, Maya." She said, taking out her phone from her pocket. My father and I looked quizzically at her as she dialed a couple of numbers before bringing it up to her ear. When either of us tried to speak up in curiosity, she would raise her finger and wordlessly demand our silence. Finally, she spoke into the phone. "Hello, this is Sarah Augustine from Human Resources. I'd like to speak to Mister Hunter immediately. Please inform him that this is an emergency and mention my name."

"Mom--" I began to protest, but her glare at me and her tense finger caused me to quickly second-guess butting into what she was about to do. Was this necessary? Liam did nothing wrong, and everything was settled peacefully with me coming home. So why did this situation demand a call? She lowered the phone from her ear and pressed the speaker button, intimidating me with her eyes to keep my mouth shut. Finally, after a couple of transfer rings, a familiar voice picked up.

"This is Louis, Liam's personal assistant. What seems to be the issue, Missus Augustine?" Louis asked, a hint of worry in his voice.

"Please put Mister Hunter on the line." My mother bluntly demanded.

"I-I'm sorry--?"

"This is regarding my daughter, Maya. Put Mister Hunter on the line now. Please."

"Mom--" I finally began to interject, standing up from the table.

However, my mother was far too intimidating to continue speaking.

"Maya. Sit down."

I felt myself sit down automatically at her words. My father was the more submissive one in the relationship, so he took a step away from my mother and towards me. Another moment of silence before another voice came up.

"Missus Augustine? This is Liam Hunter speaking. What seems to be the problem?" Liam's voice inquired. My mother took a breath before answering.

"What are your intentions with my daughter?" I stared incredulously at the woman demanding such an answer. Seriously? Intentions?? Why was she pressing herself into this?

"I intend to get to know Maya and potentially become close with her if she would allow me to," Liam replied plainly. It was really nice to hear him say such, a doubtful shadow that was lingering in my chest vanishing at hearing the words from his voice.

"May I have your word on that?" My mother pressed.

"Absolutely. If you'd like, we can discuss this in my office. I can clear my schedule to ensure this is resolved to your satisfaction at your earliest convenience." Liam responded. Wait, what? Why would he clear his schedule for this? To talk about me??

"I would appreciate that. Tomorrow morning would be great. I will be bringing Maya with me if you do not mind. Please know that I will also bring documentation to this meeting to review and sign upon closure."

"What the fuck, mom?!" I couldn't take it anymore. What the hell was she thinking? I wasn't becoming his slave or anything of the sort. I was just having dinner with him. Why was it so vital for her to be involved?!

"I understand completely, Missus Augustine. Louis will be with me to transcribe and confirm the documentation." Liam said, surprising me. Why was he on board with this?! "I will be in my office for your arrival."

"Thank you." My mother bluntly hung up before pocketing her phone and walking out of the kitchen toward the room she and my father shared. I followed, red in the face myself at the entire incident.

"What was that?! Why did you do that-- why is this happening?!" I practically barked. This situation made me regret answering her question if this was how she was going to react. I would have rather dealt with the police than this, but as my mother pulled out a suit and button-up top from her closet, I stopped. The particular suit she brought out was one she only used for legal issues in the company. It helped her weed out problematic employees from Labryintelligence, and she deemed the threads her good luck charm. "Mom?"

"Maya. While you are an adult, Liam Hunter is the man I work for. Do you understand the complications that would come up if it became public that he was intimate with my daughter?" My mother explained, the same cold tone in her voice. My brain put two and two together pretty quickly with her blunt question.

She was a woman in a man's business world trying to climb the corporate ladder. She had worked with Labryintelligence for only a short while, proving herself to be a valuable asset, enough to reach a high position in Human Resources. But, even if she had nothing to do with my choices, if people knew who I was, it would have been misconstrued that she was using me to gain promotions. The business world was cruel enough on its own, but it didn't care for details and nuance. It was far too saturated to care about the truth.

"I have to make this clear with him and in writing that your relationship with him has nothing to do with me. If it was your father working for him, no one would bat an eye. In fact, he'd probably be congratulated for 'getting a pawn in the game,' as ridiculous as that is." My mother continued, making the weight on my shoulders even heavier with her words. "But I already have enough people questioning my promotional status. Too many damn younger employees lacking motivation always think their betters don't deserve their place, and enough older peers are too set in their ways to imagine a woman getting anywhere in the world."

"I... I'm sorry. I didn't think about that." I honestly didn't. I thought of myself and what I wanted without remembering my mother's position. It was idealistic and practically ignorant to assume that nothing would happen, that things were being blown out of proportion. However, I wasn't a businesswoman like my mom; she dealt with the worst of it on her own, enough to know better than I ever would.

"And it's not your job to think about that." My mother stopped preparing her suit and sighed, turning and walking towards me. She placed a gentle hand on my cheek before petting my hair. "You can do whatever you want. You know that. Your father and I will always support you as we always have. But please understand my position on the matter. It's a business issue."

Follow along.

Well... at least I was going to see him again.

Chapter 8

Binding

The trip to Labryintelligence wasn't long despite the main office being located in the heart of Chicago. My mother was born and raised in Chicago, so she knew every side road and secret path to get around the traffic that often plagued the city's asphalt veins. One flash of her office ID and we were safely parked in the private lot beneath Labryintelligence's building. I had never been in the facility before, so I followed my mother closely to ensure I didn't get lost. We had to go through multiple checkpoints with body scanners, metal detectors, ID checks, and the like. Unsurprisingly, the guards stationed at each post knew my mother and greeted her politely with a nod to me out of respect.

Into an elevator we went, and up we ascended towards I only assumed the top floor of the building. It was cliche for the boss to be at the physical top of the building, but I wasn't going to complain as such. Perhaps it was just a traditional business thing that every company followed, a physical symbol of the hierarchy. I couldn't imagine myself in such a place.

As the elevator stopped and the doors slid open, we took in the sight of a sizeable studio-like office. Windows made up three of the four walls, and the space was large and open enough to accommodate a practical party of people. However, it was nicely decorated with modern furniture and a welcoming atmosphere.

Liam sat at the desk across the room with Louis at his side, both in mid-conversation over something presented on Louis's tablet. A couple of steps from me and my mother caused Liam to lift his head from the conversation and look over. He locked eyes with me and smiled that warm smile that made me return it in kind. Still, I kept a step behind my mother as she approached the center of the room and watched as Liam stood from his desk, adjusted his suit jacket, and followed to meet us in the middle. Louis followed behind his boss, and we all stopped, flanking a coffee table and two very comfy-looking sofas.

"Missus Augustine. Maya," Liam greeted us, adding a slightly adoring flair to my name with his voice before locking his attention on my mother. "I'll do my best to clear this up to your satisfaction."

"I appreciate that, Mister Hunter," my mother replied before sitting down and laying a small folder of paper she had been carrying with her onto the coffee table. Not wanting to stand the entire time, I moved to sit beside my mother and kept my eyes on Liam, curious as to what terms they would discuss regarding the relationship Liam and I would likely pursue.

Liam followed suit and sat down across from us on the opposite couch, reaching over and opening the folder to see blank sheets of paper. Interesting start, mother. As if he expected to see such, Liam nodded and leaned back. Louis walked over to stand behind Liam and the couch with his tablet up to transcribe the conversation about to occur.

"I, Sarah Augustine, would like a clear definition of what you, Liam Hunter, intend to be to my daughter, Maya Augustine, for documentation and reference for Human Resources," my mother began. Louis immediately started to tap his fingers against his tablet, writing every word that fell out of my mother's lips. Liam nodded once again before replying, causing the terms to become apparent.

"I, Liam Hunter, intend to seek a friendship with Maya Augustine. Should she desire it, I would be open to pursuing more intimate relations with her upon her consent." Liam's words were so to-the-point that I could imagine my jaw hitting the floor from how surprised I was. This was really a straight-and-narrow business world, and I was watching a word-based chess game between the man I was attracted to and the woman I had to thank for bringing me into the world.

"I, Sarah Augustine, mother of Maya Augustine, acknowledge these terms and would like to submit to this documentation that I have no involvement with the relationship in question. The relationship in question shall not hold legal or corporate weight or advantage upon my position in Labryintelligence." Everything seemed too natural and almost heartless to think about. Was a potential business scandal really how my relationship was going to be seen by Labryintelligence's company?

"I, Liam Hunter, understand and agree with the statements laid out by Missus Sarah Augustine. Anything relating to Maya's involvement with me, Liam, shall be seen as separate from the company and will not be used professionally or legally by any entity for advantage or scrutiny." My mind began to wander. This was pretty much laying out that everything was good for Liam and my mom, but what about me? I was more of an asset here, defined and dissected in a business arrangement. It was almost similar to how people would treat a business gift or the like... and it irked me.

"I, Sarah Augustine, agree with the statements listed by Liam Hunter." This was crap. I knew why this had to happen, but it was crap nonetheless. It was 2021 for chrissake. What kind of boomer would even think of seeing me as an asset for promotions rather than a regular woman in a potential relationship with the man who owned a practical Fortune-500 company?

...on second thought, there were plenty of boomers and younger idiots who would think of negative conclusions if I defined it like that.

Let them settle their problem. Patience.

The back and forth continued into detail, defining that legal action was permitted should an accusation of bribery or fraud be pursued by any Labryintelligence employee. Defamation protection, in essence. At least my mother was safe now. As the talks ended, a sigh was exchanged all around.

"Well, are you satisfied with our agreement?" Liam asked,

leaning back on the couch he graced. My mother nodded, gathering her notes and folders.

"Very much so. I do wish to clear up one more thing." My mother replied, standing and leading Liam and me to do the same. Liam nodded before my mother looked at me. I raised an eyebrow, confused at her gaze. As she turned her face back to Liam, her expression became dark. "Hurt her in any way, and I will ensure your company burns to the ground."

Goddamn, Mom.

I stood stunned as I watched her walk around the couch and towards the door. Louis was equally surprised, but Liam grew a smile before calling out to her. "I'll hand you the match personally."

My mother opened the door before she looked back at me. "I work until 4. If you are still here, I'll drive you home." It was obvious that I had to speak to Liam after her talk with him, so I was thankful that she let me have my chance alone. I nodded to her and waved.

"I'll be okay, mom. See you at home," I assured her. I watched her leave before falling back down onto the couch in relief. So much legal jargon was passed around that my head could barely take it. Louis moved towards the shelf by Liam's desk as the boss himself walked around the coffee table and sat beside me, his elbows to his knees in his own exhaustion.

"Are you okay?" Liam asked, earning my nod in reply.

"It was just a lot, you know? I mean, sure, I get it. She works for you, and it looks kinda bad when her daughter is, well..." I trailed off. Did this mean that we could be a couple? If he was interested in me, was this the sign to say go for it? It was another lucky shot, but was my luck running out on something he viewed as a pleasureful exchange instead of a truly potential relationship? I didn't know.

He wanted to be friends and potentially more, but was it as a lover or as a romantic partner?

Louis appeared beside us and lowered a small tray of drinks onto the coffee table before taking one himself to sip on. "I told you she was a good hire."

"She is indeed," Liam commended before taking the remaining two glasses and holding one up to me. "Now I see where you get your professionalism from."

I couldn't help but laugh a bit as I took the offered drink and raised it in a toast. "She actually inspired me to pursue being a food critic. 'If you can speak your mind, do. If you can't, learn to.'"

"Wise words to live by," Liam commented before sipping his drink. I took a taste of my drink, surprised at the refreshing taste of water and citrus. Part of me believed it was alcohol to ease off the tension that previously consumed the room. The water was nice, though.

I let out a content sigh at the taste, leaning back against the couch and relaxing. "Can't lie: that meeting reminded me of this one book I read, but the meeting in that book was about a BDSM contract. The same kind of silly, you know?" I joked only to be greeted with a curiously raised eyebrow from Liam. Louis covered his mouth with a smile, obviously knowing what I meant, but what was on Liam's mind?

"Do you find BDSM silly?" Liam inquired.

"I mean, no. I just meant the scene where they meet to talk about the contract was goofy, you know? Same kind of tension, lots of legal jargon, stuff like that." I replied. Truthfully, BDSM was interesting, but I only ever read about it in smut during my passing breaks. Handcuffs and ball gags weren't part of my sexual life.

"Would you ever consider exploring BDSM for real?"

Wait, what?

I stared at Liam, stunned. Did he seriously ask me about BDSM? Was he into BDSM? What kind of BDSM was he into? Was he secretly a hardcore dom or some sort of submissive bottom? My mind began to swirl faster than it did when my mother was in the room.

Louis released an exasperated sigh of defeat before setting his now empty glass down and walking towards the door. "I am taking my lunch mega-early, and I don't care." He announced, clearly not wanting to be in the room. Didn't blame him. I watched him leave the room and close the door before turning to Liam, who still had his gaze fixed on me.

What did he want me to say? Yes? No? We fucked once. This was a little bit on the deep end for exploring our relationship or lack thereof, especially when we weren't official in any capacity. Still, I had to say something.

"I mean, I'm not opposed to it. I'm willing to try everything once." I answered, using my mentality of food critique to my sex life. After all, how could I have claimed it wasn't for me if I didn't try it? It was interesting enough to consider at least one or two chances.

Liam took another sip of his drink before slowly standing and walking over to his desk. I couldn't help but follow, curious as to what was on his mind now that I had answered his question. He walked around his desk and started to move things around, clearing the surface as he spoke. "I'm glad. I would have been a little disappointed if you swore off trying it before continuing to be close to me."

"Are you into BDSM, Liam?" Part of me wasn't surprised. He was charming and held a dominant aura without really trying, yet the other part of me could barely see a sweet man like him having a riding crop or a cat o' nine tails.

Liam nodded before looking up at me and reaching into his desk drawer. He pulled out something and placed it on his now clear desk. I didn't want to pull from his gaze, but I did to see what he wanted to show me.

It was a collar, but it clearly wasn't made for any cat or dog. Soft fur embroidered the inside of the leather ring while the outside was polished with an almost mirror-like shine. It had intricate ruby studs and a ring latch on both the front and back. What drew my full attention was the tag that was attached to the front latch. It had a small circle and a plus symbol at the center, embellished in sparkling gemstone glitter.

It's stunning, isn't it?

It was gorgeous, and I felt a little breathless staring at it. But how would it feel around my neck? Would I be able to unlatch it on my own, or would he have to be the one to take it apart?

Maybe I was more interested than I thought.

I looked up at Liam to see him examining my expression. How did I really feel about the collar? Why did he have it in his desk in the first place? Was he waiting for me? The latter question made no sense, as it seemed custom-made, and we barely had over a month of knowing each other with only a handful of meetings.

"Would you like to try it on?" Liam asked. I didn't hesitate and nodded. If my feet were in the water, I might as well dive in to see if it was worth the swim. As he made his way to me from around the desk, a small voice in my head worried about the collar fitting around my neck.

My worries were quelled, however, when Liam softly wrapped the collar around my throat from behind and latched it closed with the ring on the back. It felt so soft on my skin, practically weightless. I closed my eyes and let out a gentle sigh at the feel of the fur lining. The collar felt extremely comfortable and fit around my neck nicely without choking me or feeling too tight.

I couldn't help but smile as he turned me to face him. He slowly wrapped his index finger around the front ring loop and ever-so softly pulled it side to side. I was forced along but letting him control the collar felt so subtle and relieving. My head bobbled softly against the direction of his tugging, and something in my brain felt satisfied.

This feels so good...

Yeah, this is something I was willing to try further.

Liam then pulled the collar towards him, and we were quickly forehead to forehead, with me staring almost helplessly up into his eyes. There was a hint of a deep desire in his gaze, but he was obviously holding back. What were his limits? Would I learn of them?

"May I remove the collar?" Liam asked politely, unable to entirely mask a darker tamber of hesitancy in his voice. I nodded, despite not wanting it to be removed so quickly. I had almost gotten used to feeling it against my skin. His hands slid around my neck and unlatched it, causing the collar to slide down and fall to my cleavage. I almost winced at the cool air hitting my exposed neck, missing the feel of the collar's fur keeping it warm. Liam lifted the collar and stepped back from me, stretching it open between his hands in a show of sorts. "This is one of many things that are part of my private life. It's a small part of my life, but one I cherish greatly."

"What other things are there?" I couldn't stop my curiosity. He took care of his collar so much that he had to have been careful with other parts of his BDSM world. He wasn't going to toss me around like the love interests of the smut I read.

A small smirk peeked at the edge of Liam's lips. "I would go further, but we should probably establish something first before going that far," Liam replied as he lowered the collar to his desk. He gently lifted one of my hands and rubbed his thumb over the back of my hand. "Are you in this for pleasure, or do you feel the same as I do?"

The question finally dropped, and I found myself unsure of how to answer.

Yes, I lusted for Liam. He was undeniably hot, and his sex was a practical dream come true. He knew how to please a woman and to brush off a chance to be his sexually was the dumbest move anyone could have made. Plus, the idea of diving into his kink life practically screamed for me to pursue pleasure above all else.

At the same time, I was still curious about him. I knew what the public knew and some private bits of info, but I practically demanded to learn more. Isn't that what a relationship is all about? Learning about someone and building a romance with them? It was a balance of compromise, understanding, and support. I was more than happy to try and support him, but was I myself ready to be supported by him and to let him in on my life? I wasn't as perfect as he described me to be at that dinner.

I gripped Liam's hand and guided him back to one of the couches before sitting down, tugging him to follow along. He abided in my direction and listened.

"I need to be honest with you: my life has pretty much been devoted to my work. During college and after, I focused on building my food blog and barely stepped outside my office. Romantic relationships were short, but I'm not ignorant of what's involved." I began, knowing that my mind needed to unfold my thoughts verbally to give Liam the answer he deserved. "I'm scared, if anything, of not being totally devoted to being a perfect partner. I can get tunnel-visioned to my work, forgetting friends and other things. I can often be seen as dense to common sense because I take more time to process things.

"Still, I really do want to know more about you. I can't say that I'm expecting romantic feelings to come quickly or not, but at the end of it all, the only way I can know if we're compatible is to give it a try. Does that make sense?" I could only pray that I didn't sound like a rambling idiot. My goal was to be clear with my thoughts and answer him with the full context of my intentions and background. It wasn't sexy at all, as logic was rarely ever, but I'd rather not play with fire ignorantly.

Liam waited for a moment, taking in my words, before gently cupping my hand with both of his and growing a comforting smile. "I'm glad we're on the same page." He stated, causing my chest to finally release the worried pockets of air I held within my lungs. Liam gave my hand a slight squeeze and tilted his head ever so slightly. "I was grateful for what you did for me, and I grew more enchanted with you at the gallery and dinner. I also want to know more about you and fall even further for you."

My face quickly began to burn, and I found myself speechless.

Was Liam that interested in me? He made it sound like he was just as intrigued by me as I was with him, and that was saying something. I quickly recalled my research on him and how obsessed I was with learning about him from the public eye. Still, it was a little refreshing to know that our interests in each other were evenly matched one way or another.

Plus, it was apparent that we found each other sexy. Liam's eyes couldn't hide his desire for me, and I wasn't witty enough to disguise mine, nor did I care to. I couldn't wait to get him in bed again, especially if he was going to let me into his world of kink. What was waiting for me?

I had to ask.

I leaned over and brought his hands to my chin with a teasing grin. "So, now that we're in agreement do you want to tell me more about your lifestyle?" I was too eager to know what else he valued. Liam could only chuckle and shake his head before lifting one hand and pressing a finger under my chin, forcing our eyes to truly align. That one action had me straighten my spine at attention.

"Over time, Maya. We just became a couple. Let's see how things go."

The ultimate tease and the biggest mystery to learn. Challenge accepted.

Chapter 9

Anticipation

I had a multi-million-dollar boyfriend. It was hard to wrap my head around, but the fact of the matter was I was dating the CEO of a multi-million-dollar company. I had achieved the ultimate fantasy that erotica readers and romance enthusiasts dared to only read or write about.

From that fateful day in his office, we exchanged numbers and could not stop talking to each other as we worked. Just because we were a couple didn't mean our lives had to stop. There were obviously breaks in time when he had something important to do, or I had to meet with sponsors for my blog, but when we were free, we asked questions about each other. He was a cat person. I liked both cats and dogs. He actually preferred fantasy over sci-fi, despite his genius in tech. I had a marathon collection of fantasy movies both Hollywood and crowdfunded.

"I know a theater we could rent out and watch those movies together."

"Now hold on: just butter and salt on the popcorn?"

"Fresh caramel."

"And if I liked cheese?"

"Then I'm glad popcorn mixes match both flavors."

How did this man exist? I was in the honeymoon phase, clearly. There had to be things that drove me away. Something. He didn't care for pickles. I hated crowds.

"Private boxes are preferred?"

"Wait, private boxes? Of what?"

"Isolated suites at concerts and sports games away from the big crowds. They are mostly found in the nosebleed sections of a stadium."

"Oh wow. I mean, those would help a lot, but I don't really go to concerts, and I'm not really a sports person, you know?"

"How about Broadway?"

"Depends on the show."

"I'll make sure to ask before I arrange anything. I think you'd enjoy going to a show."

We were alike, preferring to stay home and listen to music. He would work out or read before bed. I would organize my work for the following morning, then read a couple of erotica book chapters before sleeping. Now that wasn't to say there weren't stark differences between us. He often met with multiple people in a day, which sometimes took him away from Chicago and sent him around the world. I had my quaint little home with my parents.

"Have you thought about one day moving out?"

"Perhaps? When I save more money, I'd like to think I'd get a place of my own."

"Any requirements that would need to be part of the amenities?"

"A good-sized kitchen. I want to eventually expand into vlogging with video tutorials and reviews, but that requires a large enough space for cameras, lights, and other things I can't even consider investing in yet."

"Very understandable. Well, what did you think of my kitchen?"

"Are you asking me to move in with you?"

"If you like the idea, then perhaps."

Every night ended with a good night and a smile on our faces. There were days of just phone calls and texts while dates were peppered between. Sometimes it was a lovely dinner. On occasions, he brought me to movies or a show. My heart pumped every time in excitement for the things he planned and managed with me. Liam was indeed a fantastic boyfriend.

And when we ended our nights with sex, I was flown to heaven every time. His touch was enough to make me shiver in need, while his kisses drove me insane. Of course, it often ended in his bed, but sometimes we were too impatient to reach the bedroom and wound up fucking on his living room couch or even in the elevator.

Five months practically flew by, and I was still happy to be Liam Hunter's girlfriend. Not even the paparazzi bothered me when they stalked Liam to the places we went to together. For a solid month, gossip blogs, social media, and magazines questioned who I was. While I would have shyly hidden my face away initially, being by Liam gave me a chance to build a sense of courage. In my gut, I knew he would protect me, so on my birthday, I took that courage and was unafraid of the first microphone that was almost jammed up to my face.

Liam had taken me to a culinary masterclass as my twenty-sixth birthday gift. What was meant to be a peaceful and enlightening evening became flooded with cameras and microphones from desperate journalists looking for the next scandal to go viral. Emily and Louis tried to stay on top of the mob, but they weren't fast enough to stop a crowd from forming around us as we left the masterclass.

"Who are you and are you really Liam's girlfriend?" the reporter barked, eager to be the first to get my answer in a digital record. Others joined in like seagulls copying a cry for food, and flashes practically threatened to burn into my sight.

Vultures. Show them no fear.

Still, I gripped Liam's hand tightly, earning a squeeze in return, and took a breath.

"My name is Maya. I run a food blog called 'Meals from Maya' where I review and share recipes for college students and low-budget families." I began. As Liam lifted my hand and kissed my knuckles, I blushed but continued. "And Liam is my boyfriend."

Another squeeze from Liam's hand distracted me from the sudden barrage of camera flashes and even more passionately curious questions. I stared up at Liam, who kept his eyes on me with a look of both pride and a little surprise. Did he expect me to say I was his girlfriend?

He was equally my boyfriend.

My site gained a massive following upon the release of the news. Many came interested in what I had to offer, while others were purely there to judge my worth. After all, Liam was a hot public bachelor. Why did he choose me out of any other woman in the world? Of course, I had my fair share of complaints, spam, and hate comments, but I always put things into perspective. They came to the site, which helped my revenue go up, and kept the site comments active, which pushed my site farther up the search engine for new viewers. Their words were made from jealousy, or else they wouldn't have been there in the first place.

Free real estate in their mind to benefit from.

What really surprised me were the sponsors that came running to my business email with offers. Each offer was absolutely in the hope of connecting to Liam through me, so sorting through them on his couch became a fun time for us. His business experience and the needs of my blog matched in vetting benefits against scams.

The closer we got, the more we laughed and opened up to each other. Liam had one go-to book: *Love and Romance, a Study of Intimacy*. Despite the book being advertised for women, he found it fascinating to glean through. I had a soft spot for pasta. Any recipe with pasta was an instant try for me, though I would reduce any portions to ensure I wasn't overindulging.

Our relationship seemed perfect and was growing to be rather picturesque. Even when we had disagreements, we both were adults with common sense. Sometimes work drove him to enter a call frustrated. Other times I was the one aggravated with life and wound up venting to Liam at his suite or even in his office on whims when I'd treat him to coffee or lunch. We anchored each other and talked out moments where tensions would fly. You would be surprised to see how many relationships would be saved with simple words and communication.

And yet two things stuck out in my mind: his schedule and the damn collar.

Sometimes, he would have to leave our calls in some sort of emergency. He'd tell me not to worry before and after taking care of the problems, but part of me knew that something else was happening. Whether it was business or something entirely different was left for my imagination to try and figure out. After all, our relationship was barely half-a-year old. Maybe I was blowing things out of proportion, and it indeed wasn't anything to worry about. It was the more minor issue between the two I carried internally.

The other issue on my mind was that collar. Sometimes I would imagine it gracing my neck again. It felt so nice to have it on, but what I didn't expect was missing Liam's tugs on it. Back and forth, my control bobbled away from me into Liam's fingers. He certainly led the sex we had, so to imagine him completely dominating me was another desire I had to quell one way or another.

Was he hiding a darker side? Maybe he was a secret dom for some underground ring of kink. He held power effortlessly, yet his smile defied any notion of him being a rough master. Liam was soft and gentle with me at every chance. He would spin me around his living room to sweet bossa nova or wrap his coat around me when it was chilly. A gentleman.

I... I almost wanted to see him break that expectation. How would he handle me if he released his limits? He had to have some control over himself to have such a dichotomy of a charming golden-retriever CEO who was also a man owning a collar meant for a person. You don't imagine his personality telling you to call him sir. At least I didn't.

I found myself lost in my erotica books again during my breaks. The men in those books were always rough and aggressive when they brought in BDSM. Maybe it was the writer wanting to push the boundaries of fiction, but it sold for a reason. Male-chasers clearly loved the idea of a fictional man taking what they wanted from a fictional protagonist and tying them down, spanking them, and screwing them in every corner of their imaginary cities.

That was not Liam. At all.

I closed the book on my lap, having skimmed through a scene I often went back to read for enjoyment and pondered. How was I going to get Liam to let me enter his world? He said to take it slow, but how slow was his pace? Did the man expect me to wait for him? Did he want me to press him about it?

Closing my eyes, I could only fantasize about Liam in my favorite smut scene with me as his submissive. I was seated on a custom-made rocking chair with my knees over the armrests, spread wide for him and unable to break the belts locking my thighs apart. My ass barely rested on the edge of the seat with my bare pussy on full display, and I was left defenseless with my arms wrapped behind the chair, handcuffed together at the wrists.

Liam was standing over me, clad in only a pair of dark jeans, and his eyes were burning in lust. He leaned forward and grabbed the front ring of my collar, pulling it and rocking the chair forward. "What makes you think you can mouth off to me?" his voice, dripping with intense power, warned me of a dangerously fun time, and I felt myself getting wet from his words alone.

"You like this mouth," I teased, knowing that I could be much more courageous in my mind. It was a pre-written script, after all. I licked my lips, expecting my scene to continue just as I had read it, only with a new leading couple. "Why wouldn't I use it?"

Liam glared with a sly grin, grabbing my hair and tugging my head back to align my eyes to his. I moaned before grinning back at him, daring him silently.

"You wanna use your mouth that badly?" Liam pressed, releasing the hand that held my collar to drag his fingers down my body. My cockiness quickly disappeared as he cupped my crotch with his hand, anchoring it down with his thumb and rolling my clit with his index and middle finger.

"F-Fuck!" I moaned out wildly, shuddering at the sensation and pulling at my restraints in earnest. I knew I would be trapped there, but the pleasure carnally pushed me to fight back for freedom. Liam pressed forward towards my face, barely feathering his lips over mine with a satisfied hum.

"Not so cocky now, huh?" Liam teased before torturously slowly moving around the chair, his hand still fingering my mess of a cunt, and leaning the chair back. It was indeed a custom rocking chair, as it managed to flip my body upside down with my face directly in line with the bulge of Liam's pants. Then, using my sex as an anchor to hold me in place, he used his free hand to release the button and zipper of his pants and let them fall to the floor. His cock, thick and delicious, sprang out of its confinement and tapped my lips in its bounce. "Open up."

I eagerly opened my mouth and let his dick in. The memory of his taste flooded my fantasy, and I practically mewled in delight. Then, as the fiction dictated, Liam groaned lowly and began to thrust into my mouth and toward my throat. I could do nothing but take him; in my mind, this was okay. I was perfectly safe to explore this wild idea.

Liam latched his lips to my slit and began to eat me out like a beast hungry for my orgasm. It was practically feral, and I adored every second of it. This is what erotica painted as a pleasureful euphoria, and I was happy to indulge my fantasy, as I had felt Liam's tongue and cock before.

We both couldn't speak, as our mouths were too busy, so only grunts and whimpers escaped us in pleasure and need. I could feel saliva and my own juices drip down my body from Liam's mouth. But it barely affected me, as my tongue was too busy licking over every inch Liam pumped between my lips.

It was drool-worthy to me, and I felt my core tightening in that beautiful and familiar build to an orgasm.

But then the phone rang.

FUCK!

I opened my eyes, not realizing my hand was deep into my panties, and shot my gaze towards my phone. It was Liam. Why now?! I quickly grabbed my phone with my free hand and answered, deciding to leave my other hand where it was for the hell of it.

"Hey, Liam!" I chirped, returning to rub my clit in slow circles.

"Hey, Maya. Am I interrupting anything?" Liam's voice was enough to bring me back to my sexual build, starting from the bottom. He did interrupt me, but he was unknowingly making up for it.

"No, I was just reading. What's up?"

"Well, I wanted to see if you'd like to come over tomorrow for dinner. I figured we both need a break from work, and I miss you." I practically cooed as I listened to his request. One flick of my finger, however, made me quiver, and I was purring into the phone microphone. "Maya?"

"Yeah?"

"Are you okay?" I stopped playing with myself. Did he hear me?

"Yeah! Totally fine. Also, yes, dinner tomorrow sounds

wonderful. Want me to bring anything?"

"Just your beautiful face."

"Body too, I'd hope?" A laugh on the other end. I continued letting my fingers dance.

"But of course. 6:30?"

"Perfect."

"Alright, see you then."

We hung up, and I relaxed back into my chair with a grin. A dinner date sounded nice. It had almost been half a year, so perhaps I would glean more secrets from Liam. Who could tell? I closed my eyes to finish my fantasy, riding my orgasm on my fingers and hoping to repeat it on his eventually.

Chapter 10

Bound

Emily had become my personal chauffeur whenever it came to picking me up for dates, and she knew exactly what to play each time. I began to learn more and more about Liam's taste in music as I prepared to be by his side. Still, it wasn't just music that entertained me each ride. Emily and I would exchange stories, like two girls gossiping about their high school love lives. Her wife continued to share her culture with Emily, expanding her tongue to flavors she never had as a child growing up in the bible belt of America. When she recalled stories of her wife, her smile made her face glow, and I caught her a couple of times swaying to the radio.

However, on the night of the dinner date, something was off about Emily. As she picked me up to drive me to Liam's penthouse, I noticed a heavy bruise on her jawbone.

"Are you okay??" I pressed, worried about her pain. Emily covered her cheek and waved her other hand dismissively.

"Oh! Don't worry about me. That's what I get when I pick a fight, haha!" Emily brushed off. A fight?! When did she fight someone?

As I got into the car and we drove off, I leaned towards the partition between us. "Emily, what happened? How did you get into a fight?" I asked, now more curious than ever at the idea of her STARTING a fight.

Emily shook her head. "It's fine. Some jackass thought he was slick, so I broke his nose. He got a nice swipe at me before I made him eat concrete." Emily replied, clearly masking something with a chipper tone. While I expected her to regale the story with a prideful smirk, I saw a deadpan expression as I looked in the rearview mirror at her. Her eyes had a coldness that made the story more darkly fascinating.

Did the jackass touch her wife? Her? Liam?? It had to have been personal for such a serious recall. I let my thoughts linger on it for a while as I became lost once again in the swing of the radio's bossa nova. Emily didn't talk again the entire ride.

I was eventually driven into the underground parking lot and made my way to the elevator. On the way up, something in the back of my mind told me to be ready for something. Did it have something to do with Emily's injury? Was I missing something important that day? Call it whatever you want, but I took note of it mentally. I'd keep an eye open.

The doors opened into Liam's suite, where the smell of garlic wafted through the air. I was practically drooling already as I walked in and followed my nose to the kitchen, dropping my bag off in the living room on the way. Liam was unsurprisingly dressed in a black silk button-up, sleeves rolled to the elbows, and dark jeans. I felt underdressed in my boho dress, but at least I was comfy, and he seemed to be as well.

Liam turned, most likely hearing my footsteps, and his face almost glowed with happiness. "Hello, beautiful."

I didn't stop the beaming smile growing on my face at the nickname, the blush following after. "Hello, handsome."

Liam wiped his hands on a nearby towel and walked over to me, taking my hand and kissing my knuckles. "I hope you're hungry. Dinner is almost ready."

"I honestly can't wait. What's on the menu? It smells great already." After releasing my hand, Liam returned to the counter and brought forward two plate bowls. The dishes: chicken parmesan over linguine. I gasped and licked my lips at the sight. "Someone's been reading my blog."

"It was a little tough deciding on what to make, but your reaction made the choice absolutely worth the trouble of choosing." Liam quipped with a wink, causing me to roll my eyes.

Like the gentleman he was, Liam carried the plates to the dining table and sat them in the same corner, one we frequented when eating together. We had the whole table to ourselves, but it was nicer seated beside each other and at least somewhat face-to-face. I quickly assisted by fetching a jug of sparkling water I knew he had from his fridge and two glasses. We both set up our dinner before Liam helped seat me.

"Always a gentleman." I joked, watching him sit beside me at the head of the table. Liam shrugged slightly.

"Well, not always." That was a first. What did he mean? Sure, he laughed at silly things and could be goofy sometimes, but he always returned to his polite and humble gentleman persona. Did it have something to do with his other lifestyle?

"You've yet to show me otherwise," I commented, hoping it would make him elaborate and prove his claim further. Maybe that night, I was meant to explore more of him. Was that what my gut was telling me?

Liam laughed a bit under his breath before taking up his utensils. "Let's eat before this gets cold. I need your approval on it."

With that, I began to eat a very nice chicken parm meal. Liam wasn't a perfect chef, but my meals weren't meant to be masterpieces for master culinarians. Nevertheless, it was delightful and only echoed how talented Liam was as a person. A man who could control technology and have a love for both reading and cooking was a rare find indeed. I made sure to thank every lucky star in the sky for my predicament.

Still, the excellent jazz music he played whenever we shared a meal together wasn't enough for me that night.

"So, do you know what happened to Emily? She has a massive bruise on her face..." I asked, hoping he would provide some answer to my inquiry.

Liam grimaced and stopped eating for a moment, looking down at his plate with an expression of shame. "She was... protecting me. I'm sorry about that."

Protecting him? Hold on.

"Wait, what do you mean? What happened?" I suddenly became concerned. Did Liam have a stalker? Did some paparazzi jerk get too close? The bruise definitely came from a fistfight, but what kind of person would throw their hands that violently?

"It was a misunderstanding. Someone thought I was someone else and tried to attack me, but Emily managed to keep him from me." Liam confessed; his voice low but not in shame. Instead, it felt like anger was shadowed in his words, and his eyes did not help in hiding it as they practically glared daggers into his plate. It took a moment for Liam to take a breath and look at me with a weary smile. "I'm sorry that we worried you. It's been handled properly, I promise."

I simply nodded. I wanted to know more, but I doubted I would glean anything else. It seemed like the situation was handled, and Liam felt guilty about what had happened with Emily. Best not to pry.

We continued to eat and enjoy our meal. The mood had slowly swung back to calm and positive with news of production happening at Labryintelligence from Liam and sponsorship updates from me. We were both growing in our individual fields and proud of the growth we had accomplished thus far.

However, my mind drifted back to the day before when I had imagined Liam as someone he was not presenting to me. His outfit practically screamed 'master' with his shirt's first three buttons undone and the rolled-up sleeves. Liam looked like he came out of an erotica movie, but he was-- or at least made himself out to be-- a golden-retriever boyfriend.

Plus, I wanted to try on the collar again.

As we finished eating, I decided to press another mental fuck-it button. I had to at least try with how it was on my mind. I stood and gathered our plates, positioning myself to where my lips were by Liam's ear.

"Let me take care of the dishes, *sir*."

I collected his plate and moved back, catching a shiver running up his spine and causing him to sit upright. Then, not wanting to be stopped, I layered my empty plate on his and pinched both of our glasses with my fingers before quickly making my way to the sink. Feign ignorance. Feign innocence. I began to lather some dish soap onto a sponge and wash each plate, emptying my mind of any wrongdoing.

When a warm chest pressed itself up against my back, and two strong arms cornered me against the sink, I stopped and felt my breath catch itself in my throat.

"Please repeat what you said to me." Liam's voice whispered into my ear, low and full of dangerous energy. Was he mad? Was I not supposed to call him that? I barely recognized his voice, only hearing its tamber when being railed by him. It was sexy and made me quiver ever so slightly despite the nervousness I had.

Feign ignorance. Feign innocence.

"I said I'd get the dishes. That's okay, right?" I replied, telling a half-truth, and continued washing the plates. So, I wasn't lying, and he couldn't claim as such. Easy.

"Of course..." Liam muttered, still leaning his head against the side of my neck and letting his breath brush against my ear. I kept my composure as best as possible, rinsing the soap off one dish and placing it on the drying rack before starting the second plate. I only jumped slightly when both of his hands grabbed my hips. "But if you intend to call me 'sir,' we need to talk."

Wait. Talk?

I stopped and turned my head to him, now very confused. I was under the impression that he was going to punish me or something. Why did we have to talk? "What do you mean?"

Liam kissed my cheek, clearly holding back judging from the tense squeeze of his hands, and burned his gaze into mine. I was silenced by it.

"Finish the dishes, then we'll talk." Liam directed before releasing me and walking away. I turned my body as much as I could to see where he went, but as he was out of my line of sight, I was left with my thoughts. I resumed washing the remaining dish and glasses while processing what he could have had in store.

Was it going to be a chat about his kink? He probably had rules and was most likely going to lay them out for me to agree to and follow through with. It was fair. I was sure the talk involved me giving my two cents on the matter. At the same time, however, my scope of knowledge was limited to what I read in fiction. I had only physically indulged in vanilla sex, so it was all trial-and-error from there.

Well. I did say I would try anything once.

After I placed the last glass on the drying rack, I washed my hands and solidified my position on the matter. Whatever Liam had in store, I would try once. No questions asked. He probably knew more than I ever would, and I was okay with being an eager student to my hot professor. Would I have to sign a contract like that cheesy scene I remembered? What would I sign away? Who knew but Liam?

Take the dive.

I took a breath. Then I turned and walked to the dining room.

Liam sat in his usual spot, but there was a notepad and pencil on the table in front of him this time. My chair was already pulled out for me, as he expected me to join him. I did such, scooting my chair in and examining his expression as his eyes met mine. They were earnest as if he was in a business meeting rather than sitting at a table with his girlfriend. Was it really that big of a deal?

"So, what are we doing?" I asked, unsure of where the conversation would begin. Liam's lips gave a slight smile curl before he tapped his pencil's eraser on his notepad.

"How familiar are you with BDSM culture, Maya?" Liam asked. It took me a moment to really cement the truth of my knowledge.

"Not totally? I've read erotica, but that's really all I know about it. Of course, I know smut can over-exaggerate and stuff, so I can't really say everything I've read would really be called knowledge."

Liam nodded as he listened, taking in my reply. "Well, I first need to clarify one thing with you: titles like 'sir' should only be granted with full consent and knowledge of the matter."

"Why? Aren't they just fun pet names in general?"

"They can be. But to me, titles like 'sir' aren't something to be taken lightly. I wouldn't want to call you a title you don't like or a name that spurs bad context."

"But do you like me calling you 'sir'?"

Another barely visible shiver up Liam's shoulders. He liked it.

"I do, but I don't think you're aware of the power behind that." Liam slowly stood and moved to stand behind my chair. I turned my head to follow, but his hands grasped my shoulders, causing me to face forward and stare at the skyline beyond the window. "Anyone you call 'sir' should be someone you see as your superior in every way." One hand slid its way up to cup my chin with the gentlest of care. I almost swooned as one of his fingers caressed my cheek. "They reward you when you please them, so you may go out of your way to obey every order they give." Suddenly, he tightened his grip on my jaw and forced me to look up at him. It didn't hurt, but he made his point clear with his gesture and gaze. "Or you do the opposite, intent on disobeying them to the point of earning punishment if you find yourself eager to seek pleasure in masochism."

I was speechless already. I really did not know anything. Pet names were thrown around and even used in jokes, but their proper weight was emphasized by his small actions. "I... I'm sorry if I offended you." I apologized, taking in the new information.

To my surprise, Liam chuckled before leaning down and kissing my forehead. He released my chin and walked back to his chair, sitting down and picking up his pencil again. "You did nothing to be sorry for, but that's why it's important for me to know what you are okay with and what you are not."

"But what if I truly don't know?"

"Then we establish rules and procedures that let you safely explore BDSM."

This sounded more like the BDSM contract scene I previously called silly. BDSM agreements were real? How would that be legally binding? Did lawyers get involved? Was it common for lawyers to be involved in other couples' BDSM?

I shook out my confusion. This was meant to be serious, and Liam was obviously trying to get me on the same page as him. I had to listen.

"Alright. Do I sign anything? Do we negotiate a contract or something like that?"

"Some people already have established contracts, but I always found more benefit in making official documents *after* negotiations. Less extraneous stuff to write and strike out, and it's personally crafted for the relationship."

"Makes sense... So how do we start?" It took me a second to realize that the jazz music was switched to a more classical playlist.

Liam gestured to me. "Well, how about we establish what we are in this agreement? Do you approve of me as your dominant?"

"Yes."

"Do you approve of being my submissive?"

"Yes." I paused for a moment. "Wait, do we have to do this like how you and my mother did your legal agreement?"

Liam shook his head and held his hand across the table to me. I placed mine in his, definitely feeling like the stupid student. "This contract is between us. It can be as casual or as professional as you want. It's purely to ensure that you feel safe."

"I always feel safe with you, though." It was the truth. He never once put me in danger, nor had I ever felt like I was in over my head. Sure, we met because of an accident, but he wasn't the cause. Regardless, when we had sex, it was a ride to heaven, not a dance with hell at my heels. I couldn't help but doubt that he would make me feel anything but safe.

Liam's eyes widened at my comment, and I could barely catch a blush on his tan skin, but he smiled in contentment. "I'm glad I make you feel safe, but this agreement is also guide me on how else to please you in this relationship."

"Like you need help doing that." We both laughed at my teasing.

"You know what I mean. It wouldn't be fun to strap you down to a fuck machine if you didn't enjoy it as much as I would watching you."

That sent a wave of intriguing pleasure to my core. A fuck machine? He had a fuck machine on hand?? He wanted to watch me be strapped to it??? My imagination quickly painted the picture of me strapped down to a chair with some sort of dildo on a piston fucking me from below my spread-apart legs, but was that what he meant? That image certainly made my body warm in anxious heat.

Guess I had to go down the list with him.

"Well then... how about you list some things you want to do to me, and I'll tell you what I'd be okay with trying?" I offered. Maybe he had things he didn't like. Me throwing around stuff from the scenes I had read was chucking darts at a board.

Liam nodded before leaning back and placing his notepad on his lap.

"Alright then. I'd like to first list some titles you can allow me to call you."

"Go for it." What names would he give me? It was bound to be more than darling and beautiful.

"Kitten."

"Okay. Yes."

"Brat."

I laughed. "I mean, if I am acting like one, sure."

"Good to know. Obedience is quite the rewarding trait in my book."

Note to self: weigh the pros and cons of being a brat with inaction testing.

"Princess?"

"I can try that."

"Pet?"

"Maybe...? Why not?"

"My good girl?"

"Absolutely yes."

Liam took a moment to write notes before looking back at me. "Are there any titles you'd like to call me?"

"Got any favorites like 'sir'?"

"My main three are 'master,' 'sir,' and 'daddy.' Would those work for you?"

I had to try it. "Okay... *master.*"

Liam's lips curled into a slight smirk. "And you say you aren't a brat. We're not done with the agreement yet, *kitten.*"

I couldn't stop myself from biting my lower lip, hearing the title, and connecting it to me. It felt good, and I could definitely have gotten used to it as a common pet name.

"Sorry. Wanted to try it."

A chuckle rumbled from Liam's chest with an understanding nod. "Then how about we talk about play limits? Bondage?"

"Sure, I'm open to handcuffs and stuff."

"How about rope bondage?"

"I can try it."

"Pet play?"

"Eh... not a fan of pretending to be an animal..."

"Alright. Would you be opposed to visual ownership? Wearing something to mark that you are my submissive?"

The collar appeared in my mind. "Like the collar you showed me when we got together?" I was a little too eager to put it back on to try it as I scooted to the edge of my seat in curiosity. Liam raised an eyebrow teasingly before reaching for the chair opposite me. I had to hold back a squeal as I watched him pull the exact collar I referenced from under the table and show it off to me.

"You mean this one? I had a feeling you liked it." Liam teased with a wink. He placed it on the table in front of me before sitting back. "Of course, this would be for when you are here. I'd get you a public collar to wear otherwise."

"Public collar?"

"A necklace. To anyone looking, it's just nice jewelry, but to you and me, it's a secret only we share."

That made me question how many people wore simple necklaces versus public collars. It was kind of cute to imagine it as a guessing game. I only wondered what mine would look like. Would he let me choose one?

I nodded. "Okay. Collars work for me."

A couple strokes of a pencil on the notepad. "I'll make sure we go to a jeweler for something personalized for you." Liam lifted his head and nodded.

We continued down a list of many items, with him explaining

terms and ideas I didn't have a clear vision of. I had said yes to light impact play, sensory play, orgasm control, and exhibition with sex toys with him as my audience. However, immediate nos were given to consensual non-consent, gagging, blood play, and age play. As for praise and degradation, I was keener to be pampered rather than scolded.

"Now, because we have a list of what you like and do not like, I need you to come up with a safe word. Something you would absolutely never say when we play, so I know to stop."

"What, like 'pickle'?" I briefly forgot that Liam didn't like pickles, so it took me a bit to understand his instinctual grimace.

"I mean if that's what you want…" Liam joked through his teeth. He was trying to lighten his reply despite his displeasure.

I quickly backpedaled. "No! No! It's fine. That's weird! I mean… What do you suggest?"

"The common term we have is 'red.' Basic stoplight terminology."

"Wait, so does 'yellow' mean slow down in that case?" A nod in acknowledgment. I shrugged, figuring that worked for me. "Let's go with those, then."

Liam continued to write down notes. "I'm sorry if this is a lot to take in."

"If this is part of the lifestyle, then I understand." It was a new world for me, so, as Liam was guiding me through, I had to keep an open and patient mind. I continuously shifted my glance to the collar and held myself back from just grabbing it and running my fingers along the fur. However, if this path would get me there without disappointing him, it had to be done.

After a moment of writing, he took a breath. "I'd like to finalize our agreement with some basic understandings. This is, in essence, an exchange of power. As your dominant, when I ask you to do something, I expect you to do it without hesitation. If there are any doubts, you must tell me before we move forward. I will teach you routines I like, and you will follow them to the point of habit." A pause to let me take in the information. He was clear enough for me. He continued. "As my submissive, you must obtain permission before doing anything yourself. Whatever you feel you want outside of basic survival needs must be granted approval by me. This includes pleasuring yourself. If you do not get my permission, you will be punished accordingly. Do you agree?"

Last chance to say no.

This was a lot, definitely less sexual than I anticipated. I thought it would be kinky sex all the time, but the way he framed this agreement was more of a lifestyle. Approval for things I typically didn't think much else of would be challenging to remember. Then again, if he was going to be my 'master,' I had to trust him.

"I agree."

Chapter 11

Graciousness

I didn't get to wear the collar that night. Liam wanted to write everything up properly for me, so we both had copies of our agreement after signing it. That way, we both were keen on what was expected and when the new dynamic would be officially part of our lives. According to him, he did not expect me to live it twenty-four-seven, but when he was with me, he expected me to abide by the lifestyle.

"Wait. Doesn't there have to be some sort of non-disclosure?"

"I trust you. Would you like me to make one?"

No. I wasn't of the mindset to be a snitch in any regard, especially if I was going to give myself to him as his submissive. It was odd to claim myself as such. Submissive. I was still me: a woman who held her own business and didn't care to bend to the whims of societal graces with fake extrovert behavior. Still, Liam would, in essence, direct my sexual life.

I stayed with him that night; by morning, he had written up two copies of our agreement. After signing both, before I could wear the collar, much to my displeasure, we left the suite, and I found myself surrounded by jewelry in one of Chicago's hidden gem department stores. The staff was friendly, and I was led around the glimmering diamonds and gems. Unfortunately, I did not know where to land my gaze, distracted by the elegant choices.

This was where I had to get my public collar? I figured a cheap necklace would have sufficed. Then again, my master was a multi-millionaire. I should have expected that he'd want something pricier to match.

Still, the importance of it weighed on me as Liam watched my every move and the staff insisted on each piece they presented. One desperate look at Liam caused him to stand beside me with his arm wrapped around my waist in support.

"Perhaps a back option. This is a very important purchase." Liam muttered, looking up at the staff member in front of us.

One second, a look of surprise. The next, a glow of glee before the staff member guided us to the back of the store and into a hidden away storeroom. In individual vaults were gorgeous pieces of jewelry I hadn't even dreamed of seeing in magazines or significant events. Some practically screamed royalty, while others were mysteriously simple with glimmers of potential undertones.

However, you could tell that these pieces would never be publicly shown or shared. Something about them felt highly exclusive.

My eyes finally tunnel-visioned in on one necklace. It looked like a ruby-encrusted chain with a decently sized heart charm in the front. The heart itself was thick, like the loops of my soon-to-wear collar, with a small rose made of ruby shards dangling from its inner point. I walked over to gaze upon it in awe.

That was it. That was the necklace.

Liam seemed to take the hint and gestured to the staff, who quickly rushed to unlock the vault for me. She gently moved the necklace to a pillow and presented it to me. I didn't hesitate to take it and cup the heart charm in my palm but jumped slightly as Liam's chest moved to lean up against my side. He took the necklace from my hands and unlatched it before wrapping it around my neck and reclasping it.

It fit so perfectly that I almost didn't need the mirror the staff member quickly brought up to show me my reflection. I could barely hold in my excitement for it, staring at the heart gracing my neck and sternum. It was beautiful, and I knew I would cherish it completely.

I didn't know how much it cost, but I was able to walk out with it adorning my neck without an issue. Even as we entered the luxury car waiting for us, Liam wouldn't tell me and we drove off.

"A wonderful choice..." Liam muttered, lifting my chin to observe the necklace as I cuddled up beside him. I was more than thankful for him getting me such a gift. He could have gotten me anything, and I would have accepted it, but he ensured that it was something I chose of my own volition.

"Thank you... *sir*." I let his new title ripple from my tongue. After signing our agreement, why wait to start using it? The car partition was closed, so Liam and I were practically alone. It was private enough, right?

Liam licked his lips slightly with a smile, running his fingers through my hair. "Anything for you, *kitten...*" This time, a shiver ran up my spine at the name. It had a weight now that he was my master, and my spirit knew to accept it as part of his love for me. His fingers caressed over my skin, physically praising me and making me swoon internally at his touch. Still, I listened as he continued to speak. "Now, unless you're showering or going for a swim, that does not come off unless I take it off myself."

"Yes, sir." Easy instructions. Maybe this lifestyle would be easier than I thought. I didn't care to think about removing my necklace. I liked it too much to even consider the thought. Taking it off before showering and swimming made sense, so it was a simple order.

"Good girl."

I definitely liked that. A little bubble of pride and joy rose in my stomach and chest at the praise. I then understood why praise was sought after in kink. He didn't need to monologize praise, but to hear acknowledgment of my obedience and attention planted the seed in my mind to seek more. How many more ways could he validate me?

A thought struck me, and I followed it.

I scooted closer to Liam and leaned my chest against his arm, catching his gaze in mine. "Can I kiss you, sir?" I was half-tempted to just do it without asking, but I had to practice until my role became a habit. Ask first. Be a brat later.

A small grin. "Yes, you may, princess."

Without hesitation, I leaned in and kissed him, running my hand along his cheek and cupping his neck. Liam wrapped his arm around my waist, supporting me as I pressed my body against his. It was slow but deep. I poured every ounce of thankful love I had for him into his lips. A small fire ignited in my chest, and I continued to feed it as part of my grateful gesture to Liam.

I didn't care to stop my hands from wandering his chest, feeling his muscles flex slightly under my touch. I was half-tempted to tear off his shirt, but I had to take it slow and really pay back the price of the necklace with every second that passed. After all, surely part of my submissive role was to give thanks, right?

As my hands brushed over the top of his pants, I pulled myself from his lips and stared deep into his eyes. The jade rings in his gaze were thin once again. I knew I had him.

"Let me thank you for the necklace, sir?" I purred out, feeling a slight power shift. I felt like making the power wobble, but as Liam cupped my neck and massaged the back of it with his fingers, I was once again at his mercy. In our almost-half year together, he figured out each of my weak spots as I had yet to find his.

Oh well.

Liam scanned my face and body with his eyes, slowly growing a smirk. Under my palm, his pants grew a bulge that I was more than happy to stroke ever so slowly. "Go ahead..." He gave his approval with a pleasureful rumble in his voice. He was definitely in his bed-mood, but something made him more... powerful? Dangerous? I had seen this side of Liam, but there was a layer of energy that felt so above me that I was almost thankful to be allowed to touch him.

Was this his dominant side? A small glimpse for sure, but I liked what I saw and felt.

I lowered myself to almost kiss Liam's crotch, ass in the air to compensate for my balance. Slowly, even for me, I unlatched his belt and undid his pants before opening the flap to see his boxer briefs. One tug and his still-growing erection readily bounced out of its cloth restraints. This would be my thanks for a gift I would treasure forever.

I licked over the tip and earned a small groan in return. The hand on my neck tightened for a second, massaging my skin and teasing me with a more powerful grip. That was definitely something I was eager to feel later, but I kept focusing on the task at hand-- or rather, mouth. Making small strokes with my tongue, I praised the head, the length, and the width of his God-given cock to make him grow harder for me. His sighs and moans spurred me on as his hand began to brush through my hair.

I took his dick into my mouth, swirling my tongue over every inch I could reach as I slowly bounced my head. He moaned my name, and I craved more of his pleasurable praise. I adjusted my legs to accommodate my moves, swaying my hips in joy as I sucked him off faster. What I couldn't take into my mouth, I used a hand to stroke the remaining length at the same pace.

That's when I felt him move his hands. His free hand cupped the top of my head while the one previously petting me slid down my back and grasped my ass cheek. I gasped with his dick in my mouth as he massaged it with his fingers.

"Such a good girl..." He praised, making a shiver quake in my core. His words and fingers spurred me even faster to lick and suck all over his now rock-hard cock. "Just like that..."

Fuck, I really liked him praising me. I wanted more. I wanted him to moan and tell me he liked what I gave over and over. As his hand switched ass cheeks to fondle, I moved to take his length deeper into my mouth and towards my throat. I had to take it slow, so I didn't gag at the amount, but my need to please for praise became my driving force.

The guttural sound that escaped Liam's lips solidified my resolve. "Take it all, kitten..."

I had to stop myself from gasping and choking as his fingers moved to cup my crotch and stroke the length of my pussy through my panties beneath my dress skirt. His fingers pushed me to keep deepthroating him, knowing instinctively that he would reward my efforts with pleasure. He reached farther and landed his fingers precisely on my clit, rolling it oh so slowly. My voice was muffled, but I was happy to moan out my delight and pleasure for his touch as I sucked him off.

We added to the jazz music playing in the car with our duet of moans and grunts. The air conditioning couldn't cut through the heat we were building. I swayed my hips in rhythm as he continued to touch me. I didn't even care if the driver was able to hear us.

I was going to make Liam cum in that car.

My throat was getting used to the head of his cock hitting it as I rode it with my mouth, licking every inch I could. My hand massaged and stroked the base lovingly, instinctively squeezing as Liam slid his fingers around the pad of my panties to stroke me skin-to-wet-skin. Finally, I had to take a breath and pull up, licking over the tip and panting at the new amount of air I could take in.

"You're doing so well, my good girl... taking my cock like that..." Liam praised as he stroked my head. "You're gonna make me cum soon..."

"Please, master..." I muttered, licking my lips at the idea. It wasn't the first time I sucked his dick, but our new relationship made this moment different. When we usually took our time to build our passion, I was practically impatient that time around. Did I want more praise, or did I really want to pay back the necklace with my mouth?

Both. A mixture of both.

I wasted no time sucking him off again, knowing from previous times how long it took to make him climax. He rewarded my obedience with a finger in my cunt, pumping it and brushing his fingertip over the spot that drove me nuts. My moans rumbled around his length, but I doubled down.

A grasp of his fingers over my hair. A quickened pace of his fingers in my cunt. A large and low groan of pleasure. His cum shooting into my throat.

I didn't know what he ate to prepare for me, but he tasted absolutely delicious that time. I couldn't help moaning and swallowing every drop as my lower half shook in the pleasure Liam was pumping into me. It wasn't hard to make me cum over his fingers, so I did gloriously, arching my back hard and crying out in pleasure. He hooked his fingers into me and kept holding the euphoria on his fingertips until I collapsed onto his lap with my legs going slack.

"Such a good girl..." Liam praised, earning one more mewl of joy from me between pants. His hand brushed over my hair with his fingertips ever so gently running through the strands and massaging my scalp. God, it was amazing as I rode down my euphoria. I practically rolled to my side, looking up at my lover with adoring eyes. As our gazes aligned, my heart skipped a beat.

This was a good man, and I was blessed to be his good woman.

Time became a mess I forgot to count, laying in Liam's lap as we were driven home. Liam escorted me back to the suite, but I could tell my thanks would continue beyond what I had done. His fingers continued to dance along my sides as he pressed his body against my back, kissing over my neck and necklace latch. Every butterfly kiss shot shivers up and down my spine. I loved every second of the elevator ride.

The moment we stepped out of the elevator, Liam nuzzled his

head against my neck with a small growl, sending a wave of pleasurable vibrations straight into my core. That sound was new.

"*Kitten*... bed." Two words from Liam's lips into my ear, and I was off, practically running. I could barely hear him follow in a slow walk, but I was already in the hall and through the bedroom door before I could care. I rushed to the foot of the bed and sat down on it, facing the door in eager anticipation. A small moment later, Liam joined me, already unbuttoning his shirt. Instinctively licking my lips at the sight, I straightened my posture as he walked up to hover over me.

"I'm here, sir..." I affirmed, obeying his two-word command. A smirk crossed Liam's lips before he lowered his hands to reach around my neck and unlatched my necklace. I almost protested, but the sight of my collar latched to his belt made me instantly shut up and re-resolve myself. Liam unlatched the collar from his belt loop and graced my neck with it, closing it in the back and running his fingers around the circumference of it.

I practically purred at the feeling of it gracing my neck once again. But, this time, it was all mine. As long as I stayed within the walls of Liam's suite, it was bound to me. It made me want to never leave just so I was never given a reason to remove it. As Liam's fingers finally traced under my chin, I opened my eyes to stare up at him. His expression was a mixture of lust and seriousness. I almost questioned it before he leaned over to brush his nose against mine and speak.

"Do you remember your safe word?" He asked, a hint of his caring golden-retriever voice lingering in his question. I nodded; it was red. I memorized it, and a part of me remained on the question. Was he going to unleash everything on me? His smirk grew before he looped his finger around the front circle of my collar and gave it a tug to assert his control. "Good. Then strip down and lay on the center of the bed for me."

I obeyed, doing as he commanded after he released my collar. I quickly threw my dress off and tossed it away as I scooted myself back to sit on the center of the mattress. I almost ripped the latches of my bra, taking it off, sliding my panties down my legs, and kicking it away. I was quickly bare, and I felt exhilarated about it. I was going to feel his total domination, and his gaze on me already spoke volumes about how much he lusted for me. The tent in his pants merely accentuated his desire.

As I finally laid back, resting my head against the pillows, Liam walked around the bed and knelt down to grab something from his lower nightstand drawer. As he came back up, I was pleasantly shocked to see an eye mask in his hands. I tilted my head before he leaned over, kissed me ever so softly, and placed it over my head to cover my eyes.

I was suddenly in darkness. Sounds around me amplified from my vision loss, but the mask was nice and soft over my eyes. Liam moved from my side and his clothes rustled with movement.

My heart stopped for a moment, hearing chains rustle. I listened in stunned surprise. It sounded like the chain was attached to some sort of pulley system as Liam seemed to pull on the slack and guide it closer to me. Then, as if lifting something fragile, he lifted my leg by the knee and wrapped a leather-feeling cuff around the bend near my thigh. While my brain was still stuck on how he hid chains from me, I was partially spread wide for him. Still, Liam continued to move, and I listened as something by the headboard was opened and a second chain was pulled. Was it in the headboard itself? He slowly took my hand and lifted it above my head, stretching it to where a second cuff was before he attached the cuff to my wrist.

I felt breathless, listening to him repeat the process on the other side of the bed with my leg and hand. I was bound by cuffs with my legs spread and arms locked above me. Still, the chains were pretty slack. I wasn't constrained fully and could move.

That was until I heard a button being pressed. The sound of pulleys slowly turning vibrated in the air, and the chains that my cuffs were attached to began to lessen their slack, pulling me wide apart ever so gently. It was slow, almost torturous, but as my legs and arms could no longer stretch, the button was pressed again, and I found myself securely spread. The air brushed against my teased, moist lower lips, and I couldn't help quivering at the feel, intensified by the darkness I was trapped to see.

"Perfect." Liam purred. I could hear him slide onto the bed and could only shudder in delight as his fingers ran over my inner thighs. I was already heated from the situation and felt his touch ripple through my lower body, so I could barely contain myself lying in his chain spread. Liam danced his fingers over my skin, running his fingertips over my thigh and tracing teasingly close to my pussy. "I hope you're comfortable..."

I only absorbed his statement for a second before his fingers suddenly jumped from my thigh to my pussy, his middle finger running up and down the slit as his thumb began to rub over my clit. I gasped, feeling every nerve down in my lower half jolt in pleasure, and instantly pulled at the cuffs keeping me spread wide. The chains rustled but did not give any mercy as they kept me down and apart for Liam's desires. He massaged and played as I could only shudder and moan at the intensified feelings, pulling my limbs in pleasure against my restraints. It was true that taking away a sense made your other senses practically triple, so every touch he placed on me lit me on fire.

"That's right, kitten... keep moaning for me." Liam commanded as if I had the ability to defy him. I was trapped in the best way and naturally obeyed his words. "God, you sound so good... let me hear more... I don't plan on stopping for a long, long while..."

He made a mess of me for what seemed like hours. It was as if he knew when I was melting into one action before he'd switch it up to surprise me and keep my heightened pleasure above my control. His fingers kept me grounded in reality yet spinning in a space of pleasure I had not felt before.

"Fuck... you're so wet for me... but I know you can keep going.

Give me more of your beautiful cries..."

I shattered over and over, sometimes on his fingers and others on his tongue. Liam kept me dripping, and my legs were quaking in ecstasy, but he ensured love to every inch of skin he could access.

When he finally used his cock, I was a blubbering mess, stimulated beyond my control and crying his name over and over in joy and ecstasy as he fucked me into the bed. I could feel every inch of his cock thrusting in and out of me, and, with how overstimulated I was, I was crying out pleasured obscenities and praises to him over and over in my moans.

He knew exactly what he was doing, and I adored it. I had lost count of how many times I came for him, but I was exhausted in the best of ways by the time he released me from my shackles and held my body to his. My mind wandered into a blissful space, relishing the aftermath of our sex and letting the warm sensations of my body roll through me without resistance. Liam continued petting my hair and massaged the places on my wrists and knees where the restraints were locked around. Each press and stretch made me practically purr and melt more into my practical coma of satisfaction.

"I love you so much, my sweet Maya..." Liam whispered to me, kissing my head. I was too tired to reply, feeling my body shut down to sleep, but my heartbeat quickened and thumped in my chest as I drifted off.

Chapter 12

Mystery

I found myself frequenting Liam's place more and more often. He treated me to a practical shopping spree of clothes, citing that if anything made me feel good, it was mine to have. I had my own section of his closet, and he even built an office for me in one of the spare rooms in his loft. Of course, I loaded my book collection into the shelves and made the room my own with bits of furniture and decor.

I practically all but officially moved in with him. Was that his intent? Lure me with gifts, clothes, and a space of my own? I wasn't against it by any means but seeing him bend for me as I did for him multiple times was cute. His goal was my comfort and happiness, so I wasn't going to second-guess his generosity. With my business on the up and up due to his support and the increase in sponsorships, I was able to start saving for the future, but if Liam opened his place to me, that savings would go toward something else.

Despite the pleasant gestures, I was also taught how to be a proper submissive to him. I had to wear my collar whenever I was awake, only taking it off when I left to return home, showered, or went to bed. I did not complain one bit. It was definitely custom-made, fashioned to be worn constantly and comfortably rather than just being decor for the neck. His instructions were just as simple when I was staying at his suite: I greeted him at the door when he texted that he was in the elevator. Easy. I was to be in the same room when he was home. Not an issue. If I was in the mood, I had to ask to be relieved so he could observe or participate. Hot.

Still, in our almost-seven months together, I was curious as to why Liam sometimes left our play. One phone call was all it took to take his attention away from me and thirty seconds into it to make Liam excuse himself. I first thought it was probably work, but it came at the most inconvenient of times. Was he on call for his job? It seemed a bit out of place, yet it would have made sense to be always available as a CEO if something needed his approval.

At the same time, his expression would change from light-hearted to almost stone-cold each time. His business was his pride, and I doubted it would have caused such a face to appear. He didn't hide his phone from me, so I indulged my curiosity by checking it once in a while. All the calls were incoming only and came from an unknown number. How did he know to pick up? He didn't entertain spam callers. Ever since I learned of the calls, some part of me was tempted to rush and answer his phone whenever I could. What if it was work? But why would he entertain it enough to break play with me?

It was quite bothersome...

"Is something wrong, princess?"

"Huh?" I quickly broke out of my thoughts. I was grating fresh parmesan and had almost gotten to my fingers if not for Liam's call. I dropped the small chunk I was holding and stared down at the pile of cheese I had made, confirming that this was bothering me enough to bring it up. "Well, uh... sort of, I guess?"

"What is it?" Liam's concerned voice danced into my ears as I listened to him walk over and felt him hug me from behind. As Liam nestled his chin against my shoulder, I released a sigh to hopefully brew up some courage. It was probably nothing.

Right?

"Master, who keeps calling you?" A flinch. Sometimes holding someone close was the worst time to try and hide something. It was important. It had to have been to earn such a physical tick from Liam in reply. Silence followed for a moment.

"May I ask why you want to know, kitten?" Liam's voice dropped, but it was of the more serious tone that he barely used. It was familiar in his nights of frustration after work and was rarely revealed to me. Was it work that called him frequently? Why was it an unknown number? It began to make less sense as I thought about it further.

"Well... it sometimes gets in the way of our time together, sir. I think I deserve to know who keeps butting in, you know?" I replied, turning my head to him as much as I could. He didn't push me away or release me, so it seemed like he was okay with at least talking to me about it. His eyes, however, became distant as he locked his gaze onto my cutting board. Was he really not going to tell me?

A sigh from his lips. His arms went slack around me, and he stepped back from me. I turned, unsure of where the conversation was going to go. When he locked eyes with me, I could sense a coldness behind his gaze. Did I say something wrong? I was his girlfriend and submissive. I had earned at least a generic explanation. Why the chill in the air?

"Maya, are you sure you want to know? You don't have to be involved..." He warned. It had to have been serious. He was hesitant, trying to maintain a friendly tone despite his tense stance. "I promise you don't have to worry about it."

"But I already am, mas--... Liam." I had to drop the play for this. I didn't have to be involved? I was already involved with whatever was butting into my romance with Liam. Part of our relationship was being open to each other; this seemed to be the last thing he was holding back from me. Why? Was it illegal? Was he involved in something shady? "If I'm going to stay with you, I don't want secrets between us. You know I'll support you no matter what, right?"

Liam's shoulders slumped as another sigh escaped him. He brought his hand up to pinch the bridge of his nose and took a breath before staring at the floor with a new resolve. A moment of silence before he finally looked up at me.

"I take calls from a man named Arthur."

"Arthur? Who is that? A business partner?"

Liam nodded and leaned back against the island counter. "Remember the car?"

Oh fuck, he was the one who owned the car? Things were coming full circle very quickly. From memory, I had recalled Liam mentioning that the car's owner wasn't the most forgiving but that he was a family friend. Arthur suddenly became the lead thorn in my side by getting between Liam and me. He wasn't Liam's father, but he held just as much power over Liam.

How was he going to greet me, the person who went to the hospital for his car, should we ever meet face-to-face?

"Arthur is... quite a character when you first meet him. He invests in trade, and he hired my father as an assistant of sorts. I met him when I was a kid, and he, in essence, inspired me to pursue technology."

"So, like an uncle of sorts?"

"If you call your father's boss an uncle, sure. My father was a simple man, tinkering with clocks and watches, but that didn't pay the bills. If anything, my parents owed our financial safety growing up to Arthur." According to just Liam's words, he was thankful to Arthur. What caught my eye, however, was Liam's grip on the counter. His fingers were attempting to dig into the marble as if he was holding back some hidden hatred.

"You... don't like him, do you?" I asked, very unclear whether or not Liam liked Arthur in any way. He went himself to get the man's car and even granted me my wish for protecting it from being stolen. Yet here he stood, physically conflicted with his words.

Liam pressed his lips together and shook his head. "It's not that

I don't like him. I owe him quite a lot. He at one point was interested in investing in my company..." Liam began before releasing one hand from the counter and holding it out to me. As he continued, I placed mine in his and let him caress my skin with his thumb. "He's just... unpredictable."

"What do you mean?"

"I wish I could properly explain... but the only way to truly understand what is going on is to meet him and see for yourself. However, that may be difficult with how he operates..."

Liam never left me hanging like this. Whenever I had a curious question or thought, he was forthright with me and ensured I understood everything. However, Arthur seemed to be the one block Liam refused to explain on his own. Was I supposed to be afraid of this man? Grateful?

It was the first time I saw Liam... submissive.

Our awkward silence was interrupted by the sound of Liam's phone going off. The ringtone was an old-school cumbia song with a female singer I vaguely recognized. I didn't linger on the thought for long, but Liam hesitated to pick it up, probably because we were mid-conversation.

"It's okay, Liam."

Liam nodded before pulling out his phone and answering before turning on the speaker phone. Whether he wanted me to hear the conversation or be part of it was another question, but I barely had time to think about which it was.

"Mom, is everything alright?" Mom?! This was the first time I was able to be in the room when his mother called, only hearing of past occurrences when Liam checked in with her. A few seconds later, a voice resonated from the device, soft and sweet sounding.

"Mijo! ¿Cuándo voy a conocer a tu novia?" her voice chirped. Liam went practically bug-eyed as he stared at the phone in disbelief. I didn't know Spanish but could only assume she asked something pretty gut-punching from Liam's reaction. His gaze shifted from me to the phone and back again multiple times. Did he think I understood?

I shook my head at him, trying to ease his worries on the matter. I thought it was about me for a moment, but it was better to be ignorant to avoid accidental stupidity if my instinct was wrong.

Liam took a breath and said, "When did you want to meet Maya?"

Hold up.

She wanted to meet me? Half a year of dating was a long time, so it was fair, but to just call about that?? That seemed out of the blue.

"You have been... cómo se dice... ahh-- texting!! About her for months!"

"¡Espera espera! Mom, could you hold on a moment!?" Liam quickly requested before muting his mic on the phone. He then turned to me and asked, "Would you like to meet my family?"

A big left turn. What did Liam's family have to do with this??

Where was this going? First, we were talking about Arthur, then his mother called, and now he wanted to introduce me to his family. The night was becoming weirder by the second.

"Kind of out of the blue, but--"

"Maya." Liam stopped my prodding with a stern call of my name. I took a breath, seeing the seriousness in his eyes. This made sense to him? Everything about this was normal? "Would you like to meet my family?"

He seemed adamant about making me answer his question before continuing further. If I argued the point, I knew I wouldn't get any closer to the answers I was looking for. This seemed to be another offer into Liam's world; the only way to open the door was to let him lead the way. He didn't seem to push me away from it.

I sighed. Might as well go along.

"Yeah. Yes, I would like to meet your family." I answered, shrugging. This was the oddest conversation to date for me.

Liam took a breath before unmuting the call and speaking. "Alright. How does this weekend sound?"

"Aye! That can work. I will let Mariana know. You tell Maya, okay? Took you long enough..." His mother teased.

"I'm sorry, but you know... priorities," Liam confessed, making me furrow my eyebrows. Priorities? What priorities? While I wasn't surprised that he didn't bring me to meet his family yet, as we had been together for less than a year, what kind of priorities would have prevented him from introducing me? This mystery was getting bigger and bigger with each passing second.

"I know. I understand. I'm only teasing." Oh, she understood??

"I know, mom. I'll let Maya know after we end the call." Liam looked at me with a nod, knowing the minor white lie would be irrelevant.

"Okay, sweetie. How about you come Friday night?"

"Sounds great, mom. See you then." They exchanged I-love-you's before hanging up with Liam locking eyes with me at last.

That was a practical whirlwind of emotions that I was not ready for. The conversation became a rollercoaster with Liam's mother calling and derailing us. While I was genuinely happy that I was going to meet Liam's mother, I wanted to get back to talking about Arthur. I needed to know more about the man that made Liam stand up straight and listen to his every word. I thought for sure that he was nothing more than a family friend back when Liam and I had our first date, but now there was more to the story.

"Did you plan to introduce me to Arthur at any point?" I inquired with a raised eyebrow. If Arthur was as close as family, perhaps he would be next on my list to meet after introducing myself to Liam's mother and sister.

Liam looked to the floor in thought before giving a slight shrug. "Only if he wanted to meet you," Liam confessed.

"If *he* wanted to meet *me*? What about the other way around?" Liam's back stiffened as he suddenly locked his gaze with mine. A ping of some sort of fear was echoed in his jade eyes, which made me question my curiosity about the man. Was he truly that fearsome? "Liam? This guy seems important in one way or another. It's not like you can hide him from me or me from him forever if he is that close to you."

Liam released a breath, whether defeated or frustrated, and shook his head. "You're right... I just..." He began to reply before pushing off the island counter and walking over to me. Liam took one of my hands and rubbed it over the top with his thumb, staring down at his gesture. "Only if you are absolutely sure... And I mean it: if you have no doubts about the matter."

From the way he spoke... doubts began to fester already. Arthur had become this enigma that intrigued me and almost irritated me. Ninety-eight percent of me wanted to see this man and see how he had such control over Liam. One percent remained doubtful of the need. The remaining percent... became fearful just from the vagueness alone.

Maybe another time.

<u>Chapter 13</u>

Warmth

I had agreed to dinner. Liam took me out to get a nice outfit for the occasion, despite it just being dinner with his family. While I was told it wasn't a steak-and-wine sort of occasion, it was still respectful to dress nicely. I found a simple dark red blouse and black skirt combination; nothing too fancy. I didn't expect much to come out of the event other than meeting Liam's family, but part of my mind was still stuck on the one man that made Liam practically bend the knee.

Who was Arthur?

I sat in the back of Emily's luxury car with Liam, contemplating exactly who the man was. Did he hold the family hostage with debt? Was he truly a savior for them? What made him unpredictable, and why was Liam beneath his foot? Unfortunately, without a last name, I couldn't do an internet search of him, and Liam kept his lips shut on the matter. Whoever this man was, I had to expect one day to meet him.

"Are you alright, kitten?" Liam asked, placing a hand on mine in concern. I gave his fingers a gentle squeeze with a nod.

"I'm fine. Just curious to see where this dinner goes, you know?" I replied with a reassuring smile. I didn't want to make Liam any tenser than he needed to be. He was already wound up about Arthur, and he did not hide that fact from me. The entire car ride up until that point was in silence, with only jazz music spinning through the air. Liam was constantly checking his phone, which was abnormal for him to begin with.

The night was going to be a game-changer.

We were driven an hour away from the city and into a large patch of land. At the fifty-minute mark of our drive, we were checked through a gate with security verifying Liam and Emily. What kind of house did Liam's mother live in for such high security?

Ten minutes after the gate, we came up on a hacienda-style mansion by a long stretch of woods. That answered my question. It was a lovely building from the front, but something told me it was much more lavish on the inside. Perhaps Liam financially supported his mother, or maybe Arthur did. I wouldn't have been surprised on either aspect.

Emily drove us around the front fountain and beside the steps leading up to the front door. Liam exited before Emily could leave the driver's seat and walked around to open the door for me. I stepped out, and the crisp afternoon air made me inhale the sweet aromas of flowers and fauna. I was glad Liam convinced me to dress up.

Emily made her way to the front door and gave the knocker two clacks before ringing the doorbell. Odd, but I didn't question it. Maybe it was a code of some kind. The security that surrounded the land was no joke. So why suspect anything as odd at that point?

After a minute, the front door opened to reveal a young woman with a multicolored blouse and high-waisted pants. Half of her head was shaved down while the other half draped itself over her shoulder like a gentle ebony curtain. She scanned her eyes over Emily, Liam, and finally me before raising an eyebrow.

"Kind of mad you hid her from me, Liam..." She mumbled before opening the door and stepping back to let us through. I blushed, slightly unsure of what she meant, as Liam led me in and Emily followed behind us.

Was this Mariana? She was too young to be Liam's mother, and they looked similar. Siblings, absolutely, or perhaps cousins if more people had shown up.

Liam squeezed my hand with his arm, making my brain stop thinking for a moment. "She's more than an art subject, Mariana." Was Liam being... possessive? This was a new side.

Mariana laughed and shook her head before closing the front door. "Touchy..." She grumbled in reply before walking over to me and extending her hand out. I took it politely and shook it with a smile of my own.

"Nice to meet you. I'm Maya." I greeted. I earned a nod back as Mariana looked me up and down in some form of appreciation.

"Mariana. The right brain of the family. You let me know if Liam bores you, okay?" Mariana replied with a grin and a wink. I felt Liam pull me back, but I found myself amused by the rivalry. She was gorgeous, but Liam had my heart and technically owned my body. The public collar I wore reminded me of such.

"You're not cute, Mariana." Liam retorted before walking with me deeper into the house. I took a moment to absorb the lobby courtyard and appreciate its splendor as a daughter of low-income. The place was humble but held itself up with pride in the architecture and decor. The tiles were practically polished as Liam walked me through the yard.

"I think I'm pretty funny, and that's all I need in my life." Mariana teased before walking up beside me and wrapping an arm around mine with a grin. "Hope you're hungry 'cause our mom made enough food to feed an army."

"When doesn't she?" Liam added with a small, appreciative smile despite his sister's actions.

I was a little nervous but hungry and eager to meet Liam's mother. She seemed very sweet and sounded like a gentle angel, the complete opposite of my own mother. As my thoughts ran along making a good impression, the smell of pulled pork and fresh tortillas entered my nostrils and made me drool ever so slightly.

"Oh wow... dinner smells amazing!" I praised, letting my nose guide me forward towards the smell. Liam and Mariana released me and followed me into the kitchen. A radio quietly played Latin-style music, and an older woman moved freshly heated tortillas into a container.

One look at me, and the woman smiled, placed the tortillas on the island counter, and opened her arms to me. "Ahhh, you must be Maya! It's finally nice to meet you!" Wow, she was friendly. I followed her invitation and walked over to give her a hug. She gave me a squeeze before stepping back and observing me with an approving nod. "¡Qué guapa estás!"

Liam's family was much too sweet. I could tell no negative words were coming from her mouth, which flattered me more than I expected despite not knowing Spanish. "It's wonderful to meet you too."

Liam and Mariana entered and made their way to the counter, where food containers sat in wait. Mariana picked up a bowl of corn salad and a second bowl of red rice while Liam took up the large pan of pulled pork. Both made their way out into another room while Liam's mother passed the container of tortillas to me. As I held it, she wrapped her arm around mine and began to guide me to where her children were.

"Tell me, Maya: does Liam make you happy?" Liam's mother asked, surprising me. Of course, that was quite the immediate question, but he did make me happy, and I could easily express such.

"He does; very much so. I'm rather lucky to have met him." I praised, earning a grateful smile from the woman guiding me.

"I would say Liam was lucky to have met you. He has never brought someone here until you, so you must be very special to him." That took me back a bit. I was the first? Really? Also, *HE* was the lucky one? There were already so many glaring issues with that statement that I hardly believed it, but then I remembered our first date.

We were both equally lucky.

I was guided to a dining room that hosted a handful of chairs and a table set like a party was to be had with more than just our paltry number of guests. There was pulled pork, guacamole dip, fish taco meat, tamales, and others whose scents melded together in the air to make my stomach growl in delight. Liam and Mariana were setting up the table as Emily, who had been silently following behind us, stood by the wall at attention.

Liam's mother guided me to sit down and actually started to make a plate of food. She took the tortilla container and placed it on an empty spot on the table before taking a fresh tortilla to create the plate arrangement.

"Is there anything you do not eat?" Liam's mother asked. The plate was for me?? I was half-tempted to stand and take the plate from her, not wanting her to serve me out of respect, but I held myself down. Maybe it was cultural? Perhaps it was his mother being friendly. No point in offending someone you had only just met.

"No. Everything smells delicious, missus Hunter!" I complimented, lost in the smells as I watched pulled pork and mixed vegetables get piled onto my plate.

"Please, mija, call me Rosa." Rosa instructed. When she finished filling my plate with delicious food, she placed it down in front of me. "Now you make sure to eat everything, alright? No one leaves my home hungry."

With everything smelling absolutely salivating, there was no objection from me. I nodded with a smile. "With pleasure!"

Rosa chuckled before filling up a plate of her own and walking over to the head of the table. Liam pulled out her chair and seated her, pushing her chair in. It was nice to see his manners stretch beyond me. After Rosa settled into her chair, Liam began to fill a plate of his own.

Mariana followed suit, stopping halfway to playfully glare at Emily. "You gonna eat or stand there?" Mariana asked, making Emily quickly glance at Liam for guidance. Liam nodded and gestured to the table, which must have allowed Emily to relax a bit. Emily walked over and began to fill a plate of her own, albeit a small one. Liam soon finished collecting his favorite portions and sat beside me with a lick of his lips. Mariana joined after, sitting at the corner near her mother, and Emily finished last, standing with her plate by the wall.

We all seemed hungry as we all began to tuck into our food and smile at the tastes we were lovingly punched by. I especially sank into the rich textures of the vegetables before they released their spice and seasonings against my tastebuds. The meat was tender and juicy, and the warm tortilla only mellowed the flavor like a soft cloud. Dinner was delightful, and I almost became lost with every bite.

"So, Liam, why'd it take you so long to introduce us to Maya?" Mariana interrogated her brother, pausing her eating to smirk at him and wink at me. "Wanted to keep her all to yourself?"

I couldn't help but smile in embarrassment. Mariana definitely flattered me, but imagining Liam being so possessive that he would hide me away was cute to fantasize about. Still, meeting his family would have happened one way or another, so he wouldn't have been able to hide me forever.

Liam rolled his eyes and stopped eating to reply, "Both of us have been pretty busy as of late, so I was not hiding her away." I nodded in agreement; glad he felt the same way. We were focused on work, cursed to remain as workaholics supporting each other. I was lucky to work a remote job, but it still took my attention away from friends and having free time. When I did have that blessing, it was spent with Liam.

Mariana shrugged and looked toward her mother with the same smirk and a raised eyebrow. "And yet it took more than half a year to meet her. Can you believe it, mama?" Mariana teased. I could hear that she wasn't being spiteful, so I giggled and paused my eating to join the conversation vocally.

"I'll apologize for that. Ever since we got together and it became public, my workload practically doubled; almost tripled." I explained, wanting to take the heat off Liam for a moment. "The last thing I'd want is to bring work with me when meeting you all for the first time."

Rosa nodded with impressed pursed lips while Mariana's expression changed from playful to surprised. "So, you're a workaholic too?" Mariana asked.

"Yeah, haha! It runs in the family."

"Really? What does your family do?"

"My father owns an auto-repair shop he built from the ground up. My mother actually works for Liam as the head of HR--"

"Hold up! For real?" Mariana went bug-eyed and turned her shocked face to Liam in curiosity. Liam nodded with an embarrassed expression. He rubbed the back of his neck before returning to eat his food, quickly exiting the conversation with a full mouth. I grinned. Might as well be a little brat.

"Oh yeah! It was quite the day the moment she found out."

"Oh, do tell. I can only imagine the scandal!"

"He and my mom had to have a big legal meeting about us being together."

"No kidding!? That must have been weird as hell! Certainly sounds like it."

"Without a doubt! It was the weirdest thing I've ever experienced, but I'd like to say it was worth it."

Then, I felt a hand lay over my thigh beneath the table. It took every ounce of control I had not to gasp and make a visual indication of surprise, knowing precisely who was touching me.

My mind became blank with the world around me fading into

darkness, focused only on the feeling of fingers dancing over the exposed skin of my thigh. They were warm, and every nerve they brushed against sent waves of excitement up my spine. The man beside me definitely knew how to make me flip like a light switch, able to turn me from thinking straight to thinking only of him. I was both mildly jealous of the power he had and eager to see more of his strength in such manners.

"Look, Liam: I knew you were weird, but did you have to make it a big deal like that? You're dating, not making a business deal." Mariana scolded, using a tortilla filled with pork to point at him accusingly before eating it.

"Her mother was concerned, so I did my best to appease her in the only way she would be satisfied. After all, I can't make Maya happy without her parents' approval." Liam explained, giving my thigh a small squeeze beneath the table and making another small shiver race through me.

Mariana swallowed the food in her mouth before waving a hand dismissively. "If dating requires contracts nowadays, I will take a vow of celibacy."

"Mariana!" Rosa politely huffed, glaring at her daughter midway through filling a tortilla. Liam chuckled as Mariana threw her hands into the air defensively.

"Mama! I'm joking!" Despite Mariana's claim, Rosa stared intimidatingly at her daughter before continuing to eat silently. Mariana let out a breath of tension and turned her gaze back to me.

"Like I said: if he ever disappoints you, I won't need a contract to make you happy."

Mariana winked at me, and I couldn't help but giggle. Perhaps in another life, I could have been one of Mariana's models. In this life, Liam made me happy and I loved him. That didn't stop Liam from crawling his fingers up my thigh dangerously towards my center, making me take in a breath. Was he seriously going to tease me during a family dinner? This erotica book cliché was impossible to hide in reality. There was no way he would have been able to hide his actions from his family, right?

I was about to speak until the doorbell rang.

Chapter 14

Unexpected

The front bell was rung. I was simply surprised at it, but the room suddenly became tense. Each of the Hunters became stiff in their seats. Liam, who had placed a hand on my thigh sitting beside me, suddenly gripped my flesh. It wasn't painful-- in fact, it was pretty damn sexy and pleasurable to me-- but it was evident that something was wrong.

"Mijo..." Rosa began, turning her head to Liam with a look of concern. Liam nodded, and I watched his expression change from worrying care to almost coldly calm. He took a breath, stood up, and walked out of the dining room.

Silence lingered in the air around us. The smell of the delicious spread before us couldn't slice through the awkward feeling everyone seemed to be experiencing. While the Hunter ladies kept their eyes to where Liam had exited the room, I tried to focus on something to relieve my own tension. I had a large gut feeling about who it was, as Liam's face gave me enough hint of the matter.

After the dreadful minute of silence, four sets of footfalls began echoing into the chamber. I looked over to spot Liam leading three other gentlemen into the room. It was at that moment I realized the weight of the situation.

Right behind Liam was an older gentleman, well within his late 60s. He had long gray hair with small streaks of black peppered through it, tied back into a small ponytail behind his head. However, his eyes made me question my thoughts; cloudy and pale aquamarines. He was dressed in a simple suit, almost matching the two men following behind him except in a navy compared to their charcoal black.

"Rosa! It's been a long while, hasn't it?" The man cheered, lifting his arms as an invitation for an embrace despite Rosa standing on the other side of the dining table. Without hesitation, Rosa walked around the table and gave the man what he physically requested, allowing him to pat her back softly in the hug.

"Que te folle un pez." Rosa greeted with a gentle voice and smile. I barely caught the smirk from Mariana in my peripheral vision but chose to ignore it for the moment.

"Always a sweetheart, Rosa!" The man pulled away and nodded before looking at Mariana. "And how is the art coming along, Mariana?" The man inquired, causing the woman in question to shrug.

"Well enough, I guess..." Mariana answered. She danced a fork along her plate, organizing different food sections while keeping her eyes on the man.

He shrugged back with a grin. "Well, if you ever need another investor, you just let me know, okay?" Was this man Arthur? At first glance, it was just a rich white guy, but on a second take, I could sense an air of power; stronger than Liam's. I had this gut feeling that this man could smile while holding a gun to your head. Was that the case? His voice seemed friendly, but his presence alone was enough to make the Hunters and even Emily tense.

The two men who stood behind who I assumed to be Arthur split up and walked to different sides of the room. They practically anchored themselves and stood like guard dogs, hands clasped in front of their bodies on their belts. As one stabilized himself into place, I caught a glimpse of a handgun in a holster. Bodyguards, for sure.

As Arthur turned his gaze to me, his expression morphed from gentle to energetically intrigued. "And you must be Maya Augustine! Am I right?" He asked, walking over to me and holding a hand out to me. I don't know what came over me, but I instantly stood and took his hand. Some part of me feared what would have occurred if I didn't cross my t's and dot my i's. The Hunters' expressions hinted at how serious I had to take this situation.

"I am. It's nice to meet you, mister...?" I replied, hoping to confirm this man's name to my thoughts and knowledge. The man grinned even wider before placing a hand over mine and giving a kiss over his own knuckles. Was it out of politeness, as I was not a woman for him to charm, or was it his taught mannerisms? It seemed like an older gesture, but one not commonly used, at least not anymore.

"You can call me Arthur, Maya-- can I call you Maya? I was

never a fan of calling people by their last names-- unless you're from Japan, where last names are preferred before earning trust to use first names because that's a cultural demand. One can't be successful without binding and bending to cultural respect, so I always check, haha! Does that make sense?" He rambled, aurally stunning me. He spoke so naturally, but his thoughts and words were wild and uncontrolled. He really was unpredictable.

"Maya is fine, thank you, Arthur," I assured with a nod. He returned it in kind, gave my hand a shake, and released it before walking around the table to plate some food for himself. Everyone in the room kept their eyes on Arthur as he hummed an unfamiliar tune and practically danced to the soft music from the radio as he walked. Finally, when his plate was filled, he moved to the head of the table opposite Rosa's seat and sat down.

"Wonderful spread, Rosa! I am famished!" Arthur practically crowed his praise before digging in. He wasn't a pig by any means, but he was unafraid of taking large bites and visibly savoring his meal with each sigh. Mariana turned away and ate silently as Liam returned to sit beside me and led me back down into my seat. Rosa returned to hers but simply watched Arthur as she sat down.

You could cut the tension in the air with a knife. The only person who seemed aloof to the feeling in the room was Arthur. Even his plus one and two were tense with their hands cupped in front of their waists; practiced posture for bodyguards. Emily remained in her place, slowly shifting her eyes between the guards like a security camera as if she was ready to tussle at a moment's notice. I decided to be the normal one and continue eating. The pork was still outstanding, as were the vegetables, so at least the atmosphere didn't ruin my meal. I was three bites into my dinner before I heard Arthur clear his throat after swallowing a bite of his own. I turned my head to see him wipe his lips with a napkin as he stared at me.

"So! Maya! You're the brave woman who stopped a thief from taking my car, if I'm right. Is that true?" Arthur questioned, leaning over the table with a curious smile. "If so, I owe you quite a debt!"

I wasn't deaf enough to not hear Liam inhale a hard breath of air beside me, but I steeled myself to Arthur's attention and smiled, waving my hand dismissively. "It was just strange timing! No need for any debt like that--"

"But I insist! A true gentleman should never have unpaid debts, and I pride myself as the truest gentleman one could possibly meet. That car was and is very special to me, so having it still at all is quite a blessing." Arthur detailed, finally leaning back in his chair with his hands bridging the armrests bookending his form. "Unless Liam has paid for it in my stead, I simply can't allow a debt to remain unpaid."

I looked over to the man mentioned, seeing him stare at Arthur with an almost emotionless gaze. Worry crossed my mind; was Liam okay? The conversation seemed normal at face value, but I wasn't well acquainted with Arthur, and Liam could have been reading between the lines into word ciphers I wasn't aware of. I couldn't help but jump to conclusions and assumptions when I was told nothing of this man or how he was able to control the room so easily with his presence. It was awful, yet I had to be the unassuming third party.

As I turned back to Arthur, I nodded. "Liam gave me the experience of a lifetime; a chance to review the Gold Nest. As a food reviewer, not many get the chance, so I consider that opportunity as payment enough." I explained. "It also gave me the chance to learn more about him personally."

"Personally? So you're serious about being with him?" Arthur asked, raising an eyebrow at me with a curl at the corner of his smile. The question was innocent, but his facial expression gave warning. I had to mark my words and present them with my chest; no room for doubt.

It was at that moment when time seemed to freeze around me. Perhaps my brain was going at a million miles a second and was trying to determine how to answer Arthur without delaying my thoughts. Maybe I was just that quick-thinking in serious situations. Regardless of the answer, I took each detail of my affections for Liam seriously.

I loved him.

It was apparent, and there was no other explanation for my devotion to him. Pushing aside anything other than who he was as a person, I was sweetly enamored with his loving side and enthralled deeply by his dominant side. He knew when to gently lead me and when to pin me down with his full strength. His kisses were addictive, and the way he spoke to me had me fantasizing about years of being his wife, him being the one I die with.

Could feelings build to such a peak in half a year? Arguments have spanned years of agreeing and disagreeing with such an idea. Of course, honeymoon states did exist after all, and soon the falling was bound to occur, but when would that be? I couldn't imagine it.

Liam and I spoke our truths to each other and were open enough to form our BDSM bond, which was deeply rooted in trust. So if I wasn't serious about being with Liam, then why was I there?

I took a breath and felt time continue forward in its conceptual speed, letting me speak aloud my thoughts.

"Yes. I'm serious about being with Liam. I love him."

A moment of silence permeated the air. I kept my eyes on Arthur, barely hearing Liam hold his breath. Rosa and Mariana kept silent, and I could feel their stares burn into the back of my head. Even the guards seemed tense with my answer. Why? Arthur, within that moment, remained locked to my gaze and returned it with a curious expression. It was at first enigmatic, innocently listening to my answer.

As the silence became uncomfortable, Arthur pursed his lips with an impressed twist in his expression and nodded before sitting back in his chair.

"Well. I'm glad to hear that. Would have had to kill you

otherwise."

What?

Liam suddenly stood from the table, but I was too stunned to react to the surprise action beside me.

Kill me?

"Arthur!" Liam barked.

Arthur lifted his hands in innocent defense. "What?! I had to make sure you weren't screwing around like the others!"

Others?

"Woah, hold on, Maya's not a prostitute!" Mariana's voice called out in offense for me.

"Didn't assume she was! Do you know how many one-night stands and casual hook-ups think they're the next missus wife for life? I've dealt with quite a few from my investments, I'll tell you what." Arthur continued to defend.

I, however, was left off-guard. Arthur was eccentric and clearly did not have a filter. However, I didn't imagine the man joking about killing someone, especially with how everyone else seemed to react as if he was earnest in the threat. Was he truly serious? Would he have killed me if I said the wrong thing? If I had doubt in my relationship, would he have seen it?

Liam must have felt my fear as he slowly placed one hand on my shoulder and his second on my hand closest to him. I could practically feel his concern emanate through his fingers into my body, but it wasn't enough to make me relax.

Why was murder on the table?

Fight back.

A familiar feeling bubbled into my chest. It appeared to take over the night I first gave myself to Liam, so feeling that surge of boldness within me wasn't surprising. I was the target of the conversation, and I barely took in the chaos barking around me in defense or offense to my reply. Was it a good idea to fight back? Especially against this kind of man? This wasn't a seduction attempt by any means. On the contrary, my words would have consequences of a potentially more lethal standing.

I decided to let the other side of me take over again.

I cleared my throat, causing the arguing around me to cease. My body slowly warmed up in confidence as I took a breath and locked eyes with Arthur.

"It's sweet that you want to protect Liam, but I'm serious in my devotion to him. Besides, I must warn you that I won't be that easy to get rid of." I spoke proudly, daring to see if the room was indeed as dangerous as Arthur made it become.

Within a second, the room became colder. Did I take it too far by playing nonchalantly along? Was his joke not meant to be replied to in such a manner? The warmth in my body didn't cool, but I could feel the air change from wild to calculated.

Arthur kept his gaze on me, obviously sizing me and my words up to see any crack or imperfection. I refused to break eye contact, stubborn as that may have been. I was bold, heat circling in my chest in confidence. There was no backing down.

Finally, after what seemed like an eternity in silence, Arthur began... to laugh. He threw his head back and let out a hearty guffaw, placing a hand on his chest and anchoring himself with his second hand on the table. There was an uneasiness within his chortle that circulated around the room to each person within it. As he slowly came back down from his giggling high, Arthur once again pinned his gaze on me and nodded before turning to Liam.

"You better hang on to her tightly, Liam. She's a good one." Arthur said with a grin before standing from his seat and adjusting his suit jacket. He gazed at his guards and nodded before stepping away from the table, leaving us all flabbergasted at the rollercoaster we had been on and how it ended. "In that case, there's nothing I need to worry about, so I will take my leave. Muchas gracias for dinner, Rosa. Emily, please escort us out."

The room fell silent as Arthur walked around the table and out of the archway exit, patting Liam on the shoulder as he passed our seats and letting Emily guide him out despite her reluctance. His guards quickly followed behind, keeping two steps behind their boss and leaving the dining room. We could only listen as their footfalls drifted away from us.

No one spoke until Emily returned and marched back to her spot, letting out a silent but powerful sigh. The confidence I had built within my body was slowly deflating as I realized exactly who I had spoken to and what I had said. What exactly happened?

Did Arthur approve of me now? Was he teasing some sort of hunt on me? Telling Liam to keep me close could have been a friendly compliment or a threat veiled with a smile.

A breath of air escaped my chest and out of my mouth, causing my body to almost fall back into the chair I was seated in. I closed my eyes for a moment before feeling Liam lift one of my hands and kiss my knuckles tenderly. Looking over at him, I could tell that Liam was mildly shaken. He gripped my hand and kept it firmly close to him, despite me not resisting. His gaze, however, remained locked on my hand. I could see an ocean of emotions swirl behind his jade eyes.

Mariana finally scoffed and chugged down the drink beside her plate before speaking up at last. "I hate that old gringo."

"Mariana," Rosa replied, a motherly warning behind the name she released from her throat.

"What? You hate him too!" Mariana shot back before looking over at Liam and me. "Are you two okay?"

Liam could only nod. I, however, allowed myself to step into the conversation. Perhaps I would glean more information about Arthur now that the man in question was no longer around.

"We're okay. Who exactly was that man?" I asked. Liam's grip on my hand tightened in impulse, but he remained silent. I knew he agreed that I deserved to know more, so his silence to my question relieved me. I knew it was Arthur, but who exactly was he?

Mariana sat back and rubbed her face before speaking again.

"Arthur is a rich guy that used to sponsor immigrants on top of his trade business. That guy helped our mom and dad immigrate here. Our dad came from Spain to chase the dumb American dream while mom called Mexico her home before the cartel fucked it up."

Rosa lowered her head in shame, but I couldn't judge her, nor did I plan on it.

Mariana continued. "They met at the same terminal, and it was apparently love at first sight. Arthur saw that and helped them move together to a neighborhood on the Southeast side of Chicago. A real matchmaker." There was a genuine appreciation in her voice, but it was plain to hear the disdain for the man in question alongside the praise. "Then, they got married and had us. Our dad worked directly with Arthur until he passed, and our mom got this casita."

"You're indebted to him?" I couldn't stop the question from running out of my mouth, but Mariana grimaced and nodded. Rosa did not react.

"Our dad took our mom's immigration debt and compiled it with his. Machismo bullshit, you know? Barely paid both off before he died, but that didn't stop that bleached asshole from invading our lives." Mariana spat before glaring up at Liam.

Why was she mad at him? Liam seemed powerless around him.

I looked over to see Liam close his eyes and let out a sigh of his own before finally releasing my hand.

"I refused his investments in my company." Liam defended.

"That gringo paid for your college tuition, Liam." Mariana spat back.

"And I've paid back every single penny."

"And fucking yet--"

A hand slammed down on the table, scaring everyone in the room except the one who caused the sound to erupt. Everyone, including me, turned our heads to see Rosa standing from her seat with a hand on the table.

"Enough. We have a guest. Behave, both of you." Rosa commanded, sharing an angry gaze between her two children. Mariana and Liam lowered their heads before Rosa looked at me, her eyes softening. "You are very brave, mija. Arthur... is not a good man."

I could only stare back, left with more questions than answers in my head.

<u>Chapter 15</u>

Truthfulness

The drive home was quiet. Liam didn't speak, probably unsure of what to say, and I was left trying to piece together answers in my head. Sure, dinner was delightful, but Arthur's arrival, comments, and departure left a strange taste in it. I was frustrated but intrigued at the same time, anxious yet surprisingly calm.

Was the confidence I had before building some sort of courage within me to withstand such strange circumstances? In the broad view, I was already living a seemingly fictitious dream of dating a millionaire to the point of meeting his family. Why not let a little mystery enter in as well? Was my mind just trying to prepare me for anything at that point?

I stared down at the partition wall in the car, trying to make sense of it all. The situation, my emotions, everything seemed otherworldly. Was this due to stepping outside of my little office in my parent's home? Did I owe life's karmic energies some boon for trying to stretch beyond just being a regular, boring food blogger?

Then again, it would have been very odd to owe life anything after rear-ending me into hospital admission.

Was this just fate, then?

"Maya?"

"Yes, Liam?" I automatically replied, slowly pausing my thoughts and turning my head to the man in question. His expression was dripping in concern and defeat, yet I knew he was holding back the answers I desperately needed to hear. Something was going on between him and Arthur; it was more than just some uncle-type protection.

Was Arthur some sort of crime lord? Was Liam involved in illegal business that bumped-off people as they saw fit? Was I living in some kind of book fantasy like the erotica I collected?

"Are you okay?" Liam asked, gently caressing my hand with his thumb in concern. He lifted another hand to cup my cheek in his palm, and I naturally melted into its warmth. I was in reality. This was the real world, and I knew better than to compare my life to a protagonist from a dark romance novel. More often than not, those girls were pretty and skinny damsels in distress or built to be as tough as the men they allowed to fuck them.

I was neither of those. I was a larger woman who ran a food blog... who happened to be dating a millionaire. I straddled the line between living a normal life and experiencing an erotica lover's dream. Besides, the men in those stories were strongly independent and often cold, feeding into the idea that communication was second to their dicks. Liam was the most supportive man I knew despite his secrets.

This was real love between us, and I knew my heart spoke the truth when I confronted Arthur. I loved Liam and felt he loved me in equal measure.

So, I had to make him open up to me completely.

"I'm okay... but is it okay if we talk? No more secrets." I laid my heart down for him. The tiny whisper that carried my question to him only emphasized my worry. Was he going to fight me on it? Would he hold back again? Arthur was a frightening man, unhinged and unpredictable as Liam had mentioned. Would even speaking about him put Liam in a bad position?

Liam remained silent for a moment, staring deep into my eyes before he nodded at last, releasing a breath of air he was keeping in his chest. "Here or when we get home?"

"When we're home. For now, can we just cuddle?" I asked, both relieved to hear an affirmative from him but suddenly scared for what I would hear in the conversation ahead. What was wrong with me? Too many emotions were dancing through my veins, and it was by far the most annoying and torturous feeling I had ever felt. I needed to be grounded and being in Liam's arms seemed the most appropriate way to do so.

Liam nodded before opening his arms for me and holding me close to his body. My anxiety counted the rhythm of his heartbeat as I laid my head against his chest. I curled up into his arms and let myself relax against him. As I closed my eyes, I let my brain shut off for the moment. No thoughts, just Liam.

Just him.

We arrived home before eleven o'clock struck, pulling into the building parking lot a few minutes before the hour came up. Liam roused me softly from my brief slumber and guided me out of the car, supporting me as we walked to the elevator. I was trying to rouse myself up, but the exhaustion of the evening was claiming hold of me now that it had its talons in my body. At some point during the ride up, Liam gently wrapped an arm around me and whispered in my ear.

"Into my arms, kitten."

I tiredly obeyed, wrapping my arms around his shoulders and hopping up slightly, letting him catch me and carry me in his arms. I wrapped my legs around his waist as he held me tightly to his body, nuzzling my neck. I knew he was tired as well, but he carried me without faltering even the slightest bit.

The elevator doors opened, and Liam carried me to his bedroom, slowly setting me down on my side of the bed with a small yawn. However, he lifted my chin with his fingers and gave me a small smile.

"Would you like to talk now over some coffee or wait until the morning?" Liam asked. I was glad he wasn't using our exhaustion to brush off my concern, so I smiled back.

"We can wait until the morning," I answered. Liam nodded in agreement before slowly removing my necklace and placing it on my nightstand. He helped me remove the rest of my clothes and offered to help me dress into one of the sleep gowns he had bought me. Despite the sweet intention, I slipped under the covers the second I had undressed down to my underwear, too exhausted to care. It was as if the day was finally forcing me down to sleep.

I couldn't keep my eyes open, but I felt Liam kiss my head with a small chuckle.

"Good night, my beautiful Maya..."

~~~

The morning brought sunshine, fresh bacon and eggs, delicious juice, and a serious vibe. Yet, even as I rose from the bed and latched my collar around my neck, I knew that day wouldn't be as relaxed as before. Liam had made breakfast, but I knew he was ready for a serious conversation when I saw him dressed in slacks and a button-up shirt instead of his casual sweatpants and tee. He somehow always made it clear that business meant proper attire as well.

Something about that made me admire him a bit more.

I slipped into a nice pair of shorts and a blouse before sitting down to eat, matching his habit to show how serious I was as well. As he served me my plate, Liam kissed my head.

"Did you sleep well?" He asked. I smiled at his consideration.

"Like a baby," I replied, leaning up to kiss his cheek before he sat down. He chuckled before finally settling into his seat beside me. We both ate our breakfast, happily enjoying Liam's cooking together and temporarily ignorant of what was to come. Only fate knew what was in store beyond the eggs and bacon on our plates.

As if our bodies knew, we ate slowly and savored every bite. We sipped our juice, taking advantage of time. Our spirits became heavy as our plates and cups emptied until, finally, we were left with clear views of our tableware. I stood and cleaned up for us, taking the plates and cups to the kitchen to wash each. I took my time, ensuring my reflection glimmered on each surface before setting each piece on the drying rack.

It was a while before I returned to the table and sat down, looking at Liam with a hard breath in my chest. However, as he looked at me, his gaze drifted to my collar and, for the first time, he frowned at the sight of it.

"What's wrong?"

"Would you... mind removing your collar before we talk, Maya?"

My heart stopped for a moment. Was our talk going to be so serious that our relationship was in question? I should have expected it, but I was still a little shaken at the idea.

After a moment, I nodded and slowly unlatched the collar from my neck, laying it on the table in obedience. I could tell both of us were not okay with this situation, but Liam and I knew we had to clear the air before determining what would happen next. It was both a blessing and a curse to have a partner willing to discuss problems rather than lash out in defiance. Something about the conversation we were about to have sparked an anxious flame within me.

"Ask me anything, and I will be as transparent as I can be." Liam began, breaking the tense silence between us. Was there already a limitation? I sat up straight in my seat, now confused. I had hoped that our conversation was going to be completely open.

"As you can be? What does that mean?" I questioned.

Liam's chest sank a bit at the realization of his words, and he rubbed his face before speaking again. "I meant it in an open manner, sorry. This... is a rather odd conversation to have, to be very honest."

"Well... I mean, if we planned on going long-term together, I'm sure this conversation was going to happen eventually." I politely retorted.

"In fairness..." Liam trailed off. He lowered his gaze to the table in thought, organizing his words, and I patiently let him. Then, finally, he locked eyes with me again. "I actually wanted to avoid this conversation."

"Avoid it? How??" I became even more exacerbated at the direction we were going. We were open, but now I was not meant to know certain things? What kind of secrets was I not meant to know? Why was Liam willing to keep this all from me?

Calm down. Listen.

I mentally took a breath and recentered myself. Liam was reasonable. He had to have a reason.

Liam grimaced and gripped his hands together, taking a breath to himself before speaking with his chest. "I was hoping that Arthur would... no longer be with us, as it were, within a reasonable amount of time, rendering this conversation useless to have."

Wait, what? Arthur had to *die* to make this conversation disappear?

"Liam, you're making no sense."

"Nothing about this will make any sense, Maya... but that's how it is, unfortunately..." Liam slowly unraveled his hands and held one out to me, a small desperate look in his eyes. "All I can ask is that you trust me."

Trust him? I had no reason not to... until that point. Arthur had become a point of doubt for me. He was everywhere; on Liam's phone, at his mother's house. Was Arthur aware of our sexual relationship? How much control did he genuinely have over Liam? Was this power enough to turn Liam against me if Arthur's back was against the wall? Too many questions flooded into my doubt and made my soul shake a bit.

Trust him.

I had to believe in Liam. He was the sweetest man I had ever been with. He had never once hurt me and did everything he could to ensure I was happy and safe. My collar was enough to prove my faith in him. I loved him and made it a point to prove as such when Arthur seemed to threaten my life.

"I trust you." I finally answered, taking Liam's hand in mine and giving it a supportive squeeze. Liam's expression eased into a face of relief yet still carried its sadness. I was steadfast, readying my heart for anything he could throw my way. Maybe he didn't pay back his debts. Perhaps he was still paying his father's debts off. But, even if Liam told me that he was some sort of secret fae prince and Arthur was his king, I was ready to listen and be open-minded.

After a long moment... Liam finally spoke his truth to me.

"Arthur... is, by legal definition, a criminal. He is the leader of an underground group of the rich elite: the Eye of Odin. They pretty much run trade, stocks, you name it. If a business runs on money, no matter where it operates, they know about it and have some thumb over it."

Holy crap, this was turning into one of the erotica stories I read really quickly.

"So... a mafia?"

"More of a syndicate, though many of the major Italian families are involved. Irish and other denominations are as well. All the Eye wants is to keep a tight leash on businesses and benefit from such organization. Harmless on paper, easily abusive in reality."

"Wait... so... do you...?"

Liam stared at me in silence, clearly knowing what I was going to ask.

"You work for him?"

"...Not by choice." Liam sighed and almost growled under his breath. While it was hot, I held myself together with the conversation dancing in my head. Liam was part of a syndicate group that had control over businesses, probably nation-wide. I could barely believe it, but I had to keep listening to the entire story and clear every doubt and question I had for Liam then.

"So... he's forcing you?"

Liam nodded. "When I was a boy, he was deeply interested in my love for technology. My father tinkered with watches and clocks while I was learning computer science. Arthur knew that technology was going to grow... so he constantly sent me books on the latest theories of computer development. Even some hacking books."

"He manipulated you..." At my words, Liam lowered his head in shame. Like mother, like son.

"I grew up adoring technology, so I went to school for it on his payroll. Of course, my father didn't like that Arthur had offered to pay my way, but I knew that my future work would bring in enough to pay back my debts to him... if only it worked out that way."

"But you said you paid him back."

"I did... some stupidly ignorant part of me believed that Arthur would leave us alone afterward. Arthur left my mother alone after my father picked up her debts, and Arthur even stopped contacting my father after he paid it all back, so there was hope... but I guess I was... I *am* too valuable for him to lose. The world runs on the internet now, after all."

I felt insanely horrible for Liam. He was a boy whose path was practically cemented for him, and he could only go forward in ignorance and bliss. It was tragic, as now Liam felt submissive to Arthur despite the debts he held over his parents and himself being wiped clean. Arthur had to have a lot over Liam to keep him at his beck and call.

Arthur was becoming more and more of a scumbag in my eyes. To do such a thing to a boy just to keep a leash on someone was horrendous.

Part of me was mentally screaming as to why he wouldn't just cut ties... but the majority of my mind knew better. Whether in fiction or in reality, you don't just leave dangerous situations without some form of plan and guarantee of safety. Even if Liam had just left for his own sake, he still had to consider the safety of his mother and sister, who were apparently in Arthur's reach at any time.

He was trapped.

I couldn't stop myself from leaning forward and pulling Liam into my arms, hugging him close and tightly to my body. He gasped in surprise against my ear and tensed up in my embrace.

"I'm so sorry..." I muttered, trying to comfort his shame on the matter. Liam clearly didn't want to confess what he had, but he opened up to me. I knew more of him, and some part of me was happy to learn, but I still felt deep pity for Liam's predicament.

A couple of seconds passed before Liam finally relaxed in my arms and wrapped his arms around me, pulling me onto his lap. I followed and held him close, letting him grip me tightly. Was this his first time revealing this verbally? It was undoubtedly painful enough to harbor internally. Did I open a bubbling bottle?

Liam took a couple of deep breaths, and I could feel him slightly shudder in my hug. He must have trusted me completely to allow himself to be vulnerable at that moment. We remained in each other's arms for a long moment before he finally relaxed his embrace and leaned back to look up at me.

"Well... there it is. I technically work for a criminal syndicate boss." Liam laid it out in summary. It was still wild to believe, but if he was genuinely open with me, I had to believe him. This wasn't something to joke about, especially in such a serious manner.

"So, waiting for Arthur to die is waiting to be relieved from it?" Liam nodded. "Does anyone else know about you working for him?"

"Emily, Louis, some of my security team, and my family."

That's why Mariana was mad at him. Did she know the full context? Also, Louis knew?? Then again, he was Liam's secretary and, in my time with Liam, I learned that they were best friends and grew up together. Emily made perfect sense; she was his bodyguard and driver. It made sense that his security would also be aware, but part of me was worried about anyone else knowing. Was it because I worried for Liam's sake, or was I gauging my own danger being with him?

"What things have you done for him?"

"Well, as he wanted me to focus on my field of study, I'm the tech man. I build safety and security for Arthur's financial assets, maintaining his connection to the tech world with stocks and the like."

I couldn't help but crack my goofy curiosity. "So, no hacking into banks or anything like that?" I let my mind playfully picture Liam in some sort of hoodie and leather gloves hacking into a bank with a grin on his face. It was cute to imagine and a slight relief from the shock the conversation had brought around.

Liam smiled and let out a chuckle before shaking his head. "Many members own the banks, so there's no need to hack into them. I mainly secure his electronic assets, so technically, I'm preventing hacks if that makes any sense."

"Can't lie: kind of imagined you in a room full of computers with codes and programs for tech-spyware and stuff, you know?" This was ridiculous. I was making light of a serious situation, but only because it was so unbelievable to be authentic. I knew some sort of criminal underground existed, but for it to be big and for my boyfriend to be involved was another story entirely. At least he wasn't some sort of mad hacker trying to take over the world or something.

Liam stared at me for a moment before giving me a little smirk. What was that for?

"Would you like to see my office?"

Chapter 16

Electricity

I swore I had been in his office at work. I opened every door in the loft and found no sight of any sort of space for him to call an office of any kind. He often worked on his laptop in the living room or bedroom, so I didn't expect him to have a second office. Where was it?

I couldn't help but nod at the offer to see it.

The next thing I knew, Liam was leading me back to the elevator. It wasn't on another floor, was it? I watched as Liam let the doors close before entering some sort of code using the elevator buttons. He practically memorized punching in the code, so I could barely keep up visually with his practiced speed, but it was at least ten-button presses. After the last button was pressed, the elevator descended two levels and opened to reveal a hallway with a large door at the end.

Liam gently took my hand and led me down the hall, stopping only at the door. Upon approaching it, I noticed it had a keypad on the side, a camera, and a sizeable biometric screen, or at least what I assumed was such from my imagination. I could only watch in awe over his shoulder as he pressed a code into the keypad, placed the fingertips of one hand on the biometric screen, and leaned his head towards the camera. Was it scanning his eye? It took a couple of seconds for the camera to register before a tiny blip echoed from the door, and some sort of lock was opened. It almost sounded like an air canister being released, but what could have possibly required such tightly sealed security?

The feeling of standing in front of a door leading into an unknown was tantalizingly fascinating. What if it was a big joke? What if it was just a desk and a computer in the middle of an empty room? As my life was slowly becoming the stories I read for fun, I couldn't help imagining rooms protagonists saw with their love interests. Sex dungeons, torture rooms, the works ran through my mind to prepare me for more wild sights beyond the now unlocked door.

Liam walked to the door and opened it a hair's length before looking back at me. "Tell me if this is in one of your romance novels."

He read my mind.

Finally, he opened the door fully for me and allowed me to step inside first. I was stunned at the sight.

The room seemed small, but that was only because the walls on each side were lined with large computer towers, assumedly server shelves. They went from floor to ceiling, leaving no space between them and practically making up the room's walls. It was mildly fascinating to see, but they weren't the highlighted parts of the area.

Towards the back of the room was a wall full of computer

screens. The computer they were connected to must have been turned on when the door opened. Each screen had a small load-up animation before revealing swaths of data and windows connected to security cameras. A large, glass desk stretched from server to server wall sat beneath the monitors with three sets of keyboards on top of it. Within it were intricate wires and electronics, all operational and lit with LEDs. An office chair was saddled on the side by a small glass coffee table, obviously used very little.

This was a hacker's wet dream. Was Liam telling the truth? Was I actually dating a wealthy hacker instead? Maybe.

I stepped inside and took everything in, hearing the mechanical electricity course through the space. The only lights in the room were the dim ceiling lights and some LED strings taped along the server towers and the desk. Liam stepped in after me and closed the door.

"Welcome to my actual office. I used to be in here a lot when I was just starting my company, building algorithms and security measures for random clients. Now it's more of a space for... Arthur's requests." Liam detailed, walking up to his desk and running his fingers over one of the keyboards.

"Are all of these towers computers or servers?" I asked, letting my child-like curiosity take over.

"Servers. The computer is actually built into the desk." Liam explained, tapping the surface of the desk with his finger. Liam then turned to face me, leaning against said desk with a small smirk.

"Imagine the world at your fingertips."

I could only giggle as I approached Liam, sliding my hand over the unoccupied leather chair beside him to feel the rich texture. The room must have had amazing ventilation because there was not a speck of dust around. It was even a comfortable, cool temperature, combating the warmth of the server towers and computers. One could get lost in this space with a practical window to the world on multiple screens.

"I can't lie. This is kind of wild, Liam. Never would I have imagined dating a man with his own dedicated floor of a building for his computer. Not even my book collection could paint a scene like this." I commented. While the room was built and used for nefarious purposes, I felt safe there. Maybe it was because I was with Liam. Perhaps I just wanted to sink into reality being less dramatic than the fiction I had imagined with Liam.

All I really cared about was feeling Liam's arms wrap around me as I leaned up against his chest with a smile.

"Perhaps that's a good thing." Liam hummed softly, leaning nose to nose with me.

"Oh? Why?" I questioned with a slightly curious purr. Liam's hands tightened around my waist with his fingers pleasurably kneading into my love handles.

"I'd like to imagine I can pleasure you better than your fictional crushes ever could..." The claim came so naturally from Liam's lips that it took a second for me to be taken aback. While I had compared him to the doms in my books before, he was undoubtedly much more than they could ever hope to be. Liam himself felt like a dream at points, knowing exactly how to make me quake in pleasure and taking care of me whenever I needed support. He was everything on top of being a businessman and tech genius.

I had the best fantasy in my arms... and I wanted him more than ever.

"You absolutely do, master... I love you..." I whispered, wrapping my arms around his neck.

"I love you too, my princess..." Liam replied, kissing me to solidify his words into my heart.

No matter who this man was, he was willing to open his heart to me and let me in. Liam was better than most men could ever dream of being, and I was the woman he chose to have at his side, in his bed, and within the walls of his darkest secret.

I couldn't help but press myself closer to Liam and deepen our kiss. His fingers softly tangled themselves into my hair as his other hand slowly slid down my body and massaged over one of my ass cheeks. I mewled against Liam's lips and melted more as Liam gently bit my lower lip with a smile and soft growl.

"Stay with me..." Liam softly growled. I could only nod, eagerly submitting to him. "Say it, baby..."

"Yes, sir..." I mewled out, unable to stop my fingers from pulling at the bottom of his shirt to pull it up from his slacks. As each button was undone, I freed them from their restraints and let my hands glide up his bare chest beneath. I could feel his heartbeat echo against his skin under my fingertips, and that only spurred me to press myself even closer to him, practically pinning him to the desk behind him.

However, Liam quickly grabbed my waist with both hands and spun me around before turning us to the desk. I planted my hands on the surface, effectively pinned by Liam's waist against mine and slightly bent over his computer.

It was hot, both erotically and physically from the computer being on. Of course, it wasn't burn-worthy, but it definitely echoed how steamy Liam was making me.

Liam leaned closer to me, nuzzling my head to the side and kissing my neck. The moan that escaped me practically spurred him to pull my blouse up and slide his hands into it, cupping my breasts over my bra lovingly. Finding the custom latch in the front, Liam released the bra from around my chest before replacing it with his hands. Again, I was weakened by his ministrations, mewling and moaning as he licked and nipped over my neck.

"You're the first woman to ever be in this room... and I plan to make you the first to cum in it..." That was a promise I was excited for him to keep.

All I could do was rub my ass against his crotch, welcoming the feel of his cock making a tent in his slacks. I desperately needed to get my clothes off; I couldn't stop myself from grabbing the sides of my shorts and shoving them down my hips. Wiggling my lower half to help my shorts slide down my thick thighs, Liam growled in my ear and ground his crotch against mine.

When my shorts hit the floor, one of his hands released the breast it was cupping to quickly escape into my panties. Liam's fingers danced over my clit, causing a pleasureful gasp and moan to escape my lips and making me grind my ass back against him in need and appreciation.

"God, Maya, I want all of you..." Liam moaned, tightening his massages to my breast and lovingly nipping harder at my neck. As Liam pinched my nipple, his fingers below slipped even further to trace over my tiny opening. He could feel how wet I was, but I knew he would make me drenched before he would have his way with me.

And I absolutely allowed it.

His desk was low enough to bend over it, allowing me to arch back and present myself to him in full surrender. The heat from the desk made me warm up even more, adding to my desire to be pleasured by my sir. Liam released my breast before I heard his belt and pants unlatching. Looking over my shoulder, I watched as Liam quickly opened his wallet with one hand and used his teeth to pull out a condom from it.

Impressively prepared.

He tossed the wallet across the desk away from us before he opened the condom, preparing himself for me. I quickly stretched my arms back to lower my panties, shuffling them to the floor and spreading my legs for him. My pussy was burning and dripping wet, but that didn't stop me from reaching between my thighs and rubbing myself in preparation for his girth.

No matter how often I took him in, he'd always stretch me out perfectly.

"M-Master..." I mewled out, arching as far as I could to angle myself for him. I heard him growl in approval, making me shudder at the sound, before feeling Liam lean over my body and wrap an arm across my chest to grip my shoulder. He buried his face into my neck as he lined up his cock to my entrance, and I could only purr in need.

"Do you remember your safe word?" He whispered hotly into my skin. I nodded, practically clawing at the desk in anticipation.

"Yes, sir..." I moaned, knowing he needed me to verbally confirm.

"Good."

At that moment, with how wet I was, Liam thrust into me all the way to the base, making me almost shout out a gasp. I was suddenly filled with him, and my body could barely take how pleasurable it was to have him inside me once again, all at once. He gyrated small circles against my ass, stretching me further inside, and I could only moan hotly at the feel, quaking underneath his body.

Before I could fully adjust to him, he slowly pulled back before ramming back into me roughly, making me yelp lovingly once again. Holy fuck, he felt amazing. He repeated his thrusts, again and again, holding me in place with his arm across my chest and his other hand on my hip. I could only take and welcome him within me, melting as he softly bit into my neck in dominance.

The room became hotter as Liam railed me against his desk. I was panting between my uncontrollable moans and gasps of ecstasy, already shaking and climbing to my climax. He knew exactly which spots to hit within me and practically slammed into them over and over, grunting into my skin in his own pleasure. My legs were practically about to give out, shuddering wildly as I was tossed over my first of many climaxes without mercy.

"That's it... cum for me!"

Liam groaned lovingly against my neck, pausing for a moment as I squeezed my pussy hard over his cock in my orgasm, but only for a moment. As I reeled from my euphoria, he returned to fucking me with the same merciless roughness. I cried out at the feeling, sensitive to the core and bound to feel him continue inside. He was nowhere near exhausted, even bringing up the speed of his thrusts within me and tightening his grip on my shoulder.

"Fuck, Maya..." Liam whispered into my ear. "You feel so good..." He emphasized his words with a bite on my earlobe, causing me to whimper from overstimulation. It was so good to feel him around me and within me, repeatedly ramming into my cunt without a hint of letting up. My legs eventually gave out, but Liam wrapped the arm previously on my hips around my waist to support me... or so I thought.

He supported my lower body, but his hand cradled my womb

with his fingers rubbing my clit. My body was officially on fire, surrendering to the touch and thrusts of my master and quickly rushing through orgasms without a sign of stopping. I was practically panting like a dog with tears in my eyes from how overstimulated my body had become.

Yet I refused to use my safe word. This wasn't something I didn't want. I adored this, and I was safe. I was just rising higher and higher into a space I craved and loved. I was nowhere near red. I was constantly pressing for green, green, green.

"O-Oh God, don't stop, master!!" I cried out between my moans, letting my pleasure rock my voice in my state of joy and desperation for more.

Liam's grip on my shoulder tightened, and he hugged me even closer to him, going even faster with his thrusts and moaning into my neck. "Mmm... such a good girl!"

The sex seemed endless, and I enjoyed every second. My pleas fueled Liam until he finally came, but not before I had broken over my own climax an innumerable number of times. My world was full of heaven that I didn't even try to count. All I knew was that my legs were jelly at the end, and Liam had to carry me back to the flat. Liam practically bathed me entirely by himself, and laid me back in bed after drying me off. Even his own exhaustion did not stop him from giving me aftercare.

There was nothing in the world that would take me from him.

Chapter 17

Slithering

Since that day, Liam and I couldn't have been closer despite the circumstances. He perused my erotica to be with me while I worked, and I cooked when he worked to support him. Our roles became symbiotic to our devotion as boyfriend and girlfriend and as dominant and submissive. My collar never felt more comfortable around my neck until that window of time, and I couldn't have been prouder.

A month had passed since that day at his mother's home. Mariana became a once-in-a-while visitor to Liam's loft purely to spend time with me. Of course, when she was over, Liam instructed that I wear my public collar instead of the one I had grown fond of. She spent the day in my office as I wrote up reviews and blog posts, taking up Liam's spot for her desire to see me. I even caught her sketching in a notepad while I worked.

The first time I saw her sketches, I was floored. She was a talented artist, for she even made me appreciate how she saw me: as someone beautiful enough to put on paper. Her appreciation of me made my confidence grow, and it showed when I spent time with Danni being more social.

"Girl, you look like you're living a fairytale with how much you're smiling. Good." Danni would complement me. It was relieving to know that she approved of my relationship with Liam and that she supported my growth. My spirit grew stronger with each act of support I got, whether it came from Liam, Danni, Mariana, or even Louis and Emily when they got closer to me over time.

With Liam's help and permission, his kitchen became my stage for recording recipes and reviews. No one had ever seen his flat, so it wasn't like anyone would know it belonged to him, but the kitchen was simple enough to not draw away from the focus of my videos. My fans and viewers appreciated it, and my numbers grew exponentially.

Everything was on the up and up with me.

As for Liam, he continued being as perfect as ever. He balanced being a respected businessman and tech genius to the world while being minimalistically involved with Arthur and his jobs. Unfortunately, there wasn't a way to force a separation between Liam and Arthur, so I could only move it from my mind. I supported Liam alone, and with how hopeful my man was in Arthur's eventual passing from the world, I could only count how much hope I had for the idea.

Our sex life had become welcome entrances into nirvana, and we stayed for hours every time. I had my fill of him each and every moment, and he continued to take every ounce of me for his desires. It was perfect.

Life was perfect.

"So, do you plan on introducing me to your father?"

Have you ever had that moment where you relished how far you had gone in your life, and something made your brain hit the brakes in shock?

As Liam asked me that question, it occurred to me. I was lounging at the kitchen island counter, watching Liam cook another lovely meal and basking in the joy we had in our lives. When the question appeared, my brain stopped.

Had... Had I not introduced them to each other?

Nope.

My face quickly turned a deep shade of red as I stumbled to get my phone out of my pocket. "U-Uh, yeah! That would be nice, wouldn't it?" I replied, quickly scrolling through my phone for my dad's contact information.

"Does he work tomorrow?" Liam inquired. I nodded before realizing he was facing away from me.

"Yeah, he's at the shop tomorrow," I confirmed, looking through the notes of my dad's contact info. I had written down when he worked at the shop when I still actively lived in my family's house. He hadn't changed his schedule since, and there was no reason to believe he wouldn't be following it then.

"Perfect. I think Emily mentioned the car needing a check. Might as well bring it over too." Liam casually dropped, making me metaphorically sweat bullets. My dad was used to ordinary cars. He had never once mentioned fixing a luxury car, so to imagine him having the knowledge of such was rather far-fetched.

Then again, were there significant differences between luxury and ordinary cars other than decor?

~ ~ ~

The next day, Liam and I made our way to my dad's auto-repair shop. He had built the business from the ground up instead of going to college, so he was pretty proud to be able to live off of something he genuinely enjoyed doing. While he was no car collector, he knew most cars inside and out, but only through learning about them when they came through his shop.

How would he react to a luxury car pulling in?

It took a while to reach my neighborhood where my dad's shop was. There weren't a lot of cars, so I could tell it was a slow day. Emily pulled the car into the lot and parked it in front of one of the open garages. Of course, it didn't take long for my father to step out of the building and walk up with furrowed eyebrows.

Liam stepped out of the car first and smiled before walking around and opening my car door for me. He reached down to offer me his hand, and I took it, stepping out of the vehicle and smiling at my at-that-moment surprised dad.

"Surprise! Hey, dad." I almost chirped. It had been a bit since I saw him, having moved into Liam's home. Sure, I made sure to text him once in a while, but nothing beat visiting him in person at that moment.

After a second, my dad finally smiled and opened his arms wide for me. "What took you so long, eh? Come here." He replied. I eagerly walked over and wrapped my arms around him, earning a good squeeze of a hug in return. "Your mother and I miss you, you know that?"

"I know, and I'm sorry. I'll visit more often. I promise!" I vowed. We held our hug for a while before we finally released each other, and my dad looked over at my boyfriend. His facial expression changed from cordial to almost blank. I could only assume that he still didn't trust Liam fully, despite how long we were together.

Then again, the last time they met was at the hospital, and I had only relayed my relationship with my dad over texts and calls. He never really met Liam beyond that...

Oops.

"So, to what do I owe the pleasure?" my dad asked, placing his hands on his toolbelt and slightly puffing his chest. Liam was a couple of inches taller than my dad, so it was mildly amusing to see him try and square up in such a manner.

Liam simply nodded his head and gestured to the luxury car. "Well, it's about time my car received a check-up, and, as Maya told me about your shop, I decided it would be best to request you to check it. She speaks rather fondly of your work and has told me of your professionalism." Liam replied humbly. While it was true that I did talk about my dad's work, I didn't remember ever embellishing his skill in such a complimentary manner.

Way to lay it thick.

His words, however, did seem to impact my dad, whose face lit up in surprise. My dad looked at me for a second before looking back at my boyfriend and rolling his shoulders back in pride. "Is that so? Where do you usually take her for her check-up?" My dad inquired. It took me a second to recognize my dad's fondness for cars by referring to them as feminine.

"Admittedly, my secretary ensures the car is checked, but today I wanted to see the check done myself with someone I know I can trust," Liam responded.

A moment of silence passed, with my dad dissecting Liam's posture with his gaze. Finally, after the silence became awkward, my dad nodded. "Alright, let's check her out. Pull her in."

Still in the car, Emily slowly drove behind us as we headed inside the garage. A couple of extra workers helped guide Emily to park exactly where the car needed to be before locking it down. As Emily exited the car, my dad took a small toolbox and held it out to Liam.

"Best roll your sleeves up." My dad instructed. I opened my mouth to protest, but Liam immediately nodded and rolled up his sleeves as directed before taking the toolbox from my dad. At that, my dad's lips pursed in an impressed expression before he nodded in approval. "Good. No hesitation. You'll be helping since you didn't have the courtesy to ask me to date my daughter."

"Dad!" I finally spoke up. I was twenty-six, almost twenty-seven at that moment. I wasn't a child who needed permission to be courted, and the tradition of asking someone's dad was outdated by many years.

"It's alright, Maya," Liam said comfortingly. "If this makes up for offending him in any way, I am more than happy to follow directions."

I could only stare at Liam incredulously as my father grinned in obvious approval. My dad then led Liam to the front of the car, leaving me standing in awe at what had occurred. While it only made sense to be a yes-man, it was still surprising to see Liam obey so quickly. Was it really to humble himself in front of my dad, or was Liam's submissive side coming out? Of course, I knew he was submissive to Arthur, so seeing such a side come out of him was not surprising.

For a moment, I considered him, for one night, being the submissive one. What would I be able to do to him? How much could he take? What would he allow?

Those were questions for another time.

I decided my time was better spent out of the way and walked into the shop's waiting area. It was a simple room with chairs, a table with magazines, and vending machines opposite a viewing window into the garage. I sat down and watched as my dad and Liam examined and went through the typical checks of the car. It was easy to tell that my dad was a little slower in checking the vitals of it, being that it was, as I expected, a car he didn't have much practice working with. Still, Liam was attentive to everything he needed, and I smiled at the sight.

"Man, this place is absolute dog-shit." A voice muttered, catching my attention and igniting a small flame of sudden offense. Who the hell was insulting my dad's shop?

I looked over to spot a man in a suit looking over the vending machine with a look of disgust. Upon just glancing at him, he looked like a model. He probably could have been perfect look-wise for an erotica book; dark brown hair, crystal blue eyes, and an unmistakable dominating aura that screamed he knew his way around the office and in the bedroom. He even had an attractive Italian (or at least some form of European) accent, despite what he said.

Still, his words were enough to turn me off from him. No matter how good someone looked or dressed, they could still be a crappy person to be around.

Stay calm. Ignore him.

He wasn't worth my anger. He was probably some asshole whose car broke down, and this was the closest shop able to help. There were two other cars in the garage being looked into. Perhaps one of them was his, and he was having a crappy day. I took a breath to calm down and quickly turned away before he noticed me.

"Maybe I should just set this place on fire."

That made me look over once again; rage quickly ignited from such a blatant threat. There was no way...

He looked at me with the cruelest smirk, like he knew his words would get my attention. He wanted me to look at him?

"Finally got your attention, huh?" He practically sang in an obnoxious tone, turning to fully face me and taking a couple steps toward me. I stood, not wanting to be caught in a chair, and mentally prepared to run or swing if he got too close.

"Who are you?" I almost spat, already sick of being in his presence.

"Someone who could fuck you much better than that boyfriend of yours, baby girl." He cooed, continuing to walk toward me with subtlety nefarious purpose. I moved to put the table between us, trying to maintain a safe distance from this increasingly dangerous problem and ignoring the disgust forming in my stomach.

"Doubt it. Crappy pick-up lines often mean crappy sex." I retorted, already unwilling to be civil with the stranger. I took out my phone, ready for anything to occur. "Now, leave me alone."

"Well, that's quite rude. Wonder what Arthur will think if I tell him Liam's little sidepiece doesn't have any basic manners." The man teased with a toothy smirk, causing me to freeze in my place. Was he one of Arthur's men? There was very little chance he was pulling names out of a hat, but where did he fall in the spectrum of Arthur and Liam's lives?

"That doesn't tell me anything, so why should I have manners?

Especially to some random guy who threatened to burn a place down like it was nothing?"

"Because manners ensure I don't just resort to other dangerous actions." With one flick of a wrist, the man moved his suit jacket to reveal a pistol, holster unlatched and attached to his belt. That silenced any resolve in me to retort again, but it also seemed to have emboldened him. "Now, I'm willing to forgive and forget your attitude if you just humbly apologize."

There was more. There had to be more. Besides, it didn't look like the gun had a silencer, so he wouldn't get away with anything unnoticed. Was bending my pride a good choice to begin with? I stared, trying to determine my options as quickly as possible.

He wasn't the patient type as he quickly reached down and pulled the gun out from the holster. My heart stopped at that moment, and the world almost entered slow motion as he went to aim out the window, most likely toward my father and Liam.

However, before he could target, a pair of hands clapped themselves around the gun and yanked it from the man's grasp.

"What the fu--?!"

The man turned, now weaponless, to see Emily holding the gun and quickly turning to aim at him with it. Thank God. The stranger, without hesitation, held his hands up in a form of surrender but maintained an angered face at the sudden surprise.

"Emily!" I exclaimed, relieved to see her despite her ice-cold expression at the stranger. She rightfully ignored me, keeping her attention where it needed to be.

"You have five seconds to step away from her." Emily threatened, moving her finger to the trigger to back up her words. The stranger did as he was told, moving to stand by the vending machine and give me an accessible route out of the waiting room. I took the opportunity to rush over behind Emily but did not want to leave her alone.

"I was just playing around~" The stranger teased, smirking at last at Emily and me.

"Shitty game to play, if you ask me," Emily responded, releasing the magazine from the gun and pulling it out. She then pocketed the cartridge, moved her hand along the top of the gun, and locked it so it looked empty. I wasn't completely familiar with guns, but seeing the stranger roll his eyes in irritation was enough to make it clear that the weapon was unusable in the state Emily placed it in.

"Now you're pissing me off." the stranger growled, lowering his hands to his sides and clenching them into fists.

"And you're lucky I was the only one who saw what happened here. Pulling a gun in front of an open window-- threatening Liam's girlfriend nonetheless... Are you really trying to piss Arthur off?"

"Like I care what that dying fossil thinks-- if he can think straight anymore. I just want Liam out of the way."

"Not possible."

"Like hell it is!"

What the hell was going on? I debated just leaving to grab Liam, but would that have made things worse? This guy had a severe hatred for Liam, enough to threaten me in a public place. The shop wasn't equipped with the best security, so anything could have happened. I was thankful for Emily's protection, but something else lingered here that worried me.

What did the stranger mean about Liam being in the way?

Emily tossed the empty gun at the stranger's feet. "As much as I would like to pay you back for the black eye you gave me months back, my priorities are protecting this woman." Emily hissed before turning to me and guiding me out of the room, turning her head to the stranger. "Leave before I make you regret sticking around."

I didn't even get the chance to see the stranger again before being walked towards where Liam and my father were. A twinge of fear lingered in my heart, but it was clear that Emily wanted to keep me out of it. Her serious expression did not allow any crack of opportunity to press what had happened. It practically clashed with Liam's smile as he assisted in changing the oil in his car.

Seeing Liam and my father's bond temporarily stamped my silence on the matter. This needed to be brought up another time. Emily's grip on my shoulders solidified as much, even as I spotted the stranger walk by out of the corner of my eye. He hid himself well behind another traveling employee on his way to the farthest car being repaired.

I made a mental note to tell my dad to close the shop for a while.

<u>Chapter 18</u>

Awakening

The car check went fine. The bonding session was successful. My father actually smiled at Liam, and I could tell that they were closer because of the surprise visit.

My mind, however, lingered on the man who threatened Liam and me. Who the hell was he, and why did he seem like a problem I had to deal with immediately? With Arthur, I had to wait it out with Liam. There was no point risking Liam's family if Arthur retaliated from a sudden leave.

With this stranger, the danger seemed much more immediate. He had some sort of hatred for Liam, and I couldn't understand it beyond just jealousy. They both worked for Arthur, but the stranger seemed to play the victim of stolen glory. How could that have been? Liam was very minimal with his work for Arthur. What could Liam possibly take beyond the bare minimum?

After Arthur passed, Liam was bound to be free, for no one else had any strings over Liam's health and safety... until that point.

"Kitten?" Liam's voice caught my attention. I straightened up and looked over at him. He sat beside me in the luxury car as we were being driven back to the loft, but now he had a look of worry on his face. Was I really that deep in thought?

"Ah! Sorry... What's up?" I dodged, putting on a smile and temporarily sweeping my mind of my worries.

"Did you want me to order dinner tonight? You seem a little preoccupied." Liam spoke, tilting his head to the side and gently stroking my cheek. "Is everything okay?"

Looking up briefly past the partition, Emily's gaze met mine in the rearview mirror as if she was curious about what I would say.

I couldn't lie to him, despite my instinct to do so. We promised to be open to each other, and he let me in on his darker side. If I demanded his truth, he earned mine.

"There was... someone at the shop." I started to regale, letting my memories bring me back to that moment in the waiting room. "Someone who knew you."

Liam's eyebrows furrowed farther, a flash of confusion crossing his jade gaze. Plenty of people knew him. He was a popular CEO that frequented social media. We had to give thanks to the paparazzi that practically stalked his every move outside of his loft. Before he opened his mouth to say anything, Emily spoke up and revealed a singular word; a name. "Giorno."

With that name, I finally had the identity of someone I had to be careful of. However, I also witnessed Liam's expression quickly shifting from worry to absolutely murderous. It was jarring to see, despite his gaze being turned to Emily. The car, cool enough from the air conditioning, became like a freezer within seconds.

For the first time... I was afraid of Liam, and I wasn't the one who angered him.

"What did he do?" Liam quietly asked, his voice as cold as the car felt.

"He cornered Miss Augustine and threatened her. He also pulled his weapon, but I was safely able to remove her from the situation without anyone's notice." Emily reported, locking her gaze to the road as she continued to drive us.

Liam lifted his head and quickly turned to look at me in shock, causing me to flinch from the sudden change in energy. He wasn't going to take anything out on me, was he? He wasn't mad at me, right? To my relief, Liam gently took my hand in his and held out his arm, opening his chest to me for an embrace.

"You're not hurt, are you? Please tell me he didn't hurt you..." Liam asked. I could hear him holding back some sort of rage, but he wasn't going to let it loose on me. I was beyond thankful, slowly shaking my head and leaning in to let myself be engulfed in his embrace.

"I'm okay. I promise. He didn't even touch me." I comforted him, wrapping my free arm around him to give his body a soft squeeze. He remained stiff, only warm for a hug and soft to keep me safe. Otherwise, with his quickened heartbeat in my ear, I knew a fire was raging within him, and he was doing everything he could to remain visually okay.

"Emily..." Liam muttered through his teeth, gently petting my hair with the softest of care.

"Louis is already on the way over to the shop to organize a watch on it. I notified him via text after securing Miss Augustine." Emily confirmed, turning into a familiar street in the city. Liam took a couple of deep breaths, but I could tell he wasn't satisfied or any calmer doing such. As he held me in his arm, he quickly moved a hand to slip his phone out of his pocket and quick-dialed a number. After Liam put the phone on speaker, it rang twice before being answered.

"I'm here. We have two on each corner with eyes on the shop." Louis's voice replied. I remained silent and listened, not wanting to interrupt Liam's methods and actions he deemed needed.

"Priorities are Mr. Augustine and the employees. I'll have eyes there soon on my end, but the second that *malparido* gets even close to there--" Liam began, practically growling. His hand on my back remained soft but quaked as if bound by harsh control to stay gentle.

"Miss Augustine, are you there?" Louis's voice called out, causing Liam to stop and silence himself. I froze up for a second, looking up at Liam in hesitation. After a second of silence, I decided to speak up.

"I'm here, Louis. I'm okay."

"Very good. Please rest assured that we'll do everything we can to protect your family and their livelihoods." Louis soothed despite my answer. I took a breath to sigh and smile slightly. While words were just words, it was good to at least hear that it wasn't just me who was protected.

"Thank you, Louis. I really appreciate hearing that." I said, nuzzling Liam's chest in an attempt to help him also calm down. I felt Liam give me a slight squeeze with the arm he had around me and lower his head to rest his chin against the top of my head.

"Emily, please join them after dropping us off home." Liam requested, earning a nod from the woman in question. "Louis, please keep me--... *us* updated."

At Liam's stumble, I turned to look up at him, catching him staring down at me with the strangest mixture of expressions on his face. I could tell he was trying to be calm and not furrow his eyebrows to indicate anger. Yet, at the same time, his politeness for my consideration barely hid his previously cold state of mind.

This wasn't a dealbreaker. It was another side of Liam I had never faced, and now that it was in the spotlight, I had to see how I would handle him and how he would handle himself now that I was at his side. A heavy part of me was worried about him, but this was something I also had to observe and adjust to accordingly.

What would he do if something went terribly wrong?

We arrived at the loft and made our way up the elevator. Despite pretending not to listen or care, I eavesdropped on Liam, confirming with Louis and Emily that they were not followed and that his security team, who answered to Louis, confirmed that the building and block were safe as well. We had a haven to stay in, at the very least.

I was thankful that my collar brought me comfort. Knowing that danger was within reach put me on edge, though I refused to show it. I couldn't add to Liam's stress, which was higher than I had ever witnessed. So instead, I closed my eyes and imagined the warm fur of the collar tingling and heating up my neck, taking my mind away on a bit of a vacation as we ascended the building.

Liam let out an audible sigh, taking me out of my thoughts. I turned my head to watch him take out his phone and open his food delivery apps. He never actually got anything delivered. He'd place his orders for pick-up, and a trusted security guard would obtain it to bring it back. We were both a little distracted to consider cooking, and he did suggest the idea of ordering in the car.

"Would you like anything specific, kitten?" Liam asked.

"Surprise me, master."

~~~

We thought the night would be uneventful.

We believed for sure that nothing terrible would occur.

Laying together in bed, Liam held me close as we slept into the night. The only thing that broke our peace was Liam's cell phone ringing. It was Emily's ringtone: the only country-rock song on his phone. Liam answered it. Being a light sleeper but moving, he also woke me, a deep sleeper, up. Instead of putting it on speakerphone, Liam kept the phone to his ear.

"Emily?" Liam answered, trying to hide the grogginess of his voice. Due to my tired state, I could barely hear Emily's voice as it was muffled by the phone and Liam's ear, but I could sense that it was frantic and panicked by how loud she was. Slowly, Liam sat up, gently removing his arm from around me, and continued to listen. Bleary-eyed, I stared at Liam's back.

"Liam? What's going on?" I muttered out, trying to fight the sleep my body wanted to return to doing. Faintly visible to my foggy vision, I witnessed Liam's bare back twitch, mildly shaking. Before I could ask again, Liam hung up the phone and placed it on the bed between us.

"Darling. Please go back to sleep. I'll join you in a moment." Liam's voice rumbled, cold as ice and threatening consequences if I disobeyed. This wasn't a playful threat. Instead, it was something that made goosebumps litter my skin and acted like a shot of adrenaline into my heart.

I was wide awake at that very moment.

Liam slowly rose from the bed, refusing to turn and look at me, and silently walked out of the room. I watched, stunned, as he closed the door behind him. It was gently handled, but something in my brain suggested that, if he was alone, the door would have been slammed shut; maybe even broken off of its hinges.

I knew how strong that man was. He held me up multiple times without breaking a sweat, and I was around two hundred and ten pounds. So, imagining him breaking a door was not as far-fetched as one would think.

I slowly took his phone from the bedsheets and unlocked it, knowing its password with permission from the owner in question. I scrolled and opened his phone history log, seeing Emily's number before calling it back.

Two rings, and Emily answered.

"Sir?" Emily asked, exhaustion and pain in that singular word alone.

"Emily? It's me, Maya." I softly responded, quickly turning the call on speakerphone.

"Miss Augustine! Did Liam leave?" Emily's voice changed to immediate concern.

"Yeah, he just left the bedroom. He said he'd be back in a moment, so..." I began, trying to dissect what was going on with the bit of information I had. Emily was with Louis at my father's shop. If something was wrong, it was obvious that something had gone down. "What happened at the shop? Are you okay? Louis?"

I listened to Emily let out a heavy sigh before taking a breath and replying. "There was an incident at the shop, and... Louis is in the hospital now."

I stared at the phone in disbelief. Louis was hurt? Over something that happened at the auto shop? My mouth opened to speak, but I suddenly forgot how to utter words, unable to form a sentence that would make sense to say aloud without conflicting with my confusion. Luckily, Emily continued.

"We couldn't save the building, but thankfully none of the workers nor your father was there."

"W--...What happened to the shop?" I muttered before hearing my phone go off. The ringtone was Danni's, a sexy house beat. She rarely called, especially not so late at night. I quickly grabbed my phone and answered. "Danni?"

"Are you okay?! Are you and your folks safe?!" Danni pressed. Emily, clearly hearing the second call, remained silent as I spoke to Danni.

"I-I'm fine! My folks should be too! What's wrong?" I asked, pretending to be more ignorant than I was of the situation.

"I'm on my way home from a club, but I just passed by your dad's shop. It's completely burnt down! The fire department is there too!" Danni revealed, making my heart stop.

My dad's shop... was gone? Burnt down?

I could barely let out a "W--What...?" as I stared out towards the opposite wall of the room in shock.

"Oh my God, I'm so sorry... Damnit... Let me hang up, and you can check on your folks. Where are you right now?" Danni spoke, but my mind refused to move past the news in front of me. The danger was more significant than I could have anticipated, even knowing what I signed up for as Liam's girlfriend.

Now my family was in danger. Was this worth it? Logically, anyone would have run to protect the ones they love. It was human nature. Why stick around and risk losing the people you care about?

My parents didn't deserve to have a target on their backs while I had Liam and his forces protecting me.; all because Liam made me happy.

Should I defy my natural instincts?

Yes. Stop doubting your heart.

Liam wasn't the problem. Giorno was. Liam was gentle and protective, able and willing to support me. He had proven to be a dedicated partner and seemed to see me in his future with how he willingly let me meet his family and learn his secret. But, on the other hand, Giorno appeared to be the epitome of a mafia gangster, dangerous and willing to destroy anything to get what he wanted.

Giorno would have been who I swooned for in fiction, which was the scariest part of all.

"Maya? Are you there??" Danni's voice called out, breaking me from my mental battle.

"Y-Yeah. I'm here. I'm gonna call my parents. Stay safe." I kept my reply simple before hanging up and calling my father's number. Three rings and an answer came.

"Sweetie? It's three in the morning. What's wrong?" My father asked, his voice weighed down from sleep having hold of him. He was safe. Good.

"Is mom with you?" I asked, trying to keep my own voice calm and collected.

"Yes? Why?" I could hear my mom rouse herself awake in the background. She was safe too. Very good. Now to explain without dragging Liam into it.

"Dad... Danni called. She was on her way home from the city and... she saw the shop. It's been burnt down."

Deafening silence replied. What was going on in my dad's mind? Was he as shocked as me? The shop was his life's work. Of course, it was a blessing that none of his workers or him got hurt, but the building stood for almost thirty years. My father's shop represented hard work, dedication, and a promise to provide.

"The fire department hasn't called me. Were they there?" My dad spoke slowly. I could faintly hear my mother asking what happened, so it was clear I wasn't on speaker.

"Danni told me they were extinguishing the flames as she went past," I reported. Another moment of silence.

"Jerry. What is going on? Was there a fire??" My mom's voice echoed in the background, forceful for an answer.

"There was a fire at the shop. The fire department is there now, but Maya's friend saw it and called her to tell her what happened." My dad answered, his slow pace now hinting at holding back despair from the choked tone of his voice.

"Oh my God..." My mother muttered, barely audible from the phone. I felt despair hearing both of my parents take in the news. I could have let them learn of their shop's fate on their own, but with me being the target of the attack, I felt... responsible, at least partially.

I heard the phone vibrate on my dad's end. It was probably the fire department.

"There they are. Let me go answer them and take care of this, okay? You go back to sleep. Thank you for letting us know and thank Danni for us." My dad instructed. I instinctively nodded. I knew I couldn't help at that moment, despite every fiber in my body wanting to run home to them.

"Okay, dad. You let me know what I can do to help in the morning, okay?"

"Will do. Love you."

And the call ended. I lowered my phone and looked back at Liam's, seeing it still connected to Emily's phone. She had to have been listening to me the whole time, but to have such patience for me was surprising.

"Emily?"

"Yes, miss Augustine?"

"...what do I do?" I was lost. I was trying to be as calm and logical as possible, but I could feel my mind begin to reel at what was going on. Any normal person would have felt this, yet I desperately clung to the idea that I was somehow stronger. Why? I wasn't sure. Maybe it was the confidence I found at Liam's side. Perhaps my rise in my work gave my boldness a deceiving but fragile milk crate to stand on.

"...It may seem like a lot is happening now, but if I know mister Hunter as well as I do, he's already working to fix this." Emily comforted me.

"Has something like this happened before?" I asked.

"Not really, but you're really special to him. Liam would do anything for you. He's probably solving it now as we speak."

It was sweet to hear such words, but my mind switched from my own worry to concerned curiosity. What was Liam truly capable of doing? What was he going to do at all? He couldn't have left, right? He said he would return shortly, so I had to assume he was still in the building. Was he going to use his computer for something? So many questions rang in my head, and all my spirit wanted, at the end of it, was to sleep. I wanted to see this night be a dream gone wrong rather than live it in real-time reality.

"...thank you, Emily," I spoke at last. "When you can, give Louis my love."

With that, I hung up. I was alone, and with my own heart and mind to deal with. It was a chaotic party for my body to endure, but the only thing I could do was wait for Liam to return. After all, what could I possibly do in retrospect? I was one woman in a world where setting fire to innocent businesses was an overnight occurrence. Where a gun was easily pointed towards people you loved without hesitation. I knew basic self-defense, but I never once wielded a gun or even imagined getting close to the actual crime world under the shadows of my reality. This wasn't one of my erotica books where I was a badass werewolf or strong heroine with magic or power.

I was just a simple food blogger, and I was scared.

Minutes passed in my silence before the bedroom door opened

again. To my surprise, Liam walked through with a calm expression. His body seemed relaxed like he had accomplished something and was now resting from it. He locked eyes with me, and I could not see a single hint of anger behind his gaze. What on Earth did he do?

"Liam?" I spoke aloud, breaking the previous silence in the room as he approached. Liam walked around to his side of the bed and sat beside me, holding his arm out to invite me into an embrace.

"Everything's alright. Let's go back to bed." Liam said, vague enough to give both comfort and confusion.

"...are you sure?" I asked, leaning into his arms as he nodded.

"I'll explain everything in the morning. Right now, we need rest." Liam insisted.

Sleep.

I could only agree. In the morning, I'd have more energy to dissect everything. Then, I'd be able to use my power to help solve this issue instead of being the messenger girl of despair to my family.

I couldn't help crying in Liam's arms. He held me as if he was aware that I knew what was going on. He didn't confront me but let me open up like a tidal wave against his chest.

After the longest cry I had till that point, tears drew me to sleep.

Chapter 19

Damages

When I closed my eyes that night, I imagined I would have woken up to a different set of news. Louis wasn't in the hospital. My father's shop was still intact. My life wasn't suddenly becoming a strange conglomeration of low-chance happenings connected to a criminal world.

How nice to hope for such.

I woke up still in Liam's arms, practically buried and snuggled against his bare chest. He was awake, proven by his hand softly stroking my hair. I could feel the puffiness of my eyes and slightly adjusted myself in Liam's embrace to stretch. As I looked up to see Liam's face, his expression was serene, like nothing was wrong. His eyes were closed as if he was focused on listening to his thoughts or petting me. It would have looked like he was genuinely asleep if he wasn't already brushing my hair with his fingers.

"Liam?" I muttered out, reaching up to cup his cheek. He slowly opened his eyes and nuzzled my hand as he made eye contact with me.

"Good morning, princess. Would you mind coming with me to the kitchen so I can make breakfast? I believe you are owed some explanations." Liam said, earning a tired but affirmative nod from me. I didn't know what Liam did to make last night seem like a passable non-issue, but he was willing to explain as he promised.

Another reminder of how lucky I was, despite the chaos surrounding us.

Liam kissed my forehead and helped me sit up in bed before sliding out himself. He walked around the bed and held out a hand to me, which I took to slowly stand as well. I took my time to the bedroom door, which Liam opened and followed me through. Finally, we reached the kitchen, and I sat on one of the island counter stools, slouched over the surface as I continued to wake up.

"Coffee?" Liam asked. I nodded. He began preparing some in his coffee machine before setting out ingredients for breakfast. I rubbed my eyes and watched as Liam slowly worked through each component to make a quick breakfast. Whatever he was thinking, it was veiled so well with his focus on cooking that he became enigmatic.

There was no music playing, so silence claimed the air, only interrupted by the sizzle of bacon, the soft pop of the toaster, and the beep of the coffee machine.

"Liam?" I broke the silence with my voice as he slid the bacon from his pan to a paper-towel-lined plate. He stopped obediently and placed the pan down on the stove before turning to face me.

"Yes, my love?" He asked. It was now or never. He was letting me determine when the glass wall of ignorance would break, so I took hold of the hammer to smash it myself.

"...can I ask what happened now?"

Liam stared at me for a moment before nodding, taking a breath before taking the coffee pot and filling two mugs with its contents. He returned the pot to the machine, turned off the stove, and moved the bowl of eggs set for cooking aside before placing one of the coffee mugs in front of me.

"Last night, there was an incident. Your father's shop was attacked, ending with it engulfed in flames." Liam started, staring at me for my reaction. I didn't have the strength to act surprised, but I had a feeling he was keenly aware that I knew. Still, it was reassuring to hear it come from him instead of him hiding the news from me. He continued, unaffected. "Louis and his team tried to stop it but wound up in a fight with Giorno's men. Louis is currently recovering in the ICU along with others, so please don't worry."

I took a breath, taking in reality once again. Everything that occurred that previous night wasn't a dream, so I had to harden myself for what we planned to do. I refused to not be involved in fixing the situation, and I would help determine what to do to protect not only my family but Liam's as well.

"Okay... what do we do?" I asked, rolling my shoulders back.

Liam shook his head, making me freeze in confusion. He then looked at the time on his phone before taking a TV remote from a drawer and turning on the rarely used TV hanging from the kitchen corner. He scrolled through channels before arriving at the city news station.

What I witnessed stunned me.

"Local authorities have apprehended seven men, who may be connected to the mom-and-pop shop August Motors fire, thanks to an anonymous tip who claimed to have seen them commit the arson. Upon arrest, all seven confessed. Confirming with the street cameras on sight identifying each suspect, these seven men are now being held for arson, assault of civilians, and potentially more." The news anchor reported. How did this happen so quickly? While I was slightly glad for the quick response, police were usually never on top of a crime so quickly. She continued. "Authorities have also taken another suspect who wasn't at the crime scene but had evidence of planning the arson. Giorno Buccialli had apparently ordered the hit, according to the confessions of each member. When the police arrived at his home, they also found drugs and other illegal paraphernalia, including computer documents listing involvement in human trafficking."

What the hell...?

I could only stare drop-jawed at the TV. All of this happened as we slept? We were given the news around three o'clock; it had been six hours since. This was insanity to imagine an arrest wrapped up so quickly, let alone see the charges Giorno had on him.

"He won't survive prison," Liam muttered, sipping his coffee as he watched the TV with an intense stare. I slowly turned my gaze to him, piecing together the underlying meaning of his words. Giorno was incredibly horrible, and it was unsurprising that he was involved with so much criminal activity... but how much of it was true?

"Liam... what did you do?" I hesitantly asked, unsure if I wanted to honestly know. Liam kept his eyes on the TV, leaning against the counter as if he was completely innocent of the arrests being highlighted.

"I sent the police video evidence of the gang attacking your father's shop, which also featured them attacking Louis and my men. From the angles I sent, Louis and my men were innocent civilians trying to stop them. I erased everything else, making it look like the cameras errored out." Liam began to explain, sipping his coffee to refresh his mouth. "I also ensured the police had every ounce of info on the men arrested, so confession was easy to obtain with typical interrogation behavior.

"As for Giorno, while he is actually involved in the drug trade, it wasn't hard to remotely connect his computer to a string of dark-web databases. With such a wide-open entrance, it was only natural for the most deplorable to inject whatever they wanted into his computer. However, I will admit to suggesting what should have been injected in the first place. With enough tracking, victims can be found and Giorno will be blamed for their disappearance."

Liam's voice was utterly natural to what he spoke. It was like he felt no remorse for getting the dark web to plant human trafficking information on Giorno's computer. Yet, there he was, laying it all out for me what he had done as if it was just him reporting that he brushed his teeth and washed his hands. While I did ask for him to be fully open with me, I did not ever expect such cruel actions to be told to me with such ease.

Even so, to go so far? Anyone who knew the criminal system knew that if your crimes involved children in any way—even if inferred... you had a significantly larger chance of dying behind bars.

Liam... had essentially set up Giorno to be murdered in prison.

My blood ran cold as I stared at Liam's neutral expression. Liam had that much power over the tech world? He could just remotely plug the dark web into a computer and fill it full of the most heinous things without caring for repercussions? He didn't seem worried, so he had to have had something to protect himself, yet I was terrified at the idea of using the damn dark web for anything. On top of such, he used it to practically sentence a man to death.

Giorno was a horrible man. He threatened my family and me, going so far as to set my family's hard work on fire. With Liam confirming his actual crimes, Giorno deserved punishment. Was death deserved? Did the end even justify the means?

I was conflicted.

I sat there, unsure of how to react or respond to the new wave of information. I expected Liam was good at tech. I half-expected him to be good at criminal work, thanks to Arthur. I did not expect him to do such deeds with little remorse.

A prolonged silence stood between us before I heard a soft sigh, causing me to look up at Liam. He placed his mug down on the counter and stared into it as if he was finding the words to say in his coffee.

"I promised to be honest with you. We both agreed to be open with each other, and I know right now it seems like you're seeing a completely different person... It's strange for me as well, but..." Liam trailed off, closing his eyes and gripping his coffee mug. "Giorno hurt you and your family, and he did it to hurt me. I wish I could say I felt some sort of regret for setting up his hell... but all I can promise is that this will only ever happen again if you are in mortal danger..."

Liam loved me enough to commit such an act of revenge for me. Part of me worried about how far his devotion for me ran, but most of my brain understood that if he wanted to do something nefarious, he would have done so by that point. He wasn't coaxing me into anything, nor was I chained to his side. Deep down, I knew he'd let me go if I wanted to leave for any reason.

His perspective also made sense. Why care what happens to someone who wants to hurt you so viciously? Liam wanted to punish him for hurting me, and this was something he deemed justice enough for burning down something my parents slaved over. After all, what if Giorno wasn't punished? He could have been emboldened to do worse to my family, to me.

All because he was jealous of Liam.

I shuddered at the thought, which made Liam's eyebrows

furrow. Taking a breath and a sip of coffee, I finally decided to respond as honestly as possible.

"I guess... I mean, I don't really know how to react, Liam... I guess I need a little more time to process this, you know?" I confessed, gripping my mug to ground myself. Was this okay? I could have just smiled and nodded as I clearly had little power, but did this deserve obedient agreement? Instead, my emotions swam, and I had to let them calm down on their own. Rationalizing everything helped while I pushed aside more minor doubts and worries to the back of my mind.

Liam nodded, taking a breath of his own. "I understand. Is there anything I can do right now to help?"

I hesitated for a moment before replying, "Could you help my dad? Is there any way you can..." I could only trail off, not wanting to sound needy for recompense.

"I've already hired a professional construction team to the shop to assess the damages and work on rebuilding it. They'll contact your father to clear anything he needs for the construction; all paid for, of course."

I nodded and took another sip of coffee despite it settling into a warm room temperature. Closing my eyes, I had to slowly accept everything as an undeniable fact and work towards getting over each and every discomfort I had.

However, the scariest part of my thoughts was my devotion, regardless of the facts. My family was attacked, and someone was in the hospital because of me... yet I didn't see these as reasons to leave Liam. Not even Liam's actions scared me to the point of running, though it did make me step back a bit in surprise. Instead, my heart continued to pound for my boyfriend and master, flickering with the hope that he would protect me no matter what. It was being in the shoes of a damsel, and it was unnerving.

Had I become that stricken by him that no wrong could tear me away? His sex made me crazy in love and his embrace had me feeling like I was the most beautiful woman in the world. Moreover, it wasn't forced. Despite never imagining trying, nothing gave me the impression that Liam was obsessively possessive of me. I could have stood up, packed my things, and walked out of the loft for the trauma Giorno caused. This was one piece of faith I had in Liam that had him stand above the erotica I enjoyed.

Yet I stayed, and I wanted to stay.

Welcome to being a criminal's girlfriend.

He was already my criminal boyfriend before this happened, thanks to Arthur.

I definitely needed time to let everything sink in.

~~~

The days marched forward with my dad texting me updates, confirming that Liam did send a team to help him rebuild. Liam took it upon himself to go over and help with the reconstruction, both to genuinely assist the team with his own hands and to give me the space I needed to digest everything. Thankfulness aside, I spent my time alone putting everything into logical perspective. Was I just trying to cope with reality or was I making excuses for not just packing up and leaving?

As Liam returned home, he continued to give me my space. I didn't wear my collar for an entire week.

One afternoon had Liam and me visiting Louis in the hospital. Emily greeted us at the car, and I could only frown at the sight of her wounds. A large bruise was painted over with concealer on the side of Emily's face, with some red burns peeking out from her shirt collar on her neck. Still, she stood tall with a firm nod to us as we approached, assisting us as we entered the car.

For the first time, Liam and I did not sit pressed up against each other. Liam clearly respected my space as I stared out the window in my thoughts. I continued to slowly rationalize and compartmentalize my emotions, grateful for Liam's respect.

"How are you feeling, Emily?" Liam asked. I couldn't help but listen in, curious as well.

"I'm alright, sir. Well enough to work." Emily replied in her professional tone.

"I appreciate your dedication, but you know--" Liam began before Emily cleared her throat.

"You don't pay me by the hour. You pay me a stupid amount of money every month to take care of you and miss Augustine. I'm okay and will still do my job, sir."

That made me turn my head to her, seeing her gaze focused on the road with a small smile. It never occurred to me how deeply devoted Emily was to Liam. Louis, too, stayed and remained loyal enough to end up in the hospital for him. Liam was a good man through and through, whether you just worked for him or loved him as a partner. More rationalizations.

Liam sighed and took out his phone, calling a number and placing the phone up against his ear. "Hello, this is Liam Hunter. My friend Louis Theriot is a patient at your hospital, and I'm calling to ask about his status," Liam inquired. "He works for my company Labry-- oh, he is awake and expecting me? Wonderful. Thank you so much."

We stayed in silence for the remainder of the drive, mostly content with the status quo of the situation. It only took us thirty minutes to arrive at the hospital Louis was staying. Looking out the car window at the building, I could hear my wallet scream again from how richly funded it looked.

Liam guided me into the front entrance, and we both signed in with the front desk, citing Louis's name. We then made our way to the elevator, riding it to the top floor, where Louis was moved to after the ICU. He was apparently stable enough for visitors, so when the elevator doors opened, and we entered his room, Louis looked over to greet us from his bed.

It was a miracle that he was awake. His head had bandages from surgery and stitch tape on his cheek, closing up a large line across his skin that almost reached his ear. Louis was in a medical gown, but one could see the bandages stretched across his chest from wounds hidden away. Even his hands were softly wrapped in gauze, but he still sat with a small smile at us.

"Liam. Miss Augustine." Louis greeted us each with a nod. I opened my mouth to speak but felt no words come out. He was there because of me, so what could I have possibly said?

Liam, however, stepped forward and placed his hands on the bed rails, lowering his head. From where I stood, I couldn't see Liam's expression, but when Louis looked up at him, he frowned at the sight and clicked his tongue.

"I'm not going to yell at you," Louis said, shaking his head.

"You should," Liam replied softly, his shoulders tensing up. Louis rolled his eyes and grabbed Liam's arm before pulling him down for a firm hug. Liam gasped but slowly returned it in kind, burying his face in Louis's shoulder.

"It was my choice to fight them. They had it coming." Louis reprimanded, patting Liam's back. "Now stop worrying about us. I'm sure you tried to get Emily to take today off too."

Liam remained in Louis's arms as Louis turned his gaze to me. I flinched, despite hearing what Louis said. Of course, he chose to fight, but he could have been spared from such a choice if I wasn't...

"Maya," Louis spoke, interrupting my thoughts and forcing me to stand up straight.

"Y-Yes?" I replied at attention.

Louis shook his head before reprimanding me. "You get whatever thoughts you have out of your head. I did what decent folk should do: give a damn about people. You're one of those people I give a damn about."

That broke me. I couldn't stop the tears from flowing down my cheeks as Louis smiled and held out an arm to me. He got hurt protecting me, and he still had a smile on his face, as if he had zero regrets. We weren't as close as him and Liam, but Louis was incredibly funny and kind to me the few times he was around. He was the only one who knew of my submission to Liam, but he didn't shame either of us for it.

The fact he cared about me was enough to solidify my own emotions for good.

I rushed over and took his hand, letting him pull me into a hug with Liam. I wrapped an arm around Liam, who returned the one-armed hug in kind while still holding Louis close. I wept into Louis's other shoulder, earning back rubs and pats from both Louis and Liam.

That lunch made me solidify my rationalizations.

Chapter 20

Eternity

Louis recalled the fight he had with Giorno's men, reciting it to us like it was a Tuesday afternoon. Even when the nurses checked him during our lunch together, he sat proud of his accomplishments. He praised the other guards who worked under him, and we made sure to visit them and give them well wishes before leaving the hospital. Each guard smiled at Liam as if they were devoted enough to not care for their own lives. Maybe it was Liam's truly kind nature, or perhaps the pay was high enough to demand loyalty, but seeing each of the men and women beam at the sight of their boss was surprising.

There was something about Liam that truly deserved or naturally brought care.

On the drive home, I sat hip to hip with Liam and relaxed in his arms. My legs were draped over his lap as I listened to Liam's heartbeat. Liam gently brushed through my hair with his fingers and simply kept me close and warm. It was peaceful in the car, with a gentle piano melody playing for us, thanks to Emily. The partition was up, and we had a moment to ourselves as we drove through the city.

"Liam?" I muttered, looking up at the man holding me.

Liam connected his gaze with mine at full attention. "Yes, Maya?" He replied.

I wanted to word my thoughts carefully. I had decided to stay by Liam's side, but I felt like I was learning about him again. It seemed almost nostalgic, dissecting the man who intrigued me beyond belief. I was set...

...but was he?

"Do you regret being with me?" I finally asked, obviously surprising Liam by the change in his expression.

"No. Not at all." Liam replied, adjusting to turn his body to me. He gently took hold of my hand and brought it to his chest, letting me feel his heartbeat. "Maya. You are by far the most wonderful woman I have ever met. At no point had I ever considered you being with me a mistake or something to regret."

"Even after... you know...?" I meekly added, earning a small sigh from the man I adored.

"When I told you that I was the lucky one, I meant it. You are dedicated, beautiful, charming, and by far the most patient and understanding woman to ever be part of my life. There are days when I think of how lucky I am to have earned your attention..." Liam explained, gently caressing my cheek and letting me nuzzle into the warmth of his palm. "The fact that you're still here only cements how precious you are to me and how much I want to make you the happiest woman in the world... that is if you'll let me."

His words sent my heart completely aflutter. He still believed me to be the blessing of the relationship when I knew he was doing his damnedest to make me happy already. What he felt I understood from his perspective as my own.

Over time, maybe there would be a way to protect and care for him as he did for me. That time would only arrive, however, if I remained at his side, and I was more than happy to continue seeing his smile every morning and support him no matter what.

"You keep forgetting what we agreed on during our first date..." I teased with a small smile.

"Oh? What did we say?" Liam chuckled.

I wrapped my arms around him, moving to sit on his lap, and nuzzled his nose with mine. "We're *both* lucky. You're strong and caring, loved by almost everyone, and for a good reason. You protect and are devoted to the ones you love, including me. No matter what has happened or will happen... I think we can pretty much survive anything together."

Liam's expression practically melted into one of deep adoration and warm joy. Wrapping his arms around me, Liam nuzzled my nose back with a smile. "My precious queen..." He muttered in admiration.

"My king..." I replied, unable to stop the cliched butterflies fluttering in my chest from influencing my words. He was almost like a king. A CEO was close enough. He ruled with a stern but humble fist, dealing punishment only as needed and supporting every part of his court to the best of his abilities.

And he called me his queen.

I had to put my faith in him. After all, his escapades into the criminal world lasted only as long as Arthur was alive. He said he would leave it after he was free, and there was no reason to believe otherwise. After all, why maintain the connection? It was a risk to his future if anyone found out. It was a risk to *my* future if he stayed, but he was willing to defend me against everything.

I would be his queen and support him no matter what as he supported me.

We held each other close, exchanging loving kisses and nuzzles until we finally returned home. Emily waved as she dropped us off before driving off, leaving Liam and me to ride the elevator back up to our loft.

For some reason, my entire chest was warm and practically shook with the beating of my heart. Liam had an arm softly wrapped around me, and I couldn't stop myself from leaning against his side. I had imagined the honeymoon phase of our romance to be long over, yet I was as giddy as when we first met. It was probably due to my new resolve and conviction to be a better partner for Liam. On the other hand, maybe I was just crazy in love with him.

Who knew?

That night, we both shared the kitchen and made dinner together. It was almost like a dance in how we managed to organize and synchronize preparing each part. Lo-fi jazz swung in the background as we chopped vegetables, seared off some steaks, and finished two gorgeous plates of dinner as the sun set over the horizon. All the while, we talked.

Nothing sexual. Nothing dangerous. Just simple things.

Favorite memories we had when we were children, like when I had played hide-and-seek too well with my parents and wound up being the champion of a two-hour hiding streak. Liam recalled a memory when he and his sister finished a puzzle late into the night, almost breaching the crack of dawn. His mother was furious, but the laughter they shared practically cemented itself into Liam's brain.

We even spoke of sad times, leaning on each other for comfort in remembrance. I was the final 'furever' home of a precious black cat named Pepper, who was only in my care for a short while. I loved her dearly, and it hurt to remember her passing. Liam still mourned his father's death. While it wasn't fresh, his father's passing still weighed heavy on him with his regrets, responsibilities, and devotion to his family.

There were so many things to connect to and speak about that we almost forgot about the world around us. It was reopening our hearts and hearing each other laugh, cry, and feel deep emotions with support between us. Since signing on with Arthur, Liam had never used his hacking abilities to their full extent. I was frustrated at how I felt useless at times, despite being blessed with loving family and friends.

We listened and accepted each other, even as we finished our meals. Our bonding did not stop. It was like we were celebrating a new milestone; a dangerous one, but one that we agreed to overcome together. A morbid thought, really, if you really sat down to dissect it. I couldn't deny the tickle of worry and fear that rumbled underneath my heart thinking of the future, but it was overshadowed by the beating my heart drummed in my devotion to pushing past whatever came my way.

As the moon rose into the sky, we slowly let our bonding walk us to the middle of the living room and guide us to dance to a simple piano melody playing from Liam's speakers. As the piece hypnotized us to a simple two-step on the marble tile, we gazed into each other's eyes with smiles on our faces.

It was like the world had disappeared again. All I could see was Liam, and it was clear that all he could see was me. His hand around my waist was firm to support me as the other hand that held mine carried my palm and fingers like precious glass. I was close enough to feel his heartbeat pounding against his chest, and I felt it beat for me, for his love for me.

This was what I wanted. Simple love. A tangible, proven devotion of passion. The loose strings and messy knots attached to it felt like mere distractions to the depths our love ran. Yet I accepted it all and felt genuine joy in Liam's hands. He had to have felt the same, holding me so close.

I stretched up and gently kissed him, lost in the depth of his gaze and eager to taste him against my lips again. It was feather-like but heavy, with the plethora of emotions swirling in my chest. Liam returned my kiss in kind, slowly lowering my hand to cup my neck and give me the same weighty love he carried through his lips. Enveloping his body in my arms, I pulled Liam closer to me and laid my vow to love him eternally in our kiss. I could feel his devotion returned to me as he tightened his hold around my waist and kept me close.

Pulling away and staring into each other's eyes, only one thing remained in our minds: each other. Could we just have this? Could everything else just melt away and let us have our time, our space? I was selfish enough to have such a treasure of a man in my arms. Could this have become my wish?

Or, perhaps, was this Liam's wish?

Without hesitation, Liam lowered his arms and lifted me up like a bride, causing me to wrap my arms around his neck in surprise. He kept his gaze on me as he walked into the hallway and through the door to our bedroom. I felt my entire body turn red in slow shyness as he carried me to my side of the bed and gently laid me down on it. Despite the lustful whisper in my body expecting him to lay over me, I watched as Liam walked around the bed and settled down beside me on his side of the mattress.

I could see the same lust in his eyes, which dilated to form their entrancing thin jade rings. Yet he simply ran his hand along my side as I rolled to face him.

He was waiting for me to decide. With all that happened, he was still patient with me and allowed me the first moves for everything beyond our dance. How was it possible to love this man further than I already did?

Let me be selfish.

I leaned in and captured Liam's lips again, this time deepening our kiss to more than a soft petal-like touch. Liam softly sighed, relaxing into the bed and wrapping an arm under and around me to pull me against him. I never wanted to be let go, pressing my body against his and gripping his shirt before I wrapped one of my legs around his waist. Liam's hand slid down my side and cupped my thigh, anchoring it against him as he trailed his kiss across my cheek and down to my neck.

"Liam..." I breathed out, shuddering at the pleasurable feel his kiss sent through my body. I slowly began to crave more. The heat within my body ignited into a small flame that wanted to grow and consume me whole. I tugged at Liam's shirt as I tilted my head back for him, opening my neck for more of his kisses.

Liam hummed against my sensitive skin, making me quiver at the feeling, before moving his hand to lift his shirt over his head. I released my grip to allow the removal but instantly began to caress and massage my hands over Liam's chest as it became exposed to me.

This man was mine and mine alone. As he claimed me as his, I would keep him and love him for as long as I could. Greed be damned; nothing was going to take him from me.

I grabbed one of Liam's hands and guided it to the hem of my blouse, closing his fingers over it and letting him infer my demand. Understanding completely, Liam slowly lifted my shirt up and off of my body, stopping his kisses only temporarily to remove it entirely before going back in again with new fervor.

"I love you so much, Maya..." Liam muttered out against my neck. Another wave of pleasure zipped into my core at his words, and I was breathless.

"I love you too..." I replied, pulling him harder against me to remove the space between our bodies. Liam obliged, rolling to lay over me. One leg settled between both of mine and a hand slipped under my bra to fondle my breast. The room got warmer with each intensifying touch we gave each other; one after the other, it became almost unbearable to keep clothes on.

With Liam at my shoulder, I lowered my hands to undo his belt and pants, lowering them as far as I could. Peering down, I watched his erection stretch under his boxer briefs to form a tent with the fabric. I moaned in approval and pleasure as Liam rolled my nipple between his fingers.

Liam lifted himself from my shoulder and leaned his forehead against mine, staring deep into my eyes as his hand traced around my body and unclasped my bra. He was talented enough to unlatch it with one hand, and I swooned as it fell from my chest, releasing my breasts to him.

His hand continued downward, tracing over the stretch marks on my stomach before teasingly feathering his fingers over my panties. I instinctively held my breath, wanting more, and stared up into his jade gaze of desire.

"Yes..." I whispered out, hoping he would obey.

Obey, he did.

I gasped as his fingers slipped beneath my panties and slid themselves over my clit and around the lips of my pussy. Arching back, I released a loving moan, urging him further to rub two fingers over my heated button. I spread my legs as far apart as I could, eager to feel him fully between my thighs.

"Maya..." Liam purred out, tucking an arm under my arched back and holding my chest to his as he slowly prodded my entrance with a fingertip, using his thumb to massage my clit. All the while, he stared down at me with the most loving and lustful of eyes. It was hypnotic, and I fell more and more into his spell with every stroke, every breath we let out in harmony.

I slid my hand down between our bodies, tracing my nails over his skin to make him shudder over me, and cupped the bulge of his erection over his underwear. At my touch, Liam groaned affectionately, fluttering his eyes closed and gently gyrating his hips against my hand. As his hard-on further hardened under my palm, I maneuvered it up and under the fabric of his boxer briefs to touch him skin-to-skin. My fingers encircled his girth, and I was rewarded with a growl of pleasureful approval from the man above me and a finger finally sliding within my core.

"Liam..." I mewled out adoringly, slowly pumping his length in my hand as I rocked my hips up to his. Liam licked his lips before his arm up beneath my back pulled my chest even closer to his, our lips barely touching and moaning into each other. As he slowly thrust his finger in and out of my pussy, I felt the burn of my arousal grow to an almost unbearable height. I echoed my desire into my rubbing of his cock, anticipating its length, stretching me to perfection again and adding to the heat within.

As Liam quickened his pace and added a finger, I could barely hang on to the teasing it brought. My body needed to be filled by this man just as much as my heart was.

I released his dick and used every ounce of force I had in my arms to roll us to the side, where I landed on top of his body. Liam stared up at me in shock, a gasp escaping his throat as I slid my hands into the pillows underneath his head.

My fingers danced over the condom we had loaded into it, knowing our desire for each other had us store a bunch in random places around the loft. Perfect.

I slid it out and left it beside Liam's shoulder before grinding over his palm, moaning at the fingers still buried within my cunt. Still, it wasn't enough. I lifted my hips, whimpering slightly as I unsheathed myself off of his fingers, and slid my panties down over my ass. I adjusted myself to remove it down my thighs and past my knees. Snapping it from around my ankles, I tossed the article of clothing to wherever the rest of my clothes were as I ground my bare pussy against his crotch.

Taking my obvious hints of lust, Liam arched his hips and ground back into me, using the movement to slide his boxers down and let his cock escape to rub against me bare. He pushed his underwear to his knees, and I slid them off the rest of the way, not wanting either of us to have clothes to tangle us.

Skin to skin, we were naturally drawn to kiss each other deeply. I rolled my hips to press my lower lips against the length of Liam's dick, practically purring against Liam's lips from the heat it shared. I was so wet that I glided over his cock with ease. My heartbeat pounded in my head, both in desperate need and anxiousness to do what I was going to do.

Liam raised a hand and grabbed the condom beside him, bringing it between our bodies to open and release the rubber within the packaging. With a nervous smile, I plucked the rubber out of his hands and scooted my body back to slide the condom over his dick. Seeing it at attention spurred me further to crawl back up and raise my hips as far as I could over him on my knees.

Embarrassing as it was, the tip was tapping the mound of my womb, unable to pass underneath me from its height. I had to push my anxiousness to the side, not wanting to break my run to nirvana, but I gasped as Liam sat up and wrapped his arms around my lower back.

"Let me help?..." Liam asked, deep desire dripping in his voice as his hands found purchase under each of my ass cheeks. I moaned as his hands squeezed over them, and I tilted my head to lean my

258

forehead against his with a nod.

With stupid ease, Liam lifted my body, practically lifting my knees and shins off the bed, and helped align his cock directly underneath me. I lowered my hand to further aim the head of his cock against my entrance, then grabbed his shoulders.

Liam slowly lowered my body, and I impaled myself on his dick, feeling every hot inch stretch me out and forcing moans to erupt from our lips. My heart sang as I settled on his lap, taking him fully from tip to base, and I opened my eyes to lock eyes with the man within me.

Liam's mouth hung open, clearly loving the feel of me sheathing his dick with my pussy, and he wrapped his arms around me to hug me close. I couldn't stop my hips from rolling in small circles, mewling as he stretched me even further and caressed every delicate part within. Gripping Liam's shoulders, I slowly began to ride him as lovingly as I possibly could.

He was perfect. He filled my heart and soul with love, and now he completed me in our lovemaking. As I raised and lowered my hips, slowly feeling his dick run through me with each dip down, I couldn't stop the chant of adoring moans from leaving my chest. Liam slid a hand down to support my ass, helping me lift and lower over him at my pace.

He knew I didn't have the best knees as a plus-sized woman, which made me swoon even harder over him; to know he supported me in life, in love, and in bed. I slowly increased my pace over him, panting and moaning over his lips and stealing kisses when I caught breaths between. Liam returned every kiss, groaning to me in his ecstasy of the ride.

"God, Maya... you feel so perfect... so tight..." Liam growled, shooting euphoric waves through my body at the sound. I gasped and practically growled myself in pleasure, slamming my hips down instinctively and making both of us cry out in ecstasy. I dug my fingernails into Liam's shoulders, indenting his skin with them, before kissing Liam deeply and wrapping my arms around his head.

I loved him. I needed him. I wanted all of him. I began to buck faster over him, trying to piston myself up to go from tip to base each time. Liam obliged to aid me, giving us both exactly what we wanted. My breath quickened, and my climax began to rise in my core with each thrust, signaled by my lustful cries against his lips and tightened muscles around his cock. Both of Liam's hands grasped at my ass, squeezing them lovingly as he lifted and dropped me on his lap at my pace. He knew I didn't want to stop, that I wanted to topple over my orgasm on him, and continued to guide me even as my hips started to give out from my weight.

When my orgasm suddenly erupted through me, I screamed against Liam's lips and let my body contract over him, quaking from its powerful waves through my pussy. He released a deep and low sigh against my lips, his hands gripping my skin harder to keep me impaled on his lap. I couldn't stop my hips from rocking over him, torturously slowly coming down from my peak and releasing his lips from mine.

I was full of pleasure and joy and wanted Liam to share in it.

"L-Liam... take me..." I begged, pressing my body against his chest and forcing him back down onto the bed. I could orgasm repeatedly and not be satisfied until he came with me. Until he felt as complete as I did.

Liam gave me a hard and deep kiss before lifting a hand to anchor my lower back and planting his feet onto the bed. As tender as I was from my release, I shuddered as Liam slowly rocked his hips to thrust into me from below. I settled my hands on his shoulders again and arched my back, giving him further ease to take and give his entire length into my body.

He spread his knees apart, keeping me wide open for him, as I let myself be at his mercy. Over and over, he filled me, and I found myself cresting over and over without any way to slow the ride down. I took it all and let every scream and orgasm rip through my body in wild abandon, plunging into his love and lust for me.

"Maya... God, Maya... I love you so much...!!"

I was breathless as he finally began to approach his end, his hips sputtering under me before pressing hard against my body as he released into the condom. I clung to his body, shuddering at the feeling and trying to catch my breath at last. He remained within me, panting and holding me close to him as he kissed my cheeks and lips.

"You're... so amazing..." Liam praised, causing me to mewl

affectionately. His praise still wrapped me around his finger, yet I happily wrapped myself around it. It only proved further that he was mine and I was his. My chest felt warm, and I couldn't stop smiling despite my exhaustion, nuzzling into Liam's chest.

This is what I wanted.

<u>Chapter 21</u>

Paralysis

I could barely register how much time had passed since that beautiful night. Liam and I found our bond had grown even more profound than ever. Every day, he found ways to prove his love with simple gestures: flowers, food, and small dates. He pampered and pleasured me to the point where I felt like I was in a dream every morning and night. I treated him to the best meals I could make and opened up his world to more genres of books to read in his spare time.

His collar felt softer around my neck, and his touch was electrifying. Perhaps the small amount of danger being with him became a disturbing tease, but the reminder of Liam's protective affection for me kept me grounded. I accepted him, and he allowed me every part of him without resistance.

My father's shop was rebuilt with the best machinery and security, with Liam privately investing in it for continued success. It didn't take long at all for my dad to accept him like a son after such generosity, and we made regular visits to him and my mother to further the bond. Liam was always hands-on with whatever my dad requested of him, whether it was helping in the shop or even carrying groceries into the house. My mother, however, took a bit to be comfortable around her boss and daughter's boyfriend.

On the other side, I was invited back to Rosa's home multiple times for food and bonding of my own. Most of the time, I went with Liam, but there were a few afternoons and evenings where I went alone, making a girl's night with my boyfriend's mother and sister. Again, my palate was blown away by more authentic Mexican cuisine, and my heart opened completely for Rosa and Mariana as they accepted me as a daughter and sister.

This life was a long-term commitment I was willing to go with.

Of course, my time with Liam wasn't completely full of roses and rainbows. With Giorno's sentencing, Liam and Louis had to give statements to law enforcement. Apparently, it was enough to let them both walk away without suspicion or any assumption of their actual involvement. Whether or not underhanded means helped in such was beyond me. I chose to remain ignorant of such, knowing that it was better to be blissful.

It was approaching a year of our official relationship, and I could tell that Liam was plotting something lavish for us. Would it be a trip somewhere or a decadent dinner at another glorious establishment? He made phone calls left and right, but only hid them from me with a smile to let me know it was nothing terrible. Anything troubling I could have imagined him calling someone about in secret wouldn't have made smiling at me easy.

I played coy, looking up to the ceiling every time I caught him in a call before returning to my work. My rules still had me present in the same room as him unless I was constrained, so it wasn't like he hid his surprise well. I simply let his conversations enter one ear and leave out the other. After all, he was good at being vague on his end of the phone so whether it was a vacation, dinner, show, or something wild was beyond me with how he worded his replies.

However, a phone call Liam didn't smile at broke our peace.

The phone rang with the ringtone indicating that it was an unknown number calling him. Liam and I froze, recognizing it for what it was.

Arthur.

He surprisingly was sparse with his calls and requests to Liam. He had called before regarding Giorno, only to say a haunting 'good job.' After that, it was brief and tiny things, such as securing his funds and settling any different accounts he had. They gave us small doses of hope, as such actions were done in preparation for retirement and death. Liam was hopefully going to be free soon.

Liam and I looked at each other before I nodded in assurance. It was probably something small, like Arthur's calls had been before. But nevertheless, something had to be done, and it would only ever take a few minutes to an hour at worst.

Liam answered at last before the fifth ring, putting it on speaker. "Hello?"

"Liam Hunter? This is Margarette calling on behalf of Mister Smith." An older woman's voice replied. Margarette? Who was that?

"How can I help you?" Liam questioned.

"Mister Smith will be passing today."

What?

If Arthur was mister Smith... then he was going to die that day? Who else could have been mister Smith? Only one person was labeled as an unknown caller on Liam's phone because he built his tech to silence and block any spam and phantom calls.

I looked at Liam to see him frozen solid in place. He stared at the phone in silence with the most enigmatic expression on his face. Of course, he would be free, but how did he feel to hear that at that moment? I was positive it was daunting and heart-relieving at the same time.

"...his health has deteriorated that quickly?"

"Yes, mister Hunter. He has requested death with dignity and has insisted that you be present."

Wait. Arthur wanted Liam to witness him dying? What kind of screwed-up bullshit was that? It was morbid to demand that someone watch another die, especially when the one dying was making the demand. What was the point?

Liam took a breath and closed his eyes. "...very well." He wasn't seriously going to go, was he?

"Very good. He also requests miss Augustine be present as well."

It took every single ounce of willpower I had not to interject in shock. Why was I involved now?! Arthur had not spoken to or about me since the dinner with Rosa and Mariana. I was more than ready to remove him from my memory after his death.

"...may I ask why, Margarette?" Liam slowly asked through gritted teeth. He must have sensed my discomfort and unwillingness to see Arthur, much less see him die in front of me.

"We have already extended mister Smith's demands to your mother and sister as well as your secretary Louis Theriot, who have all agreed to be present. As Miss Augustine is an important part of your life, her presence has also been deemed necessary."

Liam looked to me, most likely for my answer. Every fiber of my being wanted to scream no into the phone for myself. Who would elect to say yes to watching someone die?

...apparently Liam and his family, as well as Louis.

It was an absurd request. It was disgusting and vile to its core to think I would have been entirely okay with the idea.

Go.

Part of me, at that moment, lingered on why. Why was I so adamant in saying no? Arthur wasn't a good man, just like Giorno. With how old he was, he was probably worse than Giorno could have ever been. After all, he forced servitude from the immigrants he helped bring into the country. He held so much power over them that it made them obedient in every way possible.

Seeing him pass would have solidified Liam's freedom. It would have been like watching the execution of a power-hungry king who manipulated his subjects for his pleasure. As twisted and fucked as it was, being present would have been my stand to ensure that I would take Liam away from the shadow Arthur had put him under for good.

Arthur's dying breath would leave him witness to Liam escaping his cage.

As crazy as it was... I nodded at Liam with a mildly shameful expression. I was partially ashamed of reaching such a sadistic conclusion. Still, another logical part of me rationalized that the request was probably not one I could have said no to regardless. At least I could agree to it for my own reason rather than be forced either way.

"...she'll be there."

~~~

We had no time to plan. No time to resolve ourselves accordingly. This was a messed-up execution and funeral for someone Liam and I couldn't wait to move on from. Luckily, I had a black maxi dress perfect for the occasion, simple and uncaring for the importance of the person passing. Paired with my mini coven hat, I was ready enough to see Liam be released from his servitude.

Arthur Smith would become a vague memory of a dream no one should have been made to suffer.

Dressed in a black suit, Liam guided me down the elevator to where Emily was already waiting for us. Emily did not look happy at all, as if she was holding back some sort of anger. However, the demand did come from nowhere, so I could only assume she was taken away from her wife to cater to us. We apologized to her as we were driven to the event, but Emily remained silent. Respecting her wishes, Liam and I kept to ourselves, unsure what to even say at the turn of events.

As we drove past the city, only faint music kept the air from eerie silence. It was easily an hour out from where we lived, but soon we slowed into a side road leading into a private forest. One pass from Emily by two armed security officers allowed us through without an issue, and we drove for ten minutes more. As the trees began to clear, I was stunned to silence to see the lavish mansion we were meant to enter.

It was clearly a multi-million-dollar mansion. Vintage cars lined the side of the driveway, guiding us to the clear space we could park in front of. I could only gawk at the architecture of the building despite knowing exactly who it belonged to.

For the first time, Liam did not step out of the car as we parked.

"Liam?" I spoke aloud, placing a gentle hand on Liam's knee in comfort. He covered my hand with his own, giving it a squeeze before locking eyes with me. I could see waves of emotions swimming through his eyes. Fear, determination, anger, relief, love, hatred. His thoughts were clearly all over, and it was taking a toll on him before we had even seen Arthur.

I waited. This was not the time to force Liam forward. It was unreasonable to insist on finishing something that lasted a lifetime for Liam. Instead, we would walk to his pace and take each moment a step at a time.

After a long silence, Liam took a breath and nodded at me, gently lifting a hand to caress my cheek.

"Thank you, Maya." He said, making me nuzzle his hand and making my heart flutter. He took the hand that covered his and kissed my knuckles before exiting the car from his side and escorting me out from mine.

Standing outside the car didn't help how small I felt standing before the mansion. It was daunting in size, with guards at every corner. It was as if they knew today was important, yet the only event happening was their boss passing away. Were they ensuring his death was on his terms?

I didn't think about it long. Liam and I ascended the stairs to the front door, where two guards visually ran their gazes over us. Then, with two affirming nods, one guard knocked on the door in a specific rhythm, clearly a code for whoever was on the other side. A couple of locks were unlatched, and the door was opened before us, ushering Liam to guide me inside. I kept my arm tight around his, safer against his side than anywhere else.

The lobby was large, practically a small house-size within itself. It was apparent that Arthur liked to show his value at the very beginning, with every wall decorated with framed coins and dollar bills. It was like he was an obsessed collector.

Two servants, dressed in clean matching suits, bowed to us before walking towards the grand staircase. Liam and I followed silently behind, knowing they were leading us to where we needed to be. We climbed the steps and circled into a long hallway. The servants guided us through a door into an unnecessarily lavish but empty master bedroom. While it had more stupidly expensive framed money littering the room, the servants pushed the bed to the side to reveal another set of stairs. They each bowed once again and stood by the entryway, letting us pass through and climb it alone. As we reached the halfway point up the stairs, the entrance was closed behind us, causing me to grip Liam harder. The stairs were illuminated with gaudy light sconces, but I did not like being caught between two closed doors.

"It's okay..." Liam soothed, patting my hand softly before slowly guiding me forward. I followed, taking deep breaths as we approached the top door. Liam stopped us at the door and knocked on it.

"Name." A gruff voice replied behind it.

"Liam Hunter and Maya Augustine," Liam replied for us. After a second, the door opened to reveal what was beyond the doorway.

The room was dark, with only a couple of lights illuminating the room. While the previous rooms and hallways were splattered with riches and exuberance, the final room seemed simple in comparison. The only fancy-looking pieces of furniture in the room were the couch, where Liam's family and Louis sat, the medical equipment that echoed signs of life in the corner, and the canopy bed that the equipment sat beside.

As we suspected, Arthur was laid in bed with the mattress perched at an angle to partially sit him up and let him see us through the door. Compared to when I had last seen him, he was much frailer and paler, as if the reaper had slowly drained the life out of him and left behind meager drops for survival. His eyes were slightly sunken, and you could see the veins under his skin. It was mildly sickening and only intensified my need to avoid him.

I lowered my gaze slightly, not wanting to look directly at Arthur. I was sure, however, that Liam had locked eye contact with him.

"Liam. At last..." Arthur chirped, waving. Liam and I walked forward into the room, letting one of the guards at the door close it behind us. As it latched shut, both guards who were standing watch stepped to stand directly in front of the door. The only other stranger in the room was an older woman in a suit, her hands softly clasped around something in front of her.

As we took a couple more steps forward, Mariana rushed to me and offered me a hug. I released Liam's arm and accepted it, giving Mariana a squeeze.

"You gonna be okay?" Mariana whispered to me. She must have known that I was forced into coming, so I nodded softly against her shoulder.

"I'll be fine," I whispered back. I made my choice and rationalized it. I wasn't going back now.

Mariana led me to the couch and sat me between her and Rosa, who also exchanged a hug with me. Louis walked over to Liam and placed a hand on his shoulder, whispering something to him before nodding and walking over to stand by us.

I watched as Liam closed his eyes and walked to stand in front of the bed, staring Arthur down with his hands clasped behind his back. Despite being bedridden, Arthur had the biggest smile, as if he was blissfully unaware that he was going to die or eagerly awaiting it.

"So, Liam... I figured now would be a good time to lay everything out in the open. Man-to-man, mano e mano, ya know?" Arthur began, rolling his shoulders back to sit up straight. "Oh, and don't worry: I'm dying for sure after this, so don't hold back. I've already arranged everything as I wanted, and it's too late for me to change anything now, haha! I'm sure you have a lot to say to me."

He had no idea.

Liam took another breath, most likely to center himself, before nodding. "I do, actually. Quite a lot." Liam replied.

Arthur gestured to Liam, ushering him to go ahead with his thoughts. After a moment of deep silence, Liam let his heart out.

"Ever since I was a boy, my parents feared your very existence. They reminded Mariana and me every day to stay out of your way and not involve ourselves with you and your business. When I met you, I thought they were crazy. My father tried to sway me from technology, urging me to follow in his footsteps instead. But you were friendly and took me seriously when it came to my interest in computers. You even gave me the resources to learn how to code and build my own tech... all assumedly out of the goodness of your heart. How naive I was back then..." Liam's hands tightened together behind him, almost shaking from the pressure formed between them as he continued. "When my father finally paid the last of his debts to you, he made me swear to him that I would never repeat his mistake. That was after I had already agreed to let you pay for my college tuition. The look on his face when I told him what I had done... still haunts me to this day.

"He and I were never the same after that. I lost my dad long before he passed away because I decided to let you into my life. Stupid and ignorant, I traded the one man who worked himself to the bone to support his family for the man who would end up using me in exchange for fake encouragement. I graduated and paid off my debts faster than anyone ever could, but you knew how to dig your fucking talons in. I was a *child,* and you fed me bullshit to ensure I'd stay put and elevate your stupid agenda to the top of the Eye. But hey, I got to go to college! I got to make a company, so it's worth it, RIGHT?!" Liam's voice slowly grew from soft anger to full-on fury as he lurched forward and grabbed the foot railing of the bed canopy. Mariana and Rosa held on to me, and I could do nothing but try to support them, staring in shock at the rage being released at last. "Your worst offense, however, was dragging Maya into this. She did nothing to you besides being a victim of circumstance, yet you decided to egg Giorno on and put her in danger. For what? I know damn well you'll take that reason to your grave, and that infuriates me most of all. You sent him to die at my hands for some sick and twisted game, knowing I wouldn't tolerate anyone harming her and hers."

Wait... Arthur influenced Giorno? How? I knew Giorno knew Arthur, but hearing that Arthur instigated everything cracked my internal calm. At the bottom of it, Arthur had harmed my family. I couldn't stop my body from shaking, feeling Rosa and Mariana hugging me between them in support.

"You have no idea how much I want to be the one to end you. For everything you have done, you only deserve the deepest of pain. My hatred for you festered for years, mutating into a sick dream to be the one draining the life from your eyes. For everything you have done, you will certainly meet many enemies in Hell, and I can only take comfort in knowing that they'll take their pound of flesh from you when they see you."

The room again became silent, with Liam's anger hanging in the air. Looking at Liam's body language, one could tell he wanted to jump over and choke Arthur out or perhaps beat him to death. It certainly would have been easy with how frail Arthur was compared to Liam. A small echo within me wanted to join him after Arthur hurt my family in such a cruel manner.

Liam deserved to be angry.

Finally, when the silence became unbearable, Arthur... laughed.

Arthur let his head fall back and began to guffaw to the ceiling at what he heard. We could only watch in deep confusion, unsure what was funny about the situation. If it weren't for the obviously armed guards at the door, I was certain Liam would have gone through with his desired promise. We remained still until Arthur came down from his laughing fit and smiled at Liam with his damnable grin.

"There it is. I knew I could find that little demon in you." Arthur practically purred proudly. "Every person has a monster they lock away in their body, and all it takes is rattling the cage at the right angle to make it break out in disobedience... at last, I found it."

The sound of guns being drawn and aimed made everyone on the couch, including me, look over to the two guards at the door. Both had taken out their weapons and pointed them at Liam's back, despite their target not caring to turn around. Louis placed stern hands on Rosa's and Mariana's shoulders, knowing they would keep me down with their now fearful holds on me.

Every single dangerous scenario ran through my head. Was Liam going to die too? Why? This was crazy. Arthur was beyond crazy, and one word could have been the trigger that ended Liam's life.

On the other hand, Liam refused to look away, as if he knew and didn't give a damn about what was happening behind him. Instead, his focus was on Arthur, who continued to grin proudly.

"Your parents did well raising you to be a good gentleman. The world loves you; handsome, charming, kind... but you and I both know that's not enough. Polite manners and good citizen crap have never satisfied anyone fully-- why do you think we drool when bad things happen in the news?! We all have a little creature eager to feed on cruelty and anger, and only the truly strong can let them be free without remorse..." Arthur leaned back against the mattress, his grin curling into a smirk. "It's nice to know your demon is a lot like mine; merciless, quick, and uncaring. I protect what's mine, and you protect what's yours. That's why I like you, Liam... and that's why I'm gonna give you a special gift as I leave for Hell."

The woman standing by the bed finally turned and maneuvered with the medical equipment. The thing clasped in her hands was a large syringe filled with a pale-yellow liquid. I could only spot her injecting it into a tube that quickly siphoned itself through the machine and into Arthur's body. Was that what was going to kill Arthur?

"Liam Hunter. For your loyalty to the syndicate, proven by the death of Giorno Buccialli and continued security of Smith assets: I, Arthur Smith, in front of your family and friends as witnesses, now bequeath you my title and seat as the head of the Eye of Odin. Everything I ever owned and had in life is now bound to you."

My heart practically stopped.

The room instantly became freezing cold in a dark feeling of confusion, surprise, and disbelief. No one could speak in fear of Liam being shot, but I could imagine everyone screaming in their heads.

Liam staggered back a step, his body beginning to shake. The look on his face dropped from anger to fear and pale shock. Arthur, on the other hand, only grew a somehow wider Cheshire cat grin as his arm began to spasm slightly across his lap.

"You may not think of me as a father... but I found a son within you. What my father passed to me will be passed to you. I just needed to make sure you could make the right choices, and you did, meeting my every expectation..." Arthur sang out, some sort of force slowly choking his voice towards the end of his words. "The Eye has already accepted my will... They know who you are... They know what you have done and what you are capable of... *It's time to stop hiding and take it all...*"

Arthur's body soon became enveloped in a shudder before freezing up as if in paralysis. His gleeful expression became like stone as he stopped breathing, spasmed from some sort of oxygen deprivation, and soon he went as pale as a ghost.

We had just witnessed Arthur die and bequeath an entire criminal empire to Liam within the same singular minute.

Rosa fainted, collapsing over the armrest on her side of the couch. Louis used both hands to secure Mariana to the sofa, fighting her need to stand and fight.

I, on the other hand, felt time completely stop around me. Everything happened so fast that I could barely register it all. We came to set Liam free. Liam was meant to get out of the shadows forever with Arthur's dying breath, but now he was the center of the darkness. If the syndicate members knew him, then there was no longer an escape for Liam. Even if he somehow did, he'd be hunted down as a dangerous adversary with what he could do with a computer. I knew what they were capable of and could only imagine how much farther they would go with Liam to silence him forever.

He was stuck. Again.

Damn you, Arthur...

Chapter 22

Helpless

The world felt frozen to me. I didn't know what would happen and was trapped in the middle of it. Arthur, the man I had grown to despise, had finally passed away but didn't leave quietly.

He had trapped Liam in one more cage, and this one had a lifelong lock.

I felt every nerve in my body want to scream and run to Liam, but I didn't know what to do with two guns still pointed at him. Even if they had to obey Liam, the guards didn't have to hold back from shooting me or anyone else in the room.

I was beyond helpless. Part of me wanted to blame myself for being in danger, which caused Liam to act as he did. Another part of me wanted to run up and hold him.

Every part of me wanted to scream, and I knew everyone else did as well.

Go to him.

...fuck it.

I quickly stood, risking everything to walk to Liam's side. He was still shaking, curling over himself and staring at the now still corpse on the bed with the purest of rage. The guards did nothing. Good.

"L-... Liam?..." I muttered out loud, only able to control my voice so much. I wanted to cry for Liam. He had gone through so much, and I couldn't turn back time to fix anything. But I needed to do something. He needed help. He needed anything to rescue him, and while I couldn't make it all go away, I was more than willing to bring him back from any brink he may fall into.

Liam slowly looked over at me, torn in what his body was meant to do. His body still shook, but it was a mixture of reeling from the news and holding back something within him. I had no doubt he wanted to scream the loudest out of all of us. No doubt, he wanted to rage and lash out in the worst of ways just to find some sort of peace. He couldn't stop tears from running down his face in the despair eating away at him.

He didn't want this. No one in their right mind would have wanted this.

I slowly reached out and took his hand, trying to help ground him. Unable to say anything, I held out my other arm, opening my body for him to take. He could embrace me, crush me within his arms, or let me shoulder him up. Anything to assist.

Liam stared before he reached out towards my body and tenderly brought me to him, wrapping his arms around me and burying his head in my shoulder. He still held back, and I was honored to know he still maintained control despite the tragedy... but today was not the day for me to be fragile.

"It's okay... I can take it. I know my safe word." I whispered to him, hugging and giving him a firm squeeze with my arms. I mentally readied myself in case he took the plunge, steeling every part of my body for anything that could have happened. I listened as Liam took a breath, and I held my own.

At last, Liam released his hesitation and tightened his embrace around my body, practically crushing me within his arms. Feeling his full strength engulf me, I winced and focused on breathing within my new constraints. He was strong, but I found a wide enough passage from my mouth to my lungs for air to continue running through despite his squeeze.

"Ears…" Liam growled against my shoulder. Despite it being one word and pushing aside the way his growl sent shivers into my body, I knew exactly what he planned to do. With the arm I had around his shoulders and neck, I maneuvered my hand to my ear and quickly plugged it with a finger, doing the same with my other ear with ease.

"Done." I signaled.

He finally screamed, burying most of his voice into my shoulder but loud still enough to echo through the room. Even through my fingers blocking the sound, I could hear his anguish and feel the rumble of pain deep within it. His legs buckled and gave out, taking us both down to the floor on our knees, but he continued to scream even as he held me up. Liam curled over my body, forcing me to arch back, and I let him continue to crush me like a stress ball as I tried not to cry for him.

My heart bled for Liam... yet some darker part of me felt intrigued at the development. It was like the left side of my brain wanted to make me think of this as a blessing rather than a curse. So many erotica heroines saw power drop into their hands when they were with their mafia men. Now that Liam had it, my life was more of the fantasies I craved and consumed. He had proven himself to be ruthless when needed, smart enough to hold power outside of crime, and was a strong dominant man. This was, by all accounts, perfect in the most twisted way possible.

But Liam didn't want power that way. He was already a successful CEO, and if Arthur had just died in silence without this cursed bequeathment, Liam could have continued to thrive in the light, free from his chains. He was already desperate to hide this world from me, waiting for freedom to fully open himself to me until Arthur forced the matter. This was probably something that kept him away from many other romantic avenues. I was blessed enough to have gotten close enough for him to accept me, but now his world was tumbling down around him. Around us. Where were we going to go from here?

I had to set my thoughts aside and be there for Liam as he had always been there for me. My concerns for our future would wait until he rose back up from the ashes of his pyre.

I listened to him scream until his voice gave out, cracking to silence against my shoulder. As his grip on me slackened, I let out a sigh of both a need for air and a release of soft pleasure from the pressure. He tried desperately to continue clinging to me, but his body had clearly given up with all his weight resting on my body to stay up on his knees.

I supported him, finally releasing my ears, and kissed his cheek. When I turned my head to stretch my neck, I saw the two men at the door. They no longer held their weapons out at Liam and instead stood at attention with their guns holstered. I glared, knowing Liam couldn't command them in his state. After all, if they were Arthur's men previously, they were now Liam's without question. That also extended to Margarette, who was most likely the woman who administered Arthur's medical death.

I turned my head over to see her standing silent in her place. Her expression was blank, just like the guards', as if none of them cared what had just occurred. That only angered me further, but my focus was not on them.

"Get some water," I commanded. I wasn't Liam, but it was obvious who the water was intended for, so I decided to grab the reins. Would I be listened to at all?

Margarette bowed her head to me before walking straight past us for the door. The guards let her through and kept the door open, allowing us to listen to Margarette climb down the stairs and out of earshot.

Louis, releasing Mariana, quickly rushed over and placed a hand on Liam's back, kneeling down to be at our level.

"We're gonna figure this out," Louis stated, determination full in his chest and voice. Liam didn't reply, keeping his head down on my shoulder in silence.

"Figure this out? Liam just became a crime boss, and you think we can just figure this out?" Mariana spat out, standing from the couch to kneel by Rosa and check her vitals.

"Well, it's not like Liam can deny this. Knowing Arthur, he made sure everything was covered so Liam would have to take his role no matter what. So, what else can we do?" Louis tried to be diplomatic. Mariana had every right to be angry, but Louis had the right of it. We had no choice but to 'figure it out' regardless of how we felt.

"I don't know! We can take him and go to Mexico. Away from this shit. Start over!" Mariana listed, desperation hitting her words. "We don't have to listen to any of this shit!"

Liam's hands tightened gently around my dress. I listened to him softly whisper a groan, strained from his broken vocal cords. He wanted to talk, but he couldn't. It was as if I understood his intentions and words just from holding him so close.

"Mariana. Louis. Please stop." I spoke, causing both parties to stare at me. "Right now... no matter how any of us feel, Liam needs us. We can talk about the how and what later... Liam comes first."

Louis and Mariana sunk in their places, probably ashamed for having fought despite the situation. They were frustrated, but Liam was the primary victim. They knew I was right, and Liam's soft squeeze of thanks around me confirmed that I had said the right thing. I was happy to assist in some way.

After a moment, Margarette arrived with a tray of glasses and a large pitcher of water. She placed it on the coffee table in front of the couch before pouring a glass full and presenting it to me. I accepted it with a nod before showing the glass to Liam.

"Drink, Liam..." I instructed. It was strange being the one giving instructions when I was the submissive, but Liam had always been attentive to my needs and wants and what I wanted at that moment was for him to drink.

Liam finally lifted his head and nodded to me, taking the glass from my hands and slowly drinking the water down. His eyes were bloodshot, but I was only able to see them for a moment before he closed them to drink. He stopped drinking halfway through his water before lowering the cup and staring down at it.

"Margarette..." Liam muttered loud enough to be within her earshot despite the strain in his voice.

"Yes, mister Hunter?" Margarette replied.

"...does his will go into effect immediately?" Liam inquired.

"Correct. With the confirmation of mister Smith's passing, you are, as of right now, the owner of this house and everyone within it as well as head of the Eye of Odin." Margarette answered, making me grimace a bit. He owned people now? Arthur had owned people like a slaver? It was disgusting to imagine, and now Liam had to deal with it all.

Liam took another moment to drink from the glass before staring down at it. The glass had only a quarter of water left.

Without looking away from his drink, Liam spoke again, this time to me. "Maya?"

"Yes?" I replied attentively.

"...Will you stay with me?" Liam asked, looking up at me at last. His eyes were filled with curiosity and worry, but he kept a calm face despite that. He had asked me this before, but despite my answer, it was clear that he had to reassure himself and have me affirm my resolve with what was figuratively cuffed to his wrists and ankles. I knew this was a lot to handle, but I had made my choice.

"I told you I would support you no matter what. I will not leave." I repeated without hesitation, giving his arm a soft squeeze in assurance. At this point, Liam had become my ride-or-die. I had learned and grown so much at Liam's side. This was a trash situation, but if this was where the road was taking us, I was ready to walk at Liam's side.

Liam stared me down, taking in every word I spoke before nodding and turning his head to Louis. "Louis?"

"You're stuck with me, just like when we were kids," Louis reassured, moving his hand from Liam's back to his shoulder, giving it a small shake. "We survived this long in the damn car. Might as well survive longer at the driver's seat."

I smiled, happy to see Louis support Liam. Liam, however, didn't have the energy to smile. It was clear why.

Liam finished his water at last before letting out a small sigh. "Louis, please call Emily and let her know what happened," Liam instructed. Louis nodded and quickly stood, taking out his phone and obeying his orders while excusing himself to the corner of the room. I supported Liam's ascent back to our feet, turning with him to face Mariana and Rosa.

Mariana understandably hung her head down in some form of shame and anger. "This is bullshit, Liam..." Mariana hissed out. "Why the fuck do we have to take this crap... from some dead gringo..."

"Manita..." Liam muttered, fully releasing me from his arms and walking slowly towards Mariana. However, he stopped when his sister held her palm out and snarled at him.

"I know we can't do shit, but that doesn't mean I have to just swallow it without bitching about it!! I'm just the dumb little sister, but I watched some colonizer tell my brother he's now some kingpin. It's not like you wanted this shit, did you?!" Mariana barked. Liam didn't even speak; he just shook his head. "Exactly! I get to be pissed off not only for you but for how mom and I have to deal with this too!"

Mariana then marched over to the bed and hocked back a breath before spitting on Arthur's pale face. Margarette and the guards made no attempt to stop or threaten her, even as she walked back to kneel by Rosa.

"Fuck!" Mariana shouted before slamming her forehead on the couch armrest beside her mother's unconscious form. I flinched, even though the couch was soft enough to not be damaging to

Mariana's head.

We stood silent, knowing that Liam had to be immediately strong despite Mariana's facts. If he faltered, the target on him would have grown more dangerous than it already had become. It wasn't unimaginable to foresee the consequences of not seeing Arthur's will through as he intended. At the same time, I could sense a wall being built between Liam and Mariana, hardened by what had just occurred. Liam wanted to protect her and Rosa while Mariana mourned losing her brother to the same force that probably killed her father.

It was a tragedy.

I stepped away from Liam's side and approached Mariana, kneeling beside her. As she sensed my presence, she looked up; eyes swollen from tears and her face red with anger.

"How can you be so calm about this too?" Mariana muttered, her anger melting to concern and sadness as she registered me as the one who approached her. I gave her a wry smile. It wasn't a good situation by any means. In fact, I was risking a lot staying at Liam's side, and I knew Mariana understood that.

I made my bed in Liam's arms, and I would die in them.

I moved to sit on my knees, took a breath, and said, "Because me being angry or sad isn't going to change what happened or what's going to happen."

Mariana stared wide-eyed at my statement, hearing something utterly opposite to her feelings. I knew I was slamming her view of me, but better to let her see my entire mind than let her anger linger. I continued.

"Liam and I have been together for almost a year. We're out of any twitter-patted honeymoon phase, and we made sure to lay out everything to each other, knowing that we probably have a future together." I looked back at the man in question, seeing him watch me in his own mix of surprise and love at my words, before turning my full attention back to Mariana. "I'm not going to lie and say that I'm not scared. I'm terrified, in fact. However, Liam has made me very happy, and I believe wholeheartedly that I would forever regret leaving him because of something out of his control.

"We have to get through this together, and I am willing to do whatever I can to help him," I swore aloud. I knew Mariana could have reacted in any way to my words. She could have called me crazy. She could have sworn me off forever. Yet, here I was, the lover, trying to be rational to the sister. Anything was in the air as she was passionate about the situation with Liam.

Mariana took a breath and slumped over herself, gently taking my hand and staring down at it.

"...You're like a sister to me already... but I don't want you to regret *staying*." Mariana finally confessed, earning a more genuinely happy smile from my lips. I lifted her hand to my chest and clasped my free hand over hers, holding it close. Mariana lowered her head and pressed it against mine, finally letting tears freely fall down her cheeks. I reached up and caressed her cheek, wiping some of her tears away.

"As you're like a sister to me too, I refuse to abandon you," I vowed. My words made something snap within her, causing her to break down into sobs. Mariana quickly wrapped her arms around me and cried into my neck. I held her close, petting her head and being the comfort she needed to release her own misery.

I knew I would have to battle my heart on the matter repeatedly down the line. Any sane person would have absconded from the situation the moment danger appeared, but I refused to do so even as the road to my future curved into a dark tunnel. Anything could happen. Knowing Murphy's Law, everything that could go wrong probably would eventually.

I had to be strong.

Liam turned to Margarette with a breath. "Dispose of his body."

"Any instructions, Mister Hunter?" Margarette inquired.

After a moment of silence, Liam gave his first direction: "Burn it."

Margarette smiled.

Chapter 23

Struggle

It wasn't an understatement to say that the transition was an obstacle. However, Liam suddenly had everything Arthur owned and more under his fingertips.

Arthur's body was burnt and continued to be used as fireplace kindling for the mansion he previously owned. Those from the estate who wanted to finally leave had Louis's assistance in either immigrating back to their home countries or using... not-so-legal means to grant them legitimate citizenship. All received financial stability for their futures and agreed to lifelong silence on the matters they had to live through with therapy services given to those who needed it.

It wasn't impossible to grant all of it with how much power Liam was non-consensually given. Many of the workers cried in thankfulness, ready to be free at last. Margarette, the two guards, and only a handful of people stayed in the mansion, unwilling to change their environment from a lush mansion life. Liam gifted the land and building to them, not wanting to own a place his groomer lived and died in. Liam was given the deeds to other plots of land and buildings, documenting them for future reference for inspection and sale.

What remained after that were the financial assets.

"How much did Arthur have?"

Liam and I stood in his actual office as he pulled up a database server synched with all of Arthur's assets. His tech genius composed a literal live count of Arthur's fortunes, as that is what Liam was tasked to keep safe. Seeing the number next to the dollar sign stretch beyond twelve digits before the cent decimal stunned me to silence, but watching it continue to go up even after Arthur's death almost made my legs give out. Liam grimaced, clearly unsurprised to see the sum of what he had helped Arthur protect.

"As you can see... Well, he was an uncontrolled numismatist. Money was the one thing he valued above all else..."

Liam Hunter jumped from being a millionaire to being one of the 0.001% in the world. He probably *was* the top percent.

Arthur didn't just have business in the United States. He had fingers dipped internationally with significant profits in every aspect he could feasibly get into. All around the world, major trade, investments, and capital control somehow connected back to Arthur Smith, even to the most minor degrees. Most of his international influence wasn't noticeable to the naked eye, having been born from a time before we were even conceived and cleverly disguised with multiple lines of defense and anonymity.

It wasn't just civilian businesses Arthur profited off of. Mafia families in major cities, gangs stretching east to west, and all sorts of danger had some connection back to Arthur. His past immigration aid birthed the most dangerous of crime lords and underground black markets. His business had to have been handed down from his father and maybe his grandfather, with how deep his investments ran before Arthur stopped helping immigrants come over. Even corrupt police and politicians fed money back to his account in gross amounts, breaking my trust further in the safety of the nation I lived in.

And now Liam had complete control of it all. He wasn't just ensuring Arthur's ever-growing wealth with his own security measures. Every cent was Liam's.

I wasn't dating a millionaire anymore. I was practically bound to one of the wealthiest men in the world. *The* wealthiest.

To think that Arthur didn't have children of his own was unfathomable. With such power, he could have had any person he wanted. He could have made a damn clone of himself with DNA using the stupid amount of money he had for top science.

Yet he claimed no children and made Liam his sole heir. Furthermore, Margarette claimed, "Arthur had no interest in sex and procreation. He always said he would have been a terrible father."

Then why Liam?

That was a question that would haunt me forever.

Liam made himself a hermit in his office. Any work he required with Labryintelligence was done remotely, but his time became heavily devoted to unraveling the mess Arthur stuck him in. He made it a priority to establish his new connections, knowing the other syndicate members were aware of who had control, thanks to Arthur. Once he settled that, he focused his attention on trying to make sure nothing fell apart with what abilities he had at his fingertips and his keyboard.

Louis spent his time at the Labryintelligence building, sorting through more security and being the communicating face for Liam. Louis was brilliant as well, having a degree in business management, so it wasn't far-fetched to imagine Louis holding the reins as well as Liam did when it came to keeping Labryintelligence afloat.

With Liam's assistance, Mariana and Rosa managed to increase their home's security. Rosa refused to leave, having spent her life being a citizen and having a home to call hers. Mariana, despite wanting to run, stayed with her mother and did her best to remain legitimate with her art. Mariana found plenty of other investors outside of Liam to fund her art pieces, though she often texted me lamenting the limitations each investor placed on her creativity.

As for me, Liam-- through a wry smile-- advised me to continue work like nothing was wrong. It was weird to give that advice, but as I dissected his suggestion, it was the best one he could make. I wasn't born in the crime world like he was. I had to imagine the syndicate was well aware of me, as I was publicly Liam's girlfriend, but to the major public: I was just a food critic turned home-cooking vlogger dating a golden boy millionaire. It was unlikely that I was going to be involved with them as Liam kept their focus on him, so I just had to do my best.

Like nothing was wrong.

I kept my parents in the dark. They didn't need to know what was happening. It was for their own good, regardless. Texts and calls kept us close, but I didn't leave the loft by slating excuses. Work became my parents' worst enemy, keeping me from visiting them. Luckily, they didn't know where Liam and I lived, so them popping in for a surprise visit was impossible. Louis and Emily took turns ensuring they were safe, which made me feel less guilty about keeping my distance.

Danni kept in touch but didn't force conversations. Instead, her texts were always friendly check-ins to ensure my parents and I weren't struggling in any way. She had even offered to bring me out to clubs and the like to keep me out of my funks. Still, I declined and left positive replies of goodwill each time. I knew she wanted to help and connect further, but with where I was, I couldn't push myself to try and reach out.

To that end, I frequented Liam's office. I was still his submissive, so I was bound by the rule he placed to always be in the same room as him. At first, he didn't enforce it, but when I made it habit, he accepted it and did not start work until I was in the office. When he had meetings, I sat in a corner under his desk, hidden away from his cameras and microphone. I had bought myself a soundless keyboard for my work laptop to ensure I could work no matter what was happening on Liam's side. I also bought noise-canceling headphones to remain ignorant of his work. Arthur dealt in crime, and Liam had no choice but to take up those mantles. I couldn't lose sleep worrying if he was going to do right or wrong with his power.

While Liam took care of himself with bathroom runs and showers, he tried to push the boundaries of no sleep too often. As a result, I only ever left the office to make meals for Liam and me, use the restroom, or drag an overworked Liam to bed.

Our sex life took a nosedive, but I couldn't be mad. Liam had more critical priorities, and I had to accept that, knowing the life and death those priorities held. To his regret and my surprise, Liam let me break a fundamental rule in our sexual relationship and contract.

"Temporarily, I'll allow you to pleasure yourself without permission. However, this is only until I can finally get this all handled."

I was given a credit card, registered to a fake name, and allowed to purchase as many toys and erotica books as I wanted. Discreet deliveries would be picked up from an address I was given to use, and I had free reign to get whatever I wanted to ensure my pleasure was taken care of. It was a considerable level of security, but it made sense why it had to be done this way.

The toys were nice. I got my pick of high-quality items and got to experiment when the mood came crawling into my core. Dildos, vibrators, even rabbit wands, and small machines. I had the world's collection of pleasure at my disposal, and I made my choices as I saw fit. Of course, I managed to make myself feel good every time, but soon it became a boring play that I almost hated going into solo.

Even the fictional men I read about in my new erotica purchases disinterested me. My daredevil Ignatio became more annoyingly unbelievable the more I tried to desire his forceful manhood. My fae king Gerolt began to fail in his seduction to make me demand to become his fae queen. Even my vanilla book boyfriend Rhett didn't entice me to be held in his arms and kissed until dawn rose.

It was stunning how well Liam ruined me in sex. What blew my mind eventually wound up making me desire Liam to take control of me instead. I wanted him to leave me helpless and at his mercy. I wanted to be held. To be kissed. To be pounded into the bed until my legs turned to jelly.

I missed Liam feverishly.

But I had to be patient. He was settling things his way, and I knew he didn't want to be chained to his computer forever. Who would? An impatient shadow in my mind suggested an under-the-desk blow, but I did not want to interrupt something that he was heavily invested in, especially if it was to ensure his and our safety.

Perhaps after. A release after extreme hard work.

I just had to wait.

And wait, I did.

But that only allowed every fear and doubt in my soul to crawl up into my head. What was once pushed away and ignored in my time at Liam's side slowly bubbled into my thoughts, and it would not relent.

Why was I there? This is beyond what anyone should stomach. I was setting myself up to die like a criminal. Love isn't worth losing your life over. What of my future? I wanted to live a simple life, talking about food and being content with no big surprises. Liam was tossed into the pit, and I didn't have to dive in after.

Every therapist who had a social media account clamored on and on about toxic relationships. I wasn't gaslit into anything, nor was I bound to any chains that kept me there, yet the popular belief was that if your partner did illegal things, it would only end with misery and social abandonment.

People were shunned and dragged through the dirt when they were found even associating with criminals. So why was I going to risk everything for something beyond my control? My parents could get hurt. My friends could get hurt. I could get hurt.

My mind screamed at me to run, don't look back and run away. Stop trying to rationalize everything and just return to simplicity.

This was stupid. Reckless. Idiotic. I was a spoiled child who would get into deep trouble if I didn't cut it out.

Leave.

Leave Liam.

Leave my love and go back to normal.

...

...but I didn't want to.

I had spent almost a year at Liam's side. During that time, I saw plenty of red flags that would have swayed anyone away from living in my shoes. Liam hid things from me until it became impossible to hide. Arthur had scared me with a smile and a threat of assassination. Giorno targeted my family and succeeded in devastation. This world wasn't kind, and I was taken along for the ride because of my choice to stay. Liam had confessed to routing the damn dark web to Giorno's computer and protecting an empire of illegal money-making.

He was a criminal, and good people didn't stay with criminals.

Did that make me a bad person?

Was I as terrible as him by staying and allowing his activities to continue? Even as a helpless witness? I could have gone to the police. I could have told them everything and been put into a witness protection program. My life would have been over, but crime would have been stopped.

That's what a good person is supposed to do. Staying and being silent made me a bad person.

At the same time, I was respected and practically pampered by Liam. He chose me as I chose him, holding my hand at every point when the world felt like crashing around me. I was allowed to scream, cry, and fight back without being scolded or bound to behave.

Even Liam's friends stood by him. They may have known him

longer, but Louis and Emily were steadfast in their loyalty, even getting hurt in his name. Emily claimed that Liam was a good man, and even after everything, there was nothing that made that claim a lie. Louis clearly had dealt with Liam's antics as his best friend and stayed even as Arthur placed his barbed crown on Liam's head.

That had to carry weight to Liam's character. Not only with his personality and charm but also with his existence as a human being. He was a man who worked hard and got to do what he wanted to do as a boy.

Liam was just a man. There were plenty of other men. Safe, civilian men.

...but I loved Liam.

In the year I had known Liam, we shared laughter, tears, and emotions beyond simple love. We had seen each other's rage, misery, and joy. When the world didn't exist, we were just two people walking through time together. His gentle touch made me feel safe to grow. His encouragement became my steps toward being a more confident and prouder woman. I listened to my heart and had a strong partner to keep me moving forward.

But what do you need?

I... I needed Liam.

Liam was the sweetest man I had ever known, kind and caring in spades. He was drop-dead gorgeous to me and let me into his world when plenty of others could have had such a blessing. I knew lust became love between us in some shape, but not every romance starts with a skipping of the heartbeat. It could begin by sleeping with each other or just catching a falling spice container in a grocery store.

I imagined alternate paths I could have taken. I could have run away when Giorno attacked. I could have never seduced Liam that night at the Gold Nest. I could have never asked for that date to begin with. I could have just ordered all the spices I needed for that curry recipe.

But I made my choices, and now my heart needed Liam.

I was crazy. I was unrealistic.

I didn't give a damn.

Isn't that what a relationship was all about? Learning and supporting each other. I started my journey with Liam, intrigued by the genius businessman's life. He let me in, and I continued to learn more while letting him fill my heart with passion and rapture. Allowing him my mind and body, Liam already had claim to my heart and handled it with the softest of care.

No criminal life could change that. It already hadn't. Through his trials and troubles, he still kept a smile for me and control of every part of his body.

If Liam wanted to hurt me, he would have. If he wanted to bring me down, he would have chained me. He had the chains to do so.

But Liam trusted me. I had trusted him that far and wasn't broken in any way. In fact, I grew more than I imagined in his arms.

So why leave? Fear? Self-preservation?

If I left, Liam would have suffered alone. The door was open. The world wasn't blocked by cell doors. He wouldn't have made me stay, and he would have buried himself in his world. I'm sure he'd also find ways to keep me safe from the shadows, but I wouldn't have been there for him, and that would have been the greatest betrayal of all.

Why would I let fear control me? Liam didn't control me. Arthur didn't control me. No one held a tight chain that forced me anywhere I did not want to go.

I alone controlled my actions, no matter the consequences of them.

Damn advice. Damn reasonable suggestion. Who cared about normalcy?

I traded my simple life when I was hit by that car. I wouldn't retreat anymore, and I refused to doubt again.

It took days to settle into my thoughts. I was tired of worrying, of doubting my path. When I finally put my foot down, my chest felt lighter than it had ever been. I had to face my own resolve by myself; it was the best choice I could have made.

I obeyed no one but my own desires.

Chapter 24

Release

Two days before our one-year anniversary, I sat in Liam's office typing up a new review on my laptop. It was about a simple dish that was easy to make, perfect for my followers. Writing it was easy, mainly as I listened to jazz through my headphones.

I didn't want to think about our anniversary, but it was a milestone. Would Liam work through it? What about the plans he was setting up before Arthur's death? I began to worry, despite desperately wanting to keep my mind on my work. There was no point in making myself stressed over something we could reschedule or celebrate on a different date.

It's not like we had a date celebrating when we first met. But, of course, that would have been strange to begin with.

I clacked through the final paragraph of my review and let out a silent sigh before looking at the time. Six o'clock PM. Dinnertime. I closed my laptop and placed it in the corner where Liam put a small battery for me to charge my computer.

He always thought of me, even as he worked.

I stood and stretched before quietly making my way out of the office and back up to the loft. Dinner was going to be easy to eat with one hand, but it required a little time to put together. Tying my hair back and preheating the oven, I went to work on preparing an individual pan pizza with Liam's favorite toppings: pepperoni, green peppers, and mushrooms.

At the same time, I thought of the million ways Liam could have plotted out our anniversary. A beautiful trip to a vacation spot, like a beach or forest cottage away from the world. An extravagant dinner with the best chefs in the world serving us. A trip across the ocean to a foreign country. He could do anything he wanted, so nothing was impossible.

Still, I shook my head. He wasn't materialistic like that and didn't spend recklessly. Liam held firm to his finances when he was just a CEO. Our dates never extended into the wildly lavish, and I knew he didn't want to flaunt money like that to me. If I knew him as well as I claimed, his ideas would be much closer to home and his heart.

Dinner at the Gold Nest, like our first ever date. That would have been lovely.

After placing both of our pizzas in the oven and setting the automatic shut-off timer for the oven, I sat at the island counter and reminisced about our very first romantic date, when he promised me an unlimited wish that led him to be mine. That night I had listened to the voice in my heart guiding me to seduce and bed him in what I believed to be the bravest way I had ever done.

From then on, I listened to my heart more and more, giving me courage and confidence. It pushed me to be strong and defiant, even when I struggled to maintain a steady grip on my composure. It brought me closer to Liam and allowed me to open myself to him completely. I accepted all of him, trauma and all, and built myself to be the partner he needed.

It was a whirlwind being by his side, and there I was making pizza for him while he ran as a new kingpin for an international syndicate.

I was so lost in my thoughts that I didn't register the elevator letting out a ding, signaling someone entering the loft. I took a breath, utterly oblivious to the sound of footsteps approaching the kitchen. I practically jumped out of my spot when I finally heard someone slump in the seat beside me.

"AH!!" I yelped, grabbing the pizza cutter I left on the counter and turning quickly to face who sat beside me.

"WOAH!!" Liam's voice yelled out in reply. I watched as Liam, who had taken a seat beside me, tilted so far back in his chair that he slid off of the stool and slammed onto the floor, onto his ass.

When it finally registered who had fallen, I tossed the pizza cutter back onto the counter and dropped onto the floor beside Liam on my knees.

"Oh my God! Are you okay??" I asked, desperate to make sure my already overworked and probably exhausted boyfriend was okay after such a surprise fall.

Liam took in a breath and stretched back, most likely trying to recuperate from the pain rippling through his legs and spine from the fall. However, after a second, he began to laugh up toward the ceiling. I stared dumbfounded as he smiled at me, his tired eyes gleaming in love before he turned to lay his head on my lap.

"L-Liam?"

"I'm sorry. I didn't mean to scare you, kitten." Liam confessed, chuckling and closing his eyes as he rested on the floor with me as his pillow. I shook my head, unbelieving that he was laughing at my inability to listen for him beyond my thoughts.

"Sorry for not hearing you come up."

"It's alright. You looked like you were in deep thought." Liam finally opened his eyes and stared up at me, his lips softening in his smile. "I didn't interrupt anything important, did I?"

I shook my head. "No. I was just reminiscing."

"Oh? What about?"

"Our first date. How far we've come from it, you know?"

Liam took a breath and closed his eyes again, his smile growing in the memory. I began to pet his head as it settled on my lap, recalling that night again with a smile of my own.

"You're as beautiful as you were when you walked in the room that night..." Liam practically purred out in a whisper. His shoulders relaxed, and, for a moment, I could have sworn the dark circles under Liam's eyes softened in their gray color. The trip down memory lane was a comfort for both of us, feeling my heart swell at remembering every step we took, every bite we consumed, and every kiss we shared that night.

And yet, curiosity struck me.

"When did you start falling for me?" I asked, causing Liam to slowly open his eyes and stare up at me in thought. Perhaps he had his answer in my eyes, but I wanted to know when his heart began to fill with me. Finally, his smile curled slightly to the side in an embarrassed expression.

"Would you believe me if I said when I met you in the hospital?" Liam confessed, making me go slack-jawed. There was no way he had an interest in me while I was trapped in the hospital bed.

Then again, thinking back on the fuzzy memory, he did seem to stare at me for longer than most would.

"Really?" I questioned. Liam nodded.

"Perhaps it's odd to admit, but your smile just wouldn't leave my mind. It was genuine and sweet. It practically lit up the room, despite the pain you must have been under." Liam said. "When I left, I felt torn. I was the reason you wound up in that bed, but still, you pushed through to smile at me-- a practical stranger-- for something that shouldn't have occurred in the first place. Yet, at the same time... that fascinated me.

"When I saw you again at that art gallery, beautiful and full of curiosity, you only entranced me even more. I had to know more about you somehow." Liam slowly rose from my lap and turned to face me with a smirk. "I began to follow your blog and witnessed your humor and open-heartedness in your reviews. As embarrassing as it is to say... I felt like a fanboy. There was no end of teasing from

Louis, especially after you finally called for that date."

"Don't tell me you were nervous..." I muttered out, still taking in the information he was freely speaking. I could barely believe what he was saying if I hadn't already sensed his interest in me during those windows of time. The way he stared at me in the gallery made it clear that he liked me somehow. I just wasn't able to read his entire mind. He was just as interested in me as I was in him. Knowing his abilities with a computer, I knew he could have dug for more information on me like I did him, but I was okay being the more inspective one between us.

Liam nodded and took my hand in his, running his thumb over my knuckles. "I wanted nothing more than to become closer to you. I was willing to wait as long as it took for you to make your wish just so I could speak to you again. When you appeared that night in that beautiful dress with that fantastic smile, I knew I would fall even harder for you."

I could feel my head heat up with my cheeks burning in flattery. As Liam stared at me, he chuckled and let his free hand come up to cup my cheek. As I nuzzled his palm, I couldn't help but smile despite the bashful energy whirling through me at his confession.

"There it is... that's the smile that captured me..." Liam whispered, making me blush even harder. It wasn't intentional, but Liam made me happy enough to feel safe and loved within his hands. I stared up at him, unsure of how to respond but lost in the smile he had for me. "This is the smile I want to protect more than anything."

"I know you will, Liam... you've worked so hard and continue to do so even now, I'm sure..." I replied, cupping my hand over his and turning my head to kiss his palm. "I'm positive that I will always be happy with you..."

My love made no sense. I was intrigued by him and definitely bit off more than one could chew. But seeing Liam smile, despite all the pain and toil he had to endure, made my heart sing. He was happy to be mine and have me near him. He had made it impossible to desire anyone else, and I had claim over every part of his body as he did mine.

Screw sense.

I leaned in and finally kissed him, needing to feel him. After seeing him struggle at work, it was torturous to have held back for so long in claiming him again. I may have been his submissive, but he was my love. I was allowed to be selfish after waiting patiently.

Liam practically moaned against my lips, clearly having missed me as well, and pulled my body against his. His grip was possessive as if I would disappear if he let me go, and I relished in his possession of me. My body wanted this, and I deepened the kiss further, needing more. The feel of his hands roaming my back and arms only teased me further from sweet romance to dark desire.

It was like my libido had been replaced by a hungry animal, desperate for any sort of meal it could get, and was presented with a practical feast to devour.

"Please tell me I can stop waiting..." I mewled against Liam's lips, gripping his shirt in desperation.

"No more waiting... take what you want of me..." Liam moaned back, pulling at my sundress in equal need. "I'm yours."

Good.

I pressed my body against Liam, knowing my plus-size weight would push him back down onto the floor if he truly meant what he said. I craved every bit of his flesh against mine. I wanted his heat, his passion, and I wanted it immediately.

He clearly wanted me as well, obeying my physical command and sliding his hands under my dress onto my thighs as he laid himself on the floor beneath me. I moved to straddle his hips, enjoying the feel of his fingers on my skin and savoring the tease of it as my lips claimed his.

I wasn't waiting to get to the room. I was going to have Liam right then and there or so help me; God would have felt my wrath.

Drowning in the new wave of lust rushing through my body, I grabbed his shirt and practically tore it open at the buttons. Some of them popped off their threads, bouncing and sliding across the marble tile away from us, but Liam only growled with a smirk at the sound. Liam looked up at me, beautiful thin rings of jade staring up at me with the darkest of desires from what I had done.

I was sure I was going to be punished for ruining his shirt, but that was future Maya's problem.

"Do you know how much you have ruined me?" I asked my sexy

master. I lowered myself to lay my chest on Liam's, touching the tip of my nose with his with a smirk of my own as his expression melted to one of curious surprise. As he raised his eyebrow at me, I licked my lips and lowered my head to line my mouth to his ear for a whisper. "There is literally nothing in this house that can satisfy me more than you..."

With my confession, I rolled my hips against his, feeling the quickly growing tent in his pants rub up against the equally accelerated heat igniting beneath my panties. Both of us moaned out at the feel, with Liam sliding his hands up my thighs to grip my ass under my underwear, massaging each cheek with his fingers and making me purr in pleasure. The beast nestled in my core was eager for more, urging me to slowly circle my hips over his to tease Liam further and rub my fingers over his bare chest. The heat that emanated from his skin was like a drug that made me that much needier.

My body could barely take the heat building underneath my skin, so I sat up to grab the edges of my dress and dragged it up and over my head. The blessing of staying inside all day meant no bra, so as the cool air finally brushed against my bare breasts, I shuddered in delight. Looking back down at Liam, I was rewarded with the heaviest expression of excitement on his face.

But I wanted more than just his lust. I wanted his fingers, his tongue, his cock. Everything. Especially where I wanted him most.

I growled with a toothy grin before slowly moving to stand.

Liam's hands wanted to grip me down, but I pushed them away before settling up onto my feet. Hooking the loops of my panties and sliding them down my legs, I took my time in revealing my aching pussy to Liam before tossing them and my dress to the side to be forgotten.

It was strange seeing him beneath me in such a manner. He was my master, yet there he was, obeying and waiting for me, watching me tease him and eating in the sight with the biggest I-want-to-fuck-you expression I had seen from him in a while. Had it really been that long since he gave me those eyes? I had the upper hand. I was the one in control.

Temporarily, but I was going to relish it.

He had taught me that if he wanted me to sit on his face, I wasn't allowed to hover. My total weight was going to straddle his head and lay upon his lips. I only had the courage to obey thoroughly once, and he didn't force me to stay on him long before granting me a sweet reward in the form of his dick.

This time, he would pay for making me wait.

I lowered myself back down over him, aiming to center my pussy directly over his lips, and brushed my clit with my fingers to entice him. I barely caught a glimpse of Liam licking his lips before the lower half of his face became hidden by the curve of my belly. Not even fully upon him, I felt his tongue teasingly tap my clit and couldn't stop myself from gasping in delight.

Fuck yes.

I finally sat down, feeling Liam eagerly gorge on the meal forced upon his chin. I shuddered and moaned in pleasure as his tongue lapped over the lips of my pussy while his hands curved around my legs and anchored me down. He ate like a man starving, savoring every lick and nibble of my heat. I couldn't stop myself from grabbing his hair and slightly tugging at it. He knew my body so well, focusing on sucking over my quickly engorged clit and switching off to prod the entrance of my pussy with the tip of his tongue.

"Y-Yes, master... make me cum... I've been a good girl... I *deserve* it." I growled out, tightening my grip on his hair and earning an even more sexy roar from the man beneath me.

I let him devour me and let myself melt into the pleasure. I arched back to the ceiling, closing my eyes and praising Liam with my moans and gasps. I was already needy for him, so it was easy to climb towards my orgasm, yet to know that all it took was Liam's mouth made my spirit quake.

My climax was glorious, ushering the most primal of cries to escape my throat as Liam gripped to my legs tighter through it. My core exploded in euphoria, finally finding the level of satisfaction it needed to break through my hunger. Liam was indeed the key to my perfect ride to heaven. It took me a long moment to catch my breath, shaking from the pleasure and feeling him lap up every drop of my orgasm. My legs barely kept me up straight, but I used every ounce of strength I had to slide off of Liam's face and lay at his side.

Liam, humming in his own satisfaction, pulled me close to him and kissed my head.

"Good girl... God, what a good girl..." Liam muttered to me, running a hand down my body and massaging my breast tenderly. I shuddered and surrendered to his touch, feeling him caress every inch of skin on my chest. The flame tempered by my climax flickered back to life at his hands exploring my body, pinching my nipples, and gripping my love handles.

What stopped us was the quick beeping of the oven, signaling that our dinner had finished cooking and awaited us to retrieve it.

Liam and I stared at each other, breaking from the heat consuming us, and took in the situation. I was bare naked on the cool marble floor, being touched and caressed by my boyfriend, who had a ripped-open shirt and a hard tent in his pants. Yet, simultaneously, I could hear our stomachs rumble in hunger for something more orally tangible than sex.

I could tell Liam dissected just as much as we both began to laugh, recognizing the silliness of the situation. I wrapped my arms around Liam as he held me, and we both let ourselves go in joyful amusement. Our laughter echoed in the loft and slowly died down to chuckles and smiles between us.

"Come on. Let's eat." Liam instructed before slowly moving to stand. As he settled on his feet, he lowered his hands to me and assisted me off the floor to my own. Despite my legs still jelly-like from our fun, I carefully balanced myself and nodded in agreement.

However, Liam then leaned in to whisper in my ear...

"Take your time eating because, afterward, I'm going to fuck you until sunrise..."

~ ~ ~

That night, he indeed fucked me until sunrise. Despite how overworked he was, he didn't falter in holding me down with his cock in my mouth. His strength was unaffected from his days in the office, proven as he pinned me to the mattress and railed me until I was screaming in ecstasy. I drowned in his love, his lust, and his pleasure. Days of denial between us finally erupted in us being skyrocketed into nirvana again and again without mercy.

It wasn't him just fucking me that night. I rode him like my life depended on his depth within me. I pinned him down at points as I toppled over multiple orgasms in a row on his lap. Our bodies knew we had to make up for lost time. I had lost count of how many times I cried out his name. My voice became hoarse, but I didn't care. Liam was my chant for my midnight prayer, and my name became his repeated psalm.

The sun was blessed with breathlessness from both of us. I curled myself into Liam's arms, and he held me against his body. Breakfast be damned; we finally let sleep take us when we were good and done.

I was finally at peace. I was more than happy to be in Liam's arms and felt safe even in my dreams. My body was satisfied. My mind pulsed steadily in contentment. The world didn't matter; only Liam and I did. The hickeys and love bruises on our bodies echoed that sentiment.

I didn't even flutter my eyes open until the afternoon, and I was still in Liam's arms. My master gently ran his fingers through my hair and watched me wake, smiling as we locked eyes.

"Good morning, my queen." Liam purred out, his voice still hoarse from the night's play. I giggled softly, clearing my throat from my own hoarseness, before reaching up to caress his cheek.

"Good morning, my king..." I replied, leaning in to kiss Liam. He wrapped his arms around my form completely and kissed me deeply and slowly, each of us pouring our love into each other's lips.

To me, it was more than a good morning kiss. It was a promise to continue giving each other kisses every morning, every night, every day. So whether we danced in the kitchen making food or battled whatever the world had in store for us, Liam had my support, and I had his.

I danced my fingers over Liam's chest lovingly. "So. What happens now?"

Liam kissed my forehead before replying, "Well, I've automated many of the systems I put in place for the syndicate's financial success. Money will keep pouring in, and, with the hundreds of security programs I have on the servers, I'll be free to get back to my own work."

"What if something goes wrong?"

"I've programmed the system to notify my phone of any hiccups in the security or any negative changes in the assets."

"So you'll go fix it when it needs fixing."

"Basically. I remain publicly the innocent Liam Hunter while my involvement with the Eye remains minimal."

"They really don't expect more from you?" I was a bit skeptical at the idea. If the high powers of the syndicate knew who their boss was, why would they be relaxed about their boss's lack of involvement? If anything, Liam had to be on his toes and ready for anything.

Liam grimaced slightly. "Well, I will have to delegate some other things, such as new business and the like. However, they have no plans to expand as of this moment. So, for now, my only needs are to keep the syndicate's pockets heavy."

"And your program will make sure nothing goes wrong?"

"It lives in my servers, powered by multiple energy sources to compensate for any outages."

"What if someone tries to hack it?"

Liam smirked. "With how I programmed everything, it would take a practical army of geniuses to even make a crack in the first couple of walls of my servers."

I pursed my lips and rolled to lay on top of Liam, raising an eyebrow. "Aren't you confident..." I muttered, tapping his nose with my finger.

Liam wrapped his arms around me and hummed quietly, staring up at me with the warmest gaze. "You give a man enough motivation, he can even do the impossible."

"And what sort of motivation drives the handsome genius that is Liam Hunter?" I giggled at the flourish but let my laughter die with Liam's loving gaze melting my cocky attitude and his hand on my cheek.

"You."

Damn his charming silver tongue. I started to blush, knowing well enough that Liam had multiple reasons to work as hard as he did. He had his family to protect, business to keep spotless, and friends to support. I was just one of those reasons, yet his tone made it seem like I was the most important reason of all. It was flattering and frustrating; I both loved and hated it equally.

But the tremble of my heart caused a smile to grow across my face.

"You're quite the charmer, mister Hunter."

That day was spent relaxing in the loft from the hard work accomplished in Liam's office. We didn't bother to cook and ordered meals from our favorite places. Perhaps it was exhaustion finally hitting Liam like a tidal wave, but he barely pulled himself out of bed to lounge in my office with me.

He may have finished his work, but mine was never-ending.

I continued to construct scripts for future videos and reviews for my blog as Liam playfully dove into my new erotica collection.

Needless to say, some books made him raise his eyebrows.

"So, you like aggressive men?"

"I like aggressive *fictional* men."

"And what makes them so... *titillating* for you?"

"Big word, mister Hunter! Though, it's not their aggression that makes them attractive. It's their devotion despite the fact."

There was no way my Liam was anything like bad boy Carlos or dragon lord Zayn... but he could have been if he wanted to. After all, I was living a life that jumped out of my mafia erotica. Who was to say that magic didn't exist? What if Liam was an incubus prince of the fantastical demon world who had to slay his tyrannical father for the throne?

...now I was going too far into my imagination.

Giggling at my own silliness, I returned my focus to my work. Liam flipped back and forth between reading through one of my books and scrolling through his phone. From the corner of my eye, whenever he went to his phone, his expression would change from relaxed to intensely focused. This didn't change as the day quickly burned down to the night.

Perhaps Liam was thinking of the following day. Our anniversary. He was on top of planning before he became a kingpin, so it only made sense that he had to catch up quickly with whatever he had in store. I could only think about it for a moment, remembering how he wanted to keep it a surprise for me.

All I knew was that it would be a wonderful day, no matter what he planned. I slept that night with bated breath, dreaming of what was in store.

Chapter 25

Surrender

It was nice to dream but better to experience joy in reality. Waking to the smell of a freshly cooked breakfast became one of my favorite ways to start my morning. However, having the smell so close to me spurred me to break free from my slumber faster than usual.

Presented on a quaint gold-epoxy tray was a full breakfast with toast, pancakes, eggs, bacon, and fruit. The handsome man holding the tray smiled as I rubbed my eyes to wipe away the sleep lingering in them.

"Good morning, beautiful," Liam greeted. I smiled sweetly back, sitting up and stretching.

"Good morning, handsome," I replied, taking a second deep sniff of the food Liam was holding. It made my stomach growl in need, and I felt myself salivating. "What an interesting way to wake me up. You've never done this before."

"Oh? Do you not approve? Well then..." Liam teased, playful offense in his voice as he pulled the tray away from me. I became dismayed as he turned around to face the bedroom door. "I guess I'll just eat this myself in the dining room then."

Before I could protest, Liam marched out of the room.

Laughing, I jumped out of bed and quickly moved to catch up with him. As I reached the bedroom door, Liam sped up his march to reach the end of the hall and turned towards the dining room to hide beyond the corner. I stalked forward, letting my hunger prod me to act like a beast wanting to pounce on her prey.

Turning the corner to the kitchen and dining room made me gasp and stare at the sight I laid my eyes on.

In the middle of the room stood a plus-sized mannequin. On it was draped a stunning dark red silk dress. It flared out at the waist, giving the curves of the dress doll a flattering look, and the skirt angled into a perfect hi-lo style to show off a pair of matching wedges on the floor beneath.

The best part: across the mannequin's chest sat my public collar. It all came together beautifully, and I knew it was all mine.

I staggered forward, taking the sight in as real, and circled around the dress to observe every detail. It looked comfortable as well as elegant, perfect for an anniversary date. I wanted to try it on immediately, but the rumble in my stomach reminded me of more healthy priorities.

"Liam..." I whispered out, finally looking over to the man in question. He had a smile painted across his expression as he set the tray down on the dining table, where a matching meal sat in his spot. He turned and walked to stand at my side, sliding an arm around my waist and pulling me close.

"What do you think?" Liam asked as I hugged him from the side with a beaming grin.

"It's absolutely beautiful, sir. I love it."

"Do you love it enough to wear it tonight?"

I raised an eyebrow. "Well, where do you plan on taking me?" I inquired, earning a chuckle from the man in my arms.

Liam turned his body to face me and wrapped both of his arms around my waist with a smirk. "I mean, I want to take you everywhere... on every surface..." He teased, leaning in for a sly kiss but earning a raspberry from my tongue and a laugh.

"Master!" I scolded, softly slapping his chest as he pulled me close. Liam's smirk returned to a smile at last.

"It's a surprise, kitten. One I hope you'll enjoy," Liam answered. "Is that alright?"

I nodded, knowing that whatever he had planned would be jaw-droppingly amazing.

"Good," Liam confirmed before kissing my forehead. "Now, let's eat. I'm sure you're starving."

Indeed, I was. Liam had improved over time making breakfast; whether it was the date or his finetuning, that morning's meal was the best I ever had. I savored every bite, enjoying my morning with Liam and the sunlight shining through the window.

I felt positive that the day was going to be amazing.

When we finished, I collected and washed the dishes as I usually did. Liam stood beside me, watching and not wanting to be away from me just yet.

"Is there anything special you'd like to do before tonight?" Liam asked.

"Well, depending on when our special secret plans are tonight, I'd like to get my hair and nails done if that's okay," I suggested. "Otherwise, I can't think of anything."

"Oh? Is that so?" Liam muttered before tapping something on his phone. I raised an eyebrow, not sure what he meant with his dodge.

"Is there a pro-" I began before being interrupted by my phone ringing in the bedroom. Danni's ringtone echoed through the hall, and I knew Liam was involved. I pursed my lips at him, watching him look to the ceiling in feigned ignorance, before rushing back to the bedroom and picking up.

"Hey, Danni!" I answered.

"Hey!! So I'm not gonna lie to you: Liam told me to meet you at 2 o'clock at this spa and salon by the Loop. Just googling the place, it's mad expensive, but the reviews are all five stars from celebrities." Danni confessed relatively quickly. I couldn't believe my ears. Liam really thought of everything.

"Really now?" I asked with a smile, crossing my arm under my chest and looking back at the bedroom door. Liam wasn't there, but I knew he was plotting more with me out of his line of sight.

"Uh-huh. We are going, right? He said it's on him, and I'm not missing a chance for a free celebrity makeover and spa day." Danni asked, clearly pressing me to agree. Why wouldn't I?

"Yes, yes. Of course, we'll go, okay?" I acquiesced. Liam had most of the day planned, and I mentally rolled through a couple of ideas of what he had in mind.

"YAS! Alright, I'll see you then!" Danni chirped before hanging up, clearly excited about the free blessing of being my friend. I laughed and locked my phone again, shaking my head.

I walked back to the main area and spotted Liam on the couch, reading one of my erotica books. I rolled my eyes and leaned on my hip, crossing my arms.

"So, are there any other surprises?" I asked aloud.

Liam turned to look down at his phone nonchalantly, moving to turn the open book towards me. It was on the literal front page, and I realized it wasn't *my* book.

A signature had been written on the back of the front cover. The author's signature.

"I may have a couple more." Liam teased, looking up at me with another one of his charming smirks. Damn him.

I rushed over and pounced onto his lap, making him laugh as I took the book and saw my favorite author's signature scrawled over the white flap. The book in question was one of my favorites, and the fact that Liam got the author to sign a copy for me was a miracle within itself with how introverted she was as a person.

Liam wrapped his arms around me and smiled up at my excited expression. "If you get dressed, I'll bring you to the rest myself."

~~~

He kept that promise. I quickly dressed in a comfortable outfit before riding down the elevator with him. Emily was beaming as she picked us up and drove us down towards the Loop. There we stopped by multiple locations, where brand representatives greeted me with gifts; high-end equipment for recording and cooking. I met YouTubers who were happy to meet the person behind my growing blog as if they were fans of it themselves. It was an ego boost, and Liam stood behind me through it all.

We had lunch at a small cafe where a selection of my favorite erotica authors somehow managed to meet up and treat me to selfies and signatures. Liam's doing, no doubt. I was ecstatic through it all, as spoiled as I was.

I felt slightly sour that I didn't have anything to give back, but Liam had one twist to his gifts that I did not expect.

"What I want from you is that wish I promised you."

"Wait, what?" I stared dumbfounded at Liam as we drove further south of the Loop.

"I'm serious. You never spent your wish, so I'd like to have it."

What was Liam going to do with it? What if he asked for something weird or dark? Knowing him, it was probably going to be something I could feasibly give, but my imagination ran wild with the unlimited wish the stipulation brought about.

Oh, why not?

"Okay. Liam Hunter, you can have any wish you want as my anniversary gift to you."

With the most serene smile he ever gave, Liam nodded and shook my hand on it. We parked at the side of a lavish building, and Danni waved me down from the entrance. Liam did not come with me, and I quickly rushed over to join my friend inside as Emily drove off with Liam as her only passenger.

What I experienced inside the building was practically life-changing. Danni and I were given a special tour and spa package, fit for practical royalty. We got massages and treatments that made our bodies feel vibrant and soft. Everything the spa offered at the top dollar we received with eagerness. They even provided snacks and live music to soothe us.

Liam probably added a colossal tip, which perhaps explained the enthusiasm.

As 5 o'clock rolled around, we were guided to the other side of the building where the salon was located. Two stylists sat us in highly comfortable chairs and let us paint pictures of how we wanted to look. Danni elected for stunning curls, as she had cared very deeply for her 3c textured hair and didn't want to heavily change it. I chose to keep my hair down but wanted it tamed to a gentle wave behind me.

As our follicles were pampered, our nails were done at the same time by nail artists. It felt odd to have both done simultaneously, but with how long we were in the chairs, it made sense to save time in such a way. Our hairs were professionally taken care of, and we stared at ourselves in the mirrors in awe of how we looked.

It wasn't surprising that the salon had also received the dress Liam got for me while I was in the spa, so as soon as I was ready, I was dressed and set for the evening.

"Damn, Maya... you look so beautiful..." Danni praised in awe, dressed in her own nice outfit to boot.

I felt beautiful. Looking at myself in the mirror, I was more than happy with my appearance. With the confidence I had built, I stood tall and was damn well proud of myself.

Soon enough, a luxury car pulled up as we exited the salon. Emily parked and opened the door to the car for me, but Liam was nowhere in sight. Dissecting Emily's knowing expression, this was to be expected. I slid into the car but was surprised to watch Emily guide Danni into the seat beside me.

"Danni?" I pressed, realizing there was more in store.

"Just relax and let it happen. Hush." Danni brushed it off with a smirk.

And I did. We drove through Chicago once more, listening to a fun jazz beat that Danni swayed to in her seat. My mind quickly wandered through more ideas that potentially waited in store, but it froze as Emily pulled up to a familiar building.

We parked in front of the skyscraper that held the Gold Nest.

My heart skipped a beat as Emily exited the car and escorted Danni out before extending her hand to me. I was slow, but I took it, taking in what was happening as Emily gave me a smile and a wink. After closing the car door, she raised her elbows to Danni and me.

"May I escort you both?" Emily inquired. Danni wrapped her arm around Emily's without hesitation before watching eagerly for me to do the same. So, I followed suit and was led up the stairs to the gold and marble doors. It was almost like Deja Vu.

We walked through the lobby, where plenty of rich folks wandered and chatted, and arrived at the same elevator we took the first time I went to the Gold Nest. Emily repeated precisely what she did with the guard at the front of it and guided us inside, where we were elevated to our destination.

The ride up did nothing to help my sudden nerves. This was a date at the Gold Nest. This was a picturesque fantasy to have as an anniversary date. But why was Danni joining us?

"Maya? Breathe, honey." Danni called out, snapping me out of my thoughts. I looked over to observe Emily and Danni staring at me with concerned smiles. Was I really that frazzled?

"Sorry! Sorry." I apologized. "This is just a lot, I guess."

Danni reached over and patted my hand, giving it a slight comforting shake. "It's a lot, but it's out of love. And there isn't anyone I know who deserves this kind of love more than you." Danni stated, backed by a nod from Emily.

I deserved this?

We finally reached floor seventy-seven, and the doors opened wide for us. Emily escorted us down the hall, where the same guards

I saw a year prior stood at attention. This time, Emily did not whisper into a mic but nodded affirmingly to the two.

They nodded back to Emily, turned, and opened both doors to the familiar room I had visited so long ago.

But this time, it had a large round table, fit for multiple people. Standing around it were people I knew and loved: my parents, Rosa, Mariana, Louis, and even Emily's wife was there. Everyone was dressed up formally, ready for a meal at the Gold Nest as I was, and I couldn't help but gasp in surprise at it all.

And at the opposite side of the table stood Liam, stunned once again at my presence with a smile on his face.

As we walked in and Emily returned to her wife's side, Danni joined my parents. Everyone besides Liam cheered, "Happy Anniversary!"

I felt love and warmth blossoming in my chest, and I had to stop myself from crying. This was so much, and Liam achieved it for me on our special day. What was I going to say other than thank you? I greeted and hugged every single person in the room, grateful for them to be there celebrating with Liam and me.

By the time I finished, I was at Liam's side, beaming up at him.

"Happy Anniversary, my queen," Liam said, lifting one of my hands and laying a kiss over the knuckles. Just like our first date.

"Happy Anniversary, my king," I replied, happier than I could have ever been. However, instead of releasing my hand, Liam gently took the other and held them both up between us.

"Maya Augustine, you have made me the happiest man in the world. You've supported me through all my trials and tribulations, and I could not think of anything more worthwhile today than showering you with the love and care you deserve. Your smile lights up the room, and your laughter is absolutely infectious." Liam began. My heart was not ready, but I listened, feeling it swell and beat hard in my chest. He continued, "No matter what obstacle came our way, you stood tall and stood at my side, unafraid to get through it. That is what makes you the most precious person in the world to me, and I want to continue making you happy. If you'll let me, I would like to use that one unlimited wish. I can't imagine any wish greater than being your husband and for you to be my wife."

The world around me faded away, muffling the flashing of cellphone cameras and squeals of delight from the other guests as Liam slowly lowered himself onto one knee. He reached into his pocket and revealed a dark red box before opening it and showing me the most magnificent ring I had ever seen. I felt faint but stood tall, unwilling to pass out at that very moment. This was a dream coming true; my heart's desire made manifest in his smile, his gaze, and his actions. There was no way in hell I was going to be weak now.

"Maya Augustine... will you marry me?"

Say it.

"Yes," I replied, holding back tears of pure joy. The room erupted in cheers as Liam's eyes began to water from his surrender to happiness. I held out my hand to him and watched as he removed the ring from the box and slipped it onto my ring finger.

A perfect fit. I wasn't at all surprised.

I laughed softly as Liam stood back up and wrapped his arms around me. As we leaned into each other and kissed at last, fireworks went off outside the building, adding to the wild energy in the room.

Liam was going to be my husband. First, he was my lover and master; now, he had vowed to be mine in matrimony. I would shoulder his future as he would mine...

And I was ready.

__Epilogue__

"So, mister Hunter. Your thoughts on the trade?"

"Well, I would like to invest in it. Perhaps we can keep an eye on its growth and see where it goes. Then, if something happens, we can pull out without issue."

"It's quite a confident move. Are you certain you won't consider opening that generosity to the NFT market? Plenty of up-and-comings are eager to make them happen."

"Only a bumbling idiot would invest in a destined-to-die medium. Besides, copy-paste exists to negate any purpose of that."

"Copy-paste? You young people with your computer terms..."

"Well, this young person is directing us on the best course. Have I led you astray thus far?"

"No, we suppose not. Arthur was right to appoint you."

"Speaking of leading, congratulations on your engagement, mister Hunter."

"Thank you kindly."

"Should we expect to meet the missus? This Maya Augustine seems quite the polished civilian. What does she do again?"

"Food reviews and the like. Very popular with the modern crowds. It would be quite the shame to hide her from us, mister Hunter."

"I don't intend to hide, gentlemen. It is a pleasure to meet you all at last."